THE OLD KIND

A STAND-ALONE ANTHOLOGY
IN THE SIBYLLINE SAGA

ANNA CACKLER

Contents

Author's Note

This book includes scenes that may be distressing to some readers. Please refer to the appendix at the back of this book for a complete list of these sensitive topics. It can also be found on my website: annacackler.com

Take care of yourselves, loves.

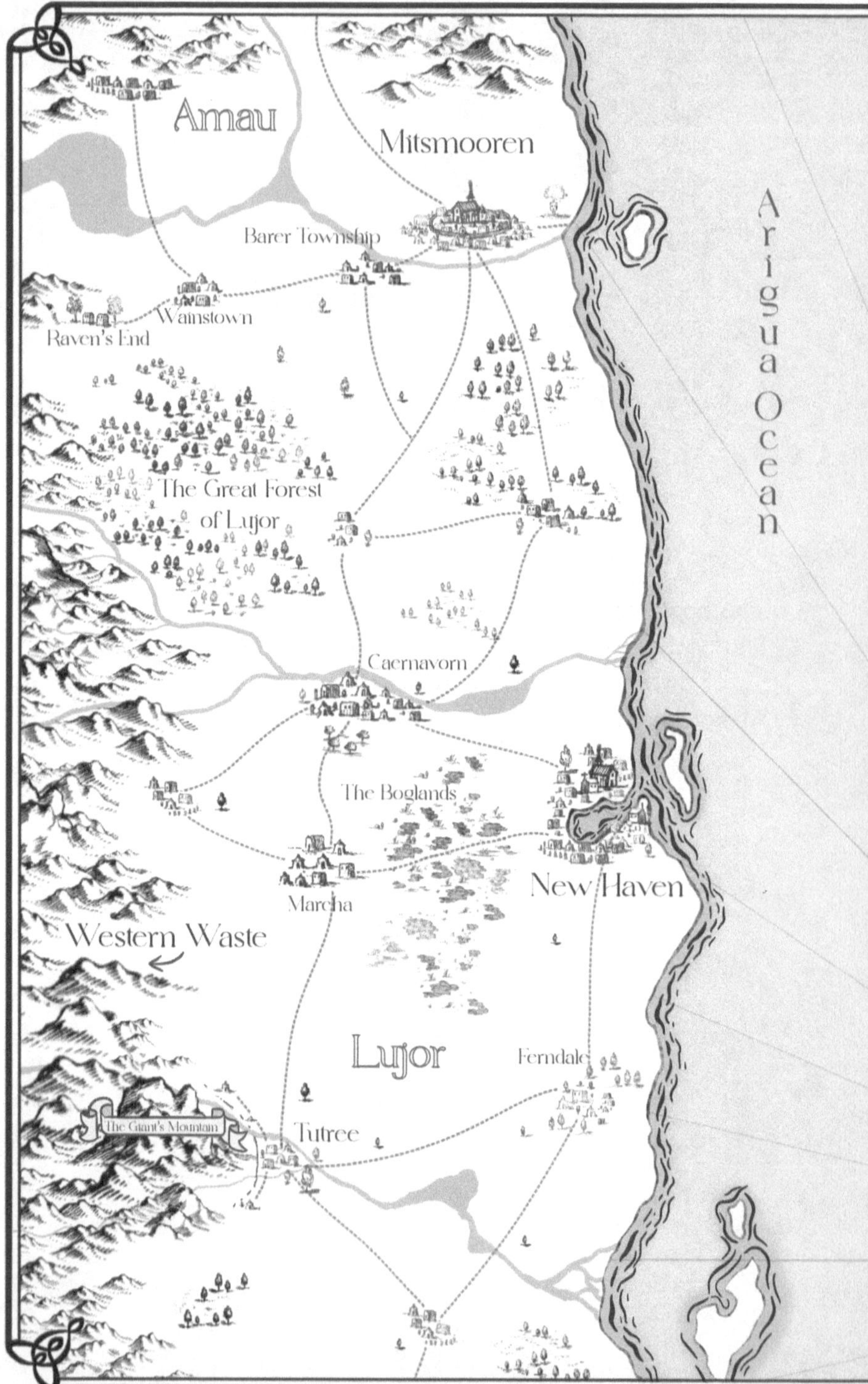

Amau
Mitsmooren
Barer Township
Wainstown
Raven's End
The Great Forest
of Lujor
Arigua Ocean
Caernavorn
The Boglands
New Haven
Marcha
Western Waste
Lujor
Ferndale
The Giant's Mountain
Tutree

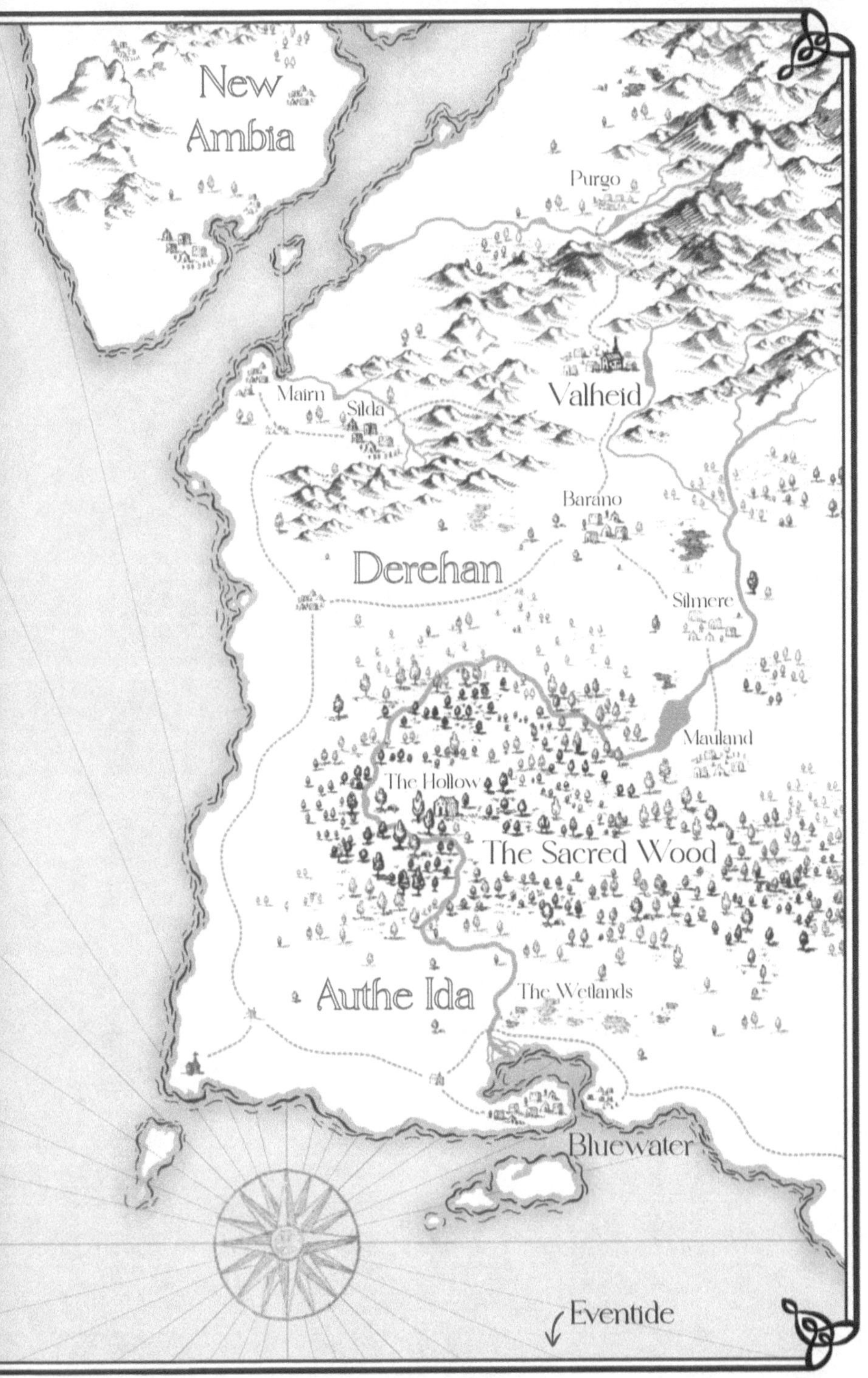

New Ambia
Purgo
Valheid
Mairn
Silda
Barano
Derehan
Silmere
Mauland
The Hollow
The Sacred Wood
Authe Ida
The Wetlands
Bluewater
Eventide

THE GLASS WHEEL

ONE

My father taught me to spin when I was five years old, and I fell in love.

"You have to hold the fiber tight, Aurora," he said in his low, smooth voice, "but not too tight. You must strike the right balance so that the fibers can draft out of the supply and twist together at the same time."

"How?" I asked.

"That's not something I can teach you, sweetheart. You have to learn that on your own. It's something you feel in your hands."

I watched in fascination as the yellow-gray flax slipped between his fingers in an endless, delicate stream from distaff to bobbin, each long fiber catching the next so that they could all twist up into thread as fine as cobweb.

"Just like every spinner has unique hands, we all find our own balance. Just the right tension and hold. Just the right method for our thread."

"Can I try?" I asked, already reaching for the thread.

My father laughed. His feet stilled on the treadles, and the wheel slowed to a heavy stop. I took his place on the padded chair, but my feet couldn't reach the treadles. He swapped out his chair and gave me a low stool to sit on instead.

"You'll grow into the big chair," he said.

I began pumping the treadles, one for each foot—left right, left right—and the wheel resumed its great circle. The drive band swung around the wheel and looped around the much smaller flier and bobbin, which spun at ten times the rate of the wheel. It whipped through the air, creating the telltale *shhhhh!!* sound that I had been listening to all my short life.

"Feed it more fiber," my father said. "Before you add too much twist. Like this."

He showed me how to pull a few fibers at a time from the supply on the distaff and direct the twist up the new thread just so. How to allow the wheel to take up the thread once enough twist had been added.

The new thread disappeared into the orifice at the end of the flier, fed through the guide hook, and wrapped around the bobbin for storage. The wheel ate up the thread like a hungry thing, always sucking, always pulling the fibers from the distaff like a long noodle. It didn't care that my thread was fat, lumpy, and full of snarls. It didn't care that it came with an uneven twist, sometimes loose enough to nearly fall apart, sometimes so tight that it kinked up on itself.

The wheel was always greedy, always pulling.

Left right, left right. Treadle, treadle. Draft. Twist. *Shhh!*

I glowered at the lumpy thread winding onto the bobbin, but my father only laughed again, his beard twitching with mirth. "You'll find your balance, Aurora. It will take time. You will spin many stricks of flax before you can produce good linen. Just think of it. With us both spinning, we will double our profits. And you'll have a real future, Aurora. Enough money to do anything we like. We can go to the seaside someday. What do you think of that? They say there's merfolk living in the water off the southern coast."

I stared up at him in wonder. "Do you think that's true? About the merfolk?"

"Believe everything you hear about the Old Kind, Aurora," he said seriously. "That way, you'll never be caught unawares."

His words sent chills down my back, but then again, mention of the Old Kind always did. But I'd been hearing about the Old Kind all my life, and no mermaid would scare me away from the salt and the sun and the sand. "When can we go?" I asked.

He laughed again and squeezed my shoulder. "One thing at a time. First, learn to spin. And once you've spun fifty stricks, then we can start selling your thread."

"But that will take forever!" I cried.

He tucked a strand of my light brown hair behind my ear. "Time flies like the wheel, Aurora."

Of all the things my father used to say to me, that was the one that stuck with me the most. *Time flies like the wheel.* I repeated it to myself any time my life ceased to be one thing and went on to be something else.

As flax farmers and spinners, change didn't come to us often, but we couldn't hide from time any better than the rest of the world. I eventually learned to spin as well as my father—better even, for I loved it more than he did.

I grew up.

Time flies like the wheel.

Our farm expanded, spilling into two more fields on our eastern border, just like Father had always dreamed about—the first step in his plan to have a better life. We brought in a man called Cael from the workhouse to help my father in the field.

Time flies like the wheel.

My father got sick. And though I tried to hold onto every moment with him as tightly as possible, they slipped through my fingers like water.

Time flies like the wheel.

When he died, time stopped for a few seconds. Just a few. For the first time in my life, the wheel stopped turning. I stood over his grave, surrounded on all sides by people I'd known my whole life: people from the village, a smattering of cousins, Mariah from down the laneway, with her white-streaked hair and stern expression.

Even Cael had come, silent and distant as always, his eyes heavy on me. He wore his best shirt, undyed linen that I'd spun myself. The pale yellow-gray contrasted sharply with his tawny brown skin.

But in those few seconds at my father's grave, those people didn't exist. Nothing existed. Not the air or the heat of the sun or our distant daydream of the seaside. The wheel stopped, and the only thing in the world was that hole in the ground and the hole in my heart.

Then the wheel resumed its turning, and my heart kept beating. And that afternoon, I went home to an empty house. My father's spinning wheel sat near the window, the distaff still half full of flax.

My wheel sat a little ways off. I'd finished my last skein of thread a few days ago and hadn't started a new one. I'd been using that wheel for years. I knew it like I knew my own hands. But those few seconds of stopped time in the graveyard had changed everything.

That was the wheel of my childhood, and that was over now.

So I sat down by the window, in the padded chair my father had promised I'd grow into. I dipped my fingers into the little bowl of water and began peddling.

Left right, left right. Treadle, treadle. Draft. Twist. *Shhh!*

But though the wheel turned, all joy had gone out of it.

Two

"Aurora?"

I jumped, sucking in a harsh breath of surprise. Morning sun streamed in through the sheer curtains and the open door. I must have fallen asleep in my father's chair.

Cael stood near the front door, his hat in his hands. Our farm hand, the one we'd taken on when we'd expanded into two new fields. He'd always been this distant, beautiful thing on the far side of the yard, a private daydream just for me. I used to watch him from this very window as he bundled up the flax to dry in tidy little towers or stood staring at the sunset.

Except now he wasn't in the field. He was in my house. I hadn't even heard him come in. He was taller than most, lean and strong from working in the fields his whole life. His dark eyes always hit me first, more than his size or his demeanor. Eyes like coals ready to light at the first spark.

I sat up a little straighter on my father's chair—no, on *my* chair. I had fallen asleep at the window, my feet on the treadles of the spinning wheel. I pulled my long braid around and began undoing it. I'd never thought much of my hair, mouse brown and boring. But my father had always loved it. "Like dark flax," he'd say.

"Did you sleep at all?" Cael asked.

I'd never seen his hands so empty. He usually had a plow or a scythe. A simple wool cap felt so small in his hands. So insignificant.

I scrubbed at my eyes and sat up a little straighter, rebraiding my hair. My back groaned in complaint at having slept in an upright chair. "A bit."

"We need to talk about the farm," Cael said. He shifted his weight from one foot to the other, and the floorboard creaked under his bulk. He was such a big man, arms thick as tree trunks after years of working in the fields.

My heart clenched at his words. The farm. All I had left. The wheel never stopped, not even for death. I nodded rapidly. "Yes. I suppose so."

"Autumn is nearly gone," Cael went on, wringing his cap between his hands. "The harvest has been soaked and dried, but it still needs scutching before it gets too cold to work outside. It should only take me a month to get through it all on my own."

I continued nodding as he rattled off the chores. I couldn't stop staring at the way he manhandled his cap. Twisting, folding, turning, over and over and over again.

"What's wrong?" I asked.

His hands froze, and he caught my eye. His eyebrows gathered in a tight bundle on his sun-darkened brow, dirt collected in the creases of his skin. His mouth pulled downward into a tight frown.

"What's bothering you, Cael?" I said again, a bit more strongly this time. My heart picked up its pace, sending adrenaline all through my body.

Whatever was on his mind, not now. Not today. Not the day after I buried my father. Please, just say everything's fine and go start scutching the flax. Come in for lunch like every other day.

"Aurora," he said, his voice low, but he couldn't continue.

I closed my eyes to brace myself. "Just say it."

"I won't be back for the sowing come spring."

For the second time in two days, the wheel stopped. Everything stopped. His words echoed in my mind again and again. *I won't be back. I won't be back.*

"I've been saving up these past two years," he continued, shifting his weight again. "Last week, I bought the field behind my house, and your father gave me a bag of seed to start working it. My own field, Aurora. My own—" His voice broke off, and silence fell between us. Smothering, aching silence.

"You can have this farm," I found myself saying. "You can have these fields. I don't want them."

He shook his head over my words. "No. This is your farm, Aurora."

"I don't want it."

"Then sell it," he said.

"I'll sell it to you."

"I can't afford it."

"I don't want it!" I said again, my voice growing more and more frantic. "I can't do it alone! I don't want it!"

Cael took three steps forward and pulled me out of the chair. I tripped over my father's wheel, and he caught me in his strong hands. His arms went around me, and for half a second, I froze.

Cael was touching me. He was holding me. At most, I'd only ever brushed his fingers when passing him a plate or a tool. I'd daydreamed of how his chest would feel, the warmth and the solidity of it. Of feeling his heartbeat under my cheek and smelling the sun on his clothes.

What a cruel twist of fate that this should be the time it finally happened. That the moment would be rooted in grief and loneliness and pain.

"You're not alone, Aurora," he said, his voice rumbling through my skin.

I nodded vaguely. He was right. I knew that. Cael only lived about twenty minutes away by foot, and Mariah only ten minutes in the opposite direction. I had friends in town, contacts in the auction house, and several dozen acquaintances that would undoubtedly lend a hand if I asked. I'd lived in Barano my entire life. One could never truly be alone in a small farming town.

But even so, the ache remained. The emptiness, the loneliness.

My fingers clutched around wads of his shirt, and the tears came. Great, wracking sobs that sent spasms through my whole body. I had been crying for days, it felt like, but not like this. Not this upturning of the world.

"Shh," he said gently. "You're not alone."

After a few minutes, when breath came easier and my face relaxed a little, I stepped away. He let his arms fall to his sides, his wool cap held casually in one hand. No more wringing and twisting.

"My father didn't love spinning like I do," I said with a throaty voice. "Flax was his mother's trade, and he grew up with it. To him, it was just a job. A way to make money. And with prices rising these past couple of years, he really thought we'd make it big, finally."

"Your father loved this farm," Cael said.

"Of course he did," I replied. "This was his home. These were his fields."

"It wasn't just a job to him," Cael insisted.

"Look," I said, moving toward the desk on the far wall. I pulled a heavy, leather ledger toward me, the page already open to the latest date. I ran my hands over the neat columns and rows filled with my father's handwriting. "He obsessed over these books. Every night, he sat for hours going over them, talking about our future, about our profits."

"Hours?" Cael asked, but I ignored him.

"He hoped to buy two more fields next year. And two more the year after that. To employ not only field hands, but spinners too. And he talked about building a workhouse for weaving. He had such big plans. We wanted to visit the seaside." But with the last word, the dream of a sunset over water faded to almost nothing. How could I ever go without him?

With a bitter frown, I snapped the ledger shut. I wouldn't have to open it again until Cael finished scutching this year's harvest. Not until his last day on the farm.

"You don't have to do any of that," Cael said. "You don't even have to think about what to do right now. You have a huge harvest, plenty to prep and spin and sell. You can hire someone in the spring. I'll help you." He stepped closer and put a hand on my arm.

I jumped at his touch. His face swam into focus before me.

He squeezed my arm. "Are you all right?" he asked.

"Of course she's not all right, you idiot!" announced a voice in the doorway.

I'd know that consternated tone anywhere. Mariah, the doctor that lived down the laneway. She'd been a close family friend since before I was born and had come nearly every day when my father was sick, to help me care for him. I should have expected her to come check on me this morning.

Mariah hadn't changed in all the years I'd known her. She'd always had that same heavy streak of gray through her black hair, the same frown lines, the same twinkling eyes. And despite her years, she still ran about town like a young woman.

"That woman has too much energy," my father liked to say when Mariah strode past our house on some unknown mission into town.

Mariah popped the fragile, happy memory like a soap bubble by barreling on as usual. "She's just lost her father! What did you expect, boy? A parade?"

Cael scowled at the older woman and let his hand drop from my arm. "Of course not."

"I'm all right, Mariah," I said in a low voice.

"No, you're not," she insisted. She scraped the mud off her boots on the front step before stomping inside like she owned the place. "When was the last time you ate something?"

I hesitated, unsure. "I..."

"If you have to think that hard about it, it's been too long," she said with finality. She plonked a covered milk crate down on the sideboard. "Here. I've brought you some cold ham, a crock of beans, and some fresh sourdough. Straight from the oven this morning. The beans are from yesterday, but they'll go down just the same. And a tin of cake."

Mariah began unloading the milk crate, then paused to stare at Cael. "Don't you have chores to get to?"

"Mariah," I began, but Cael cut me off.

"No, it's fine," he said. "She's right. I'd better get to work."

He held my eyes for three full seconds.

One.

Two.

Three.

Then he turned and slipped out of the door with a creak of floorboards and a satisfied sniff from Mariah.

A few weeks—just as long as it took for one man to scrape the fibers out of one barn's worth of dried flax stalks. Then he'd be gone.

"Here," Mariah said, passing me a bowl of cold beans with a bit of bread.

I accepted the food and scooped a spoonful into my mouth. Even cold, Mariah's cooking would outrank anyone else in town. It was something about the way she smoked the pork. Not quite sweet, but almost.

Mariah watched me eat, hands on hips. Her expression melted from consternation to worry. "It's awful shit what happened, love," she said. "Losing your father like that."

Some hideous, half-dead part of me let out a laugh at her phrasing. She always knew how to say the wrong thing in just the right way. But it was too soon. The sadness swallowed up the laugh almost immediately.

Mariah's half-formed smile melted, and she wiped under one eye before her own grief could take hold. She loved my father too. Probably second only to me. They had been best friends since childhood and had been as close to me as family for all my life.

Mariah squeezed my shoulder and sniffed again. "I'll stay a couple days. Help you finish your pickling and whatnot. Get your winter garden going. You still getting eggs?"

I swallowed hard and nodded, thinking suddenly of the hens probably desperate to get outside by this time. I had forgotten about them.

"Good, good," Mariah said. "Sounds like we got plenty to keep us busy."

The next few weeks passed in a blur. Mariah pushed me hard, preparing the house for winter. We filled up my larder with jars of beans, jams, and preserves, all lined up in tidy rows on the narrow shelves. We cleared out the old potatoes in the cellar and restocked it with apples, salt, and grain.

And when we ran out of things to do in the house, Mariah dragged me out to the barn to help Cael scutch the flax. We took it one step each. Cael beat the dried stalks with paddles to break up the stems, his muscled arms glistening with sweat in the afternoon sun. Mariah combed out the shorter, lower quality tow fibers. I threw the long, desirable line fibers on the hackle—a series of combs that separated out the last of the chaff.

It was hard work, but Mariah was right to make me do it. My mind dwelled on the soreness of my arms, the growing calluses in my hands, the pricks on my fingers from the sharp hackle. I rarely thought of my father and the empty house, or the dwindling pile of dried flax that Cael was working through.

When that pile was completely finished, he'd leave. Mariah would leave. I'd be alone.

No, Aurora. Don't think of that.

I pulled a handful of fibers through the finest hackle, shining and sturdy. These I twisted into a coil—a strick ready for spinning—and added it to the growing pile on my left.

I should be spinning. I should be spending my evenings turning these stricks into thread. Or at least, I should be selling this fiber to someone else to spin. I should be doing something.

But I wasn't. I couldn't bear to even look at the prepped fiber. Just the sight of it brought back the hole in my heart where my father had been.

Every night, Cael and I loaded a cart full of prepped flax fibers into burlap bags for storage. These we piled up in a large closet in the back of the house.

And every night, I shut that door and turned my back on it.

And every night, Cael hesitated by the front door as the sun sank in the west, until Mariah shooed him away home.

It was better that way. If he was going to leave me when the scutching was done, then he should just go.

Day by day, the pile of dried flax dwindled, until one afternoon, Cael scraped up the very last few stalks off the canvas, broke up the stems, and passed them to me to comb. Then he folded up the canvass and placed it on a shelf on the back wall to be used again next year.

I refused to look at him while I dragged the flax through the hackles. Throw, pull. Throw, pull. Until the fibers lay long and straight. I twisted them up into a bundle and placed it with the rest. A golden-brown mound of shining fiber, just waiting to be used.

A cart full of stricks like this used to fill me with joy. They were beautiful, all tidy and ready to go. A beginning to a new batch of spinning. Proof that we had worked hard all year and had been successful.

But now, all I could see was my father's life's work moving on without him.

THREE

That night, the three of us ate dinner together at my dining table, a ghost of the celebrations we'd have at seasons end in previous years. Cael helped Mariah cook while I loaded the last bags of flax into the closet. They made pork pies with mushrooms, carrots, and peas. And while they baked, we played a round of cards, sipping on a dusty old bottle of wine my father had brought home from the capital in his younger days.

We ate in silence. Not even Mariah could think of something sharp to say.

Afterward, she wrapped herself up in her heavy shawl and hugged me tight. "Are you sure you'll be all right alone tonight, love?" she asked. "Now we're all done, that is."

I gave her my best smile and waved the half-empty bottle of wine at her. "Don't worry about me. I've got company."

She laughed, for a moment sounding like her old self. She patted my arm and opened the door. A blast of cold wind pushed in around her. "Don't you keep her up too late boy," she called over her shoulder. "It's already started snowing. You should get home, too."

"I'm coming, Mariah," Cael said in a patient tone.

She cast him one disbelieving look and pulled the door shut behind her.

Cael and I stood in the empty house, the silence beating in around us. I twisted my fingers together around the neck of the wine bottle.

Finally, I could bear the quiet no longer. "Thank you for all your help this season."

Cael nodded away my thanks. "In the spring, let me know when you're ready to hire a new field hand. I'll help you find someone. Show them how things run around here."

"Okay. I will."

He nodded again, eyebrows furrowed, just like that day three weeks ago when he'd told me he was leaving. Then he took a step forward, hands up as if to reach for me. "I had a plan, Aurora," he said in fervent tones.

"What?"

"I had a plan. I *have* a plan. To make something of myself, to prove to myself that I can stand on my own two feet."

"Okay?" I said, unsure.

"When you grow up like I did in the workhouse..." he pressed on, his eyes darting around the floor at my feet. "When you're beat down and told you're nothing, day after day, it gets easy to believe it. But your father, he took me in. He gave me work, taught me a trade. I owe it to him—to myself to make something that is my own."

"I know, Cael."

He closed the last of the distance between us, actually taking my hand in his. I stared at our hands in shock.

"So, you understand?" he asked. "It breaks my heart to leave you here like this. You weren't supposed to be here alone. Your father...But I have to do this. I have to go, Aurora."

It took several long seconds for his words to find meaning, but with understanding came the slow burn of hope.

"What are you saying?" I asked.

"Aurora," he breathed.

I tightened my grip on his hand. "Speak plain, Cael," I said. "Don't make me guess or assume. What are you saying to me?"

He took another step closer, his chest heaving in and out as he searched for words. "I care about you, Aurora," he said. "I—"

But that was all the confirmation I needed. I leaned up on my toes and kissed him. He sucked in a breath of surprise, but after a second's hesitation, his fingers threaded into my hair, and he kissed me back.

I put everything into that kiss. My daydreams as I watched him in the pink glow of a sunset in the flax fields. The happiness I used to have before my father died. My hope for a little light, a little love.

And as he wrapped me up in his arms, pressed me close against his body, and kissed me with all he had, I thought for a few seconds that I might get it. That this might be it—the light and happiness that I had lost in the past few weeks. It swelled in my chest like an ember that finally caught the dry tinder and burst into flame.

But then Cael stopped the kiss and held me away from him, breathing hard.

I stared up at him, confused. "What is it?" I asked.

"It's too soon," he said.

"Too soon?" I said.

"Your father just died. You're not thinking straight."

"What does my father have to do with how I feel about you?" I asked.

He shook his head. "You're grieving. You're lonely."

I grabbed the front of his shirt in both hands. "I've wanted this for years," I said, and I leaned up to kiss him again.

But he leaned away, and the fire in my chest fizzled.

"I have a plan, Aurora."

"What, for your farm?" I asked, even more confused.

He put my hands away from him, and the ember went out completely.

"I have to make something of myself. I have to do this on my own."

"Do *what* on your own? Live alone? Why?" The ember turned to ice in my chest, jagged, painful, and cold.

"You don't understand what it was like for me growing up," he said. "I need this, Aurora. I need to build something for myself. Where I don't owe anybody anything."

"You owe my father," I spat.

"I earned everything your father gave me," Cael shot back, his voice cold.

I shrank away half a step. My heart pounded in my chest with an anger that I didn't know how to quantify. It vibrated in my fingers, took away my breath, drew up my top lip. It took away all reason, all caution.

Cael advanced a little, hands raised in a placating gesture. "Aurora, please. You're upset. These things you're feeling for me, they're not real."

"Don't you dare tell me what I'm feeling, Cael!" I shouted. "As if you're some expert!" Mariah's mostly empty wine glass caught my eye, and I dove for it before I could think.

"Aurora..." He ducked as the wine glass hurled through the air at his head. It shattered on the wall behind him, splattering glass shards and deep purple droplets all over him.

Cael stared at me, at a loss. "Your father wouldn't have wanted..."

"Don't talk about my father! You don't know what he would have wanted." I pointed toward the door with a shaking finger. "You want to leave so badly, then go!" When he still didn't move toward the door, I jabbed with my finger and screamed again. "Get out, Cael!"

This time, he didn't hesitate. He grabbed his cap and coat off the hook and slammed the door behind him.

The empty house closed in around me. My anger filled it up. Anger, confusion, grief, rejection. It vibrated through my body and into the house around me. The lamplight glowed too brightly. The fire burned too hot. The buzzing in my ears drowned out the silence.

I careened from one corner to the next. To the bed. *No, can't sleep.* To the wheel. *No, can't spin. Can't sit.* To the sideboard. *No, can't eat.* I raised the half-full bottle of wine to my lips, but the memory of Cael's wine-soaked breath nauseated me. I shrieked and threw the bottle to the ground, where the contents gurgled out onto the woolen rug. The purple stain spread like blood over the simple striped pattern, and that made me even angrier.

My father had left me. Mariah had left me. Cael had left me. The only thing I had was a closet full of flax and that gods damned spinning wheel.

I couldn't breathe. I couldn't think. Couldn't stand to look at my wheel or my bed or my ruined rug. I crammed my feet into my boots and stumbled out the front door and onto the frigid porch. The cold air brought instant relief. It smacked into my skin and brought back a little clarity. For a second, I could think again.

Breathe, Aurora. Just breathe!

I glanced back at the warm lamplight spilling out of my front door. My father's house. The place where Cael had wrapped me up in his arms and kissed me—then pushed me away.

I staggered down the front steps, away from the life I should have had, and out into the thickly falling snow. It already dusted the yard and coated the roofs of the various buildings around the house: the main barn, various sheds, and the coop. The fields stretched out to the south, nearly purple in the early twilight.

My farm. Mine. My entire world, all visible from where I stood in our front yard. The boundaries of my life came closing in just like the walls of my house. I had to get out, had to get away.

My feet began moving to the east toward the dusky tree line on the border of our property, the snow crunching under my boots. I stumbled past the sturdy elms and oaks, past the little creek that fed our irrigation system, and toward the great boulder I used to lie on and daydream when I was a little girl.

Maybe it was the gathering snow or my desperation, or the angry tears that blinded me, but the boulder wasn't where it should have been. I paused, turning this way and that. Maybe I had gone a little too far north. I veered to the right and continued on, but all the landmarks I expected never appeared.

The snow fell in heavy swaths through the bare tree limbs, reflecting the last of the twilight so that everything stood out in sharp detail.

I stopped again and turned a complete circle. These were the right trees. I was sure of it. Elms, oaks, hickories. Towering sycamores and squat little dogwoods. All naked for the winter. Sleeping, silent. The snow rustled down, encasing everything in peaceful stillness.

These were definitely the right trees. And yet...

"Why do you cry?"

I whirled around with a choking gasp. "Who's there?"

My eyes darted from tree to tree, peering through the snowfall. The last of the evening sun, diffused through the heavy clouds, bounced off of everything, illuminating every branch and twig in the semi-darkness.

Nothing. There was no one.

"'Tis only I," said the voice again, smooth and cool as ice.

Four long fingers appeared around a hickory tree about ten feet away. They wrapped around the rough bark slowly, lying down one at a time with graceful precision. And then, from behind the same tree appeared a face.

At first glance, it appeared to be the face of a young woman. Smooth complexion, long delicate nose, pert mouth. Her flowing hair was only a few shades darker than her ice-white skin, pulled back into an efficient braid that would have looked boring on anyone else.

And yet, something about that face set my heart racing. My palms began to sweat, despite the biting cold.

As the figure came fully into view, that unknown uneasiness solidified into fact. She was too tall. Impossibly tall. She towered at least ten feet high, with long, narrow proportions. Her sheer, sleeveless dress showed off her lean figure in every incredible detail. It hung about her in tatters—ripped, torn, and worn through to almost nothing.

Not human. Not human.

I backed up a step.

This was not human, but one of the Old Kind. A creature of magic long gone. I didn't have to go to the seaside to meet one after all. Here one stood, right in front of me in my own woods.

"I've gone mad," I breathed, taking another step backward.

The creature smiled kindly down at me. "No, child. You are not mad."

"What are you?" I asked in a shaking voice.

She bowed her head in greeting. "I am called the Weaver. What is your name?"

I couldn't take my eyes off her. "Aurora."

She extended one long hand toward me. "Come, Aurora, and tell me why you cry."

Every instinct screamed at me to run. All my life I'd heard warnings about the Old Kind, crones, sibyls, unnatural children, and witches. *"Beware, beware!"* they all said. *"Run!"*

And yet, my feet stayed planted in the slowly gathering snow. What did I possibly have left to lose?

"My father died," I said. "And the man who I thought...Well, he left me too."

The Weaver frowned in compassion. "Poor little thing," she said. "That is very hard."

I nodded.

She held out her hand to me again, and this time, I took it. Her skin was pleasantly warm against my fingers. But this time, when my instincts screamed *"Run,"* the warmth of her hand smothered the fear like a familiar blanket. All pain fled. All sadness. And in its wake came relief. For the first time in more than a month, I felt okay.

Blissful emptiness.

The Weaver's hand became an anchor, and all the uncertainties melted away. I let myself revel in the fact that—for right now—I didn't have to be sad anymore. Deep down, I knew she must be bewitching me, but I didn't care anymore.

"You live on that farm there?" The Weaver pointed with her free hand, and between the trees, my farm materialized, snow-blanketed and familiar.

"Yes. We grow flax."

"You're a spinner," the Weaver confirmed.

"How did you know?"

"I have been watching you, little Aurora," the Weaver said. "Your sadness has been calling to me. I wish to help you. And maybe you can help me too."

"How?"

The Weaver held out the tattered folds of her dress. Where the layers gathered the thickest, a faint glow could be seen coming from the thin material.

"My cloak is very old," she said. "The time has come to make a new one. But I need thread."

"Can you not spin it yourself?" I asked.

She shook her head sadly. "No. Only human hands can spin the thread for my cloak. It is the balance of my magic, that I must rely on the kindness of man. I will pay for your work by granting a wish. Perhaps I can make your man come back to you. The handsome worker."

"No," I said sharply. "No. Love is given freely. I will not ask you to force him."

She bowed her head. "You are very wise, child."

An image of my father's ledger books flashed through my

mind. All the plans he had for us. The weaving house, the extra fields. Our visit to the sea. Bounty he would never get to see. "Money," I said. "Riches. I want to be wealthy."

The Weaver smiled, sending a tingle down my spine. She released the folds of her dress and turned her hand over, revealing several ingots of shining gold the size of plum stones in her palm. "Very well," she said. "I will provide you with my own wheel for one year and one day. And for every fifty yards of thread you spin on it, I will pay you an ingot of pure gold. You may have these now, to seal the bargain. Free and clear."

She extended the fistful of gold toward me, but I hesitated. She still held my hand softly, warmth and safety radiating from her touch. The snow fell on my exposed skin like gentle brushes, no trace of cold at all.

Somewhere deep down, where my body remembered I stood in the snow with no cloak, with a magical creature trying to bargain with me, I heard my father's voice. *"Go home, Aurora."*

And Cael's voice too. *"Go home, Aurora. Go spin your flax, and in the spring, I'll help you hire someone new."*

"Time flies like the wheel, Aurora."

No. Not this time. Everyone had left me. They didn't get to tell me what to do anymore. This time, I decided. And it was time for the wheel to stop. Time for me to break away from this crushing sadness. This was my way out.

"A year and a day?"

The Weaver nodded, her smile growing.

I extended my hand, and she poured the heavy gold into my palm. Five lumpy ingots. More than I could earn in a year from selling my linen. I stared at them, amazed.

"Why your wheel?" I asked, slipping them into my pocket. "Why can't I use my own?"

"It is a special wheel. It will help you produce finer thread than any human is capable of. I need the very best to weave my cloak." The Weaver ran her hand over her tattered dress longingly. A shimmer followed in the wake of her hand, the last traces of an old magic nearly worn out.

My eyes followed the shimmer as it rippled through the fabric. It glowed like the moonlight on the snow, like starlight in a cloudless sky. Like the gold in my pocket.

"When shall I start?" I asked.

But only silence met my words. I looked up at the empty, snowy forest around me. The Weaver had gone, just as swiftly as she had arrived. No footprints marred the snow, and my hand had gone cold once more. I examined the tree she had stood next to and the snow on the ground. Nothing.

FOUR

"A dream," I breathed. "Only a dream." I was exhausted. Or drunk. Maybe both. Too much wine, too much confusion.

I turned to my left, and there stood my farm. Only a few trees stood between me and the south field. I had gotten so turned around. I'd only dreamed of getting lost and meeting one of the Old Kind in the woods. I'd just gone a little ways south. The snow could be so disorienting.

My shoulders slouched, and I tucked my cold hands into my pockets. But when the fingers of my right hand brushed something warm and hard inside, I jerked my hands back out. Tentatively, I drew out the shining gold ingots.

They were real. Right there, in my hands, The Weaver's gold shone in the moonlight that glowed through the clouds.

With a jolt of anticipation, I clutched the gold in one hand and ran toward the house. I threw the door open without bothering to kick the snow off my boots and went straight to my wine-soaked rug. The sweet, acrid smell hit my nostrils, but I no longer cared about the stain or the mess. My eyes fell on the spinning wheel that stood in the center of the room.

The Weaver's wheel was made entirely of glass. The treadle, the wheel, the flier—all of it perfectly clear, beautifully blown glass. Not a bubble or imperfection anywhere. The legs and distaff looked like pristine icicles freshly plucked from the eaves. The wheel, with its delicate spindles, shone in the lamplight, casting shadows and glimmers all around the room.

I moved toward it, unsure. The Weaver had said it was special. This must have been what she meant. The wheel was utterly beautiful. Delicate, clear, otherworldly. I touched it with the barest fingertip, expecting it to be cold as ice. Cold enough to bite.

But it was cool only. Unremarkable. Slick and perfect. I ran my fingers down the knobs of the distaff, then turned the flier experimentally. It spun easily, dragging the main wheel around a tenth of a turn. The refracted lamplight swung around the room in perfect time with the wheel.

My fingers traveled downward over the mother-of-all, to the table. There, stored on delicate spindles, sat four empty bobbins waiting to be filled. All of it, perfect glass.

Judging by The Weaver's tattered dress, I'd have to spin my finest thread. Doing a few quick sums in my head, I judged I could earn at least two of The Weaver's gold ingots per day. After a year and a day, that would be...

By all the gods in heaven. Even if I only spun a few days a week, after this year I'd never have to work again. I could build my father's fabric empire, or I could do something else. Anything. I could travel, or buy a fancy house in Valheid, or stay here and do nothing at all. I could go south and spend the rest of my life sea bathing and eating crabs with lemon.

With shaking hands, I ran to the storage closet at the back of the house and selected a strick of flax from the topmost bag. I spread it out on the worktable in a delicate fan. I gently removed the glass distaff from its socket and dressed it with the prepared flax, tying it all up with a long, blue ribbon with a pattern of roses.

Then I lit all the lamps I had, dragged my father's chair—no, *my* chair. I dragged *my* chair over to the glass wheel and inserted the first bobbin into the flier. I tied a new leader onto it, attached my first strands of flax, and began treadling.

Treadle, treadle. Draft, twist. Shhh!

The fiber snaked away from the distaff and toward the wheel, guided by my expert hands. And as it slid past my fingers, it happened. That beautiful glow, the shine of moonlight on snow, infused the fiber. It glowed twenty times brighter than The Weaver's old cloak. Full of life, joy, and spirit. Fresh, new magic.

It slipped around the guide hooks and began wrapping around the bobbin in a glowing filament, finer and smoother than I thought I could produce. Too perfect, too beautiful. The Weaver had been right. This glass wheel did make all the difference. I'd never be able to spin like this on my father's—on my wheel.

I spun for several hours, entranced by how easy it was. Even when the odd snarl came off the distaff, as soon as it passed through my fingers, it smoothed out into a perfect, glistening thread. I didn't have to stop or adjust, didn't have to wet my fingers and correct. It just worked. I fell into an easy pattern, eyes on the window as snow fell in steady drifts.

But eventually, the fire burned low, and my eyes grew heavy. I'd been spinning into the early hours of the morning after a hard day's work. Had we only just eaten our end-of-season dinner a few hours ago?

Finally, I let the glass wheel slide to a stop, and I got up, stretching, to crawl into bed. I walked right through the wet, wine-soaked rug without pausing and went to sleep.

It took me two days to finish the first skein of thread. I spun from dawn till late in the night, stopping only to eat and care for the chickens. I marveled in its glow as I washed the completed yarn in the basin.

Usually, I'd boil a skein in wood ash to soften it, but The Weaver's thread didn't need it. I ran my hands over it, already soft as the finest silk.

Usually, I'd hang thread outside to dry, but not now. This thread would catch the eye of anyone who happened to walk by. Thread wasn't supposed to glow. So instead, I hung it up over my bath to catch the drips and stood back to admire it.

That right there was worth two ingots of gold. A year's worth of income in just two days.

I put my hands on my hips but jerked them away with a hiss of pain. A sharp ache ran up my hands when I bent them too far in the wrong direction. I'd been spinning too long.

"Time for a break," I said with a sigh.

And so began my routine. Two days of spinning followed by a day's worth of housework and rest. And aside from a little aching in my hands toward the end of a round of spinning, everything seemed to fall into place very easily.

About two weeks after I began spinning for The Weaver, Mariah came striding up my laneway. I saw her from the window as I sat spinning and instantly went into a panic. Mariah would never approve of a deal with one of the Old Kind. She wouldn't understand.

I scampered to the table and snatched up three skeins of glowing linen thread and threw them into the cupboard. Then I ran to the bed and hastily draped a sheet over the glass wheel, careful to remove the fragile distaff and lay it on the ground first. The dense linen completely obscured the glowing thread on the bobbin just as the heavy *thunk thunk!* of Mariah's snow-covered boots against the lintel rang through the house.

"Hello, my dear," Mariah said as she strode inside. "I just wanted to check on you, see how things were doing."

"Hello, Mariah," I said, still breathing hard. "How are you?"

She stared at me, eyes narrowed at my lost breath. Then her eyes darted to the lumpy object hidden under my sheet by the window where my father's wheel usually sat. "What are you doing? What's that?"

She strode forward, one hand extended to uncover the wheel, but I stepped in front of her, causing her to stop short.

"It's just a project I'm working on," I said.

"May I see?"

"No."

She glanced over at my father's wheel, which now stood by the back wall. She had no way of knowing that the flax on it was nearly two months old now. I hadn't touched it since the day we'd buried him.

"Have you been working?" she asked.

"Yes," I answered truthfully. "Probably too much." I shook out my hands, trying to ease the low ache that never quite went away anymore.

"You shouldn't be alone like this," Mariah said. "Not every day. Have you considered taking a boarder? Maybe Cael could..."

"No!" I said sharply.

Mariah cut her eyes at me, then finished her sentence with grim judgment. "...could help you fix up your father's room to make it ready to rent."

I shifted my weight, unable to meet her eye. Why wouldn't she just leave? The glass wheel called to me, the flax ready to go. I needed to get her out of here.

"What is going on with you two, by the way?" Mariah asked. "I noticed plenty of sideways glances when we were doing the scutching. It was rather hot in the barn as the two of you beat the ever-loving shit out of that flax to release the fibers. And I'm not talking about the weather."

"Mariah!" I barked, my face coloring.

She ignored me and powered on. "You're welcome for that, by the way. I'm not a farmer, you know. I'm a doctor."

"Everyone's a farmer here," I said. "You just don't sell your crops."

"No, I eat them!" she said stoutly. "And sometimes, I bring

them to you. And sometimes, I help you scutch your flax. What is wrong with you, Aurora? Is it your father?"

I sniffed heavily. I hadn't thought of my father once in the last two weeks. All I could think of was the glass wheel. I should be spinning right now. I shook out my hands again, stretching them forward, backward, bending my wrists as far as they would go to ease the soreness.

"What's wrong with your hands?" she asked.

"Nothing," I said, relaxing my arms. "Like I said, I've been spinning too much."

"You need to take care of yourself, girl," she said. "I'll bring you some tinctures to help with the pain tomorrow."

"I just need time, Mariah," I said. I took her by the arm in as comforting a way as I could. "I'm fine. You don't need to worry about me."

She let me guide her to the door. Her usually sharp expression softened to worry and compassion. Her mouth turned down at the corners. "Aurora..."

"I'm fine, Mariah. I promise. Thank you for stopping by."

And I shut the door in her face. A pang of guilt made my heart skip. I'd just sent Mariah away, my father's oldest friend. *My* oldest friend. I'd just kicked her out of my house.

But as the knock of her boots moved away from the door and down the steps, followed by the crunch of snow, I felt only relief. I moved to the cupboard and pulled out the three shining skeins of linen. These I laid out gently on the table so that I could see them from my chair.

And then I carefully uncovered the glass wheel and replaced the distaff in its socket. Then I sat down and resumed spinning.

Mariah came back every week after that. I'd see her coming from my window, and I'd run to hide away the evidence of what I was doing. Then I'd get rid of her as fast as I could before she could comment on the state of my house, which grew steadily worse as the project wore on.

My resting days shrunk to nothing. At first, I'd spend half the day on the housework and take the rest of the time to rest. Then, after about a month, I'd stop resting and simply resume spinning after the housework was done. Then, a few weeks after that, I started doing only the bare minimum around the house so I could get back to the wheel as quickly as possible. I cleaned just enough dishes so that I could eat again and ignored the growing clutter completely.

Every moment I spent spinning meant more gold. More success. This would be the only opportunity I'd ever get in my entire life to make money like this. I couldn't waste even a single minute.

And if ever I started to doubt my logic, I'd simply get out the five gold nuggets The Weaver had given me. I laid them out on the windowsill in an orderly row and let their shine fill me with renewed purpose.

Mariah eyed the towers of dishes, the haphazard piles of clothes and tools and rubbish. But I'd always shoo her out again like an angry goose before she could start in on me. After a while, tired of hearing her scolding and worrying about the state of me and my house, I stopped answering the door when she knocked. And after that, she stopped knocking altogether. She simply came, dropped off a milk crate of fresh bread and smoked pork, then turned around and left again.

Weeks turned to months, and I barely noticed. All I could think about was the glass wheel and the steadily growing pile of glowing linen thread. I emptied the contents of my wardrobe out into the corner and instead used the shelves to store the thread in orderly rows. I twisted them into tidy hanks to prevent tangling and laid them side by side.

I liked to stare at the thread. Something about it eased the ache in my arms. It brought a little light back into the darkness that crowded in at the corners. They were beautiful, glowing with life and vitality.

The Weaver would be pleased. Her new cloak would be glorious.

FIVE

Cael came back in spring, just like he'd promised. I saw him from my window, trudging up through the last of the muddy snow. He was as broad as I remembered, just as rugged and strong. The sight of him triggered a pang of longing that I had entirely forgotten about.

I froze at the glass wheel, unsure of what to do. I had fallen into an easy routine with Mariah. I didn't have to speak to her at all. She didn't even try anymore. But Cael would be different. As determined as Mariah was, she could be held back. Cael? He didn't take no for an answer.

In a panic, I ran to hide the wheel the way I used to do with Mariah. I laid the distaff on the ground to keep it safe, then draped my sheet over the whole thing. I closed the doors of my wardrobe, hiding the glow of the finished linen, then moved toward the kitchen and began nervously straightening up.

Not that it would do any good. I needed several hours of dedicated scrubbing to get this place in order.

Cael paused at the threshold, fresh, spring air blowing in around him. He stared around at my house, which I realized was in shambles.

"Hello, Cael," I said without turning around. I stretched out my arm to relieve the aching that had crept up from my hands toward my shoulders. Even my ankles had started complaining from all the treadling, but it would all be worth it when The Weaver bought my linen.

"Hello again, Aurora," he answered. "I'm just stopping by to see how you're doing. It'll be time for the sowing soon. Have you started looking for a new field hand?"

"Oh, uh," I hesitated, reaching for another dish. "No, not yet. I will soon."

"Aurora," he said.

I stayed facing the sink, dipping my rag into the water and scrubbing the old beans off of a plate. "Yes?"

"Why won't you turn around?"

I put down my dishes and turned to face him with a pleasant smile. I wiped my hands on my apron and shrugged. "I'm just doing the dishes."

Cael gasped when he saw me. "Aurora, what's happened? Are you sick?"

I frowned. "No. Just a little sore. I've been spinning." I rolled my shoulders.

"Have you been eating?"

"Of course!" I gestured at the piles of dishes around me. But he couldn't know that these dishes were weeks old. I had taken to eating the cold, unseasoned vegetables directly out of the canning jars. It was faster, and I could get back to work.

He narrowed his eyes at me, taking in my jutting collar bone and the way my shirt hung off of me at least two sizes too big. I hadn't noticed these things until I saw the way he looked at me. I must have grown very thin over the past few months.

"Mariah's worried about you," Cael said. He ran his hand through his dark hair, looking around. "And now I can see why. I was giving you space after our argument, but that may have been a mistake. I shouldn't have left you alone for so long. I'm so sorry."

"You didn't give me space," I said, hackles rising. "I told you to leave."

He stared at me in shock at my outburst. "Aurora, what is wrong? Wait...what is that?" He moved toward the window, his boots clunking across the wood floor.

Horror dropped my stomach to the floor. The gold. I had left The Weaver's gold ingots laid out on the windowsill, where I could stare at them as I spun. I darted after him, more sluggish than I used to be. Maybe I'd been sitting too long. I'd grown weak.

I should really take time to eat. I couldn't spin if I wasted away to nothing.

"Is this gold?" Cael picked up one of the ingots and turned it over in his grubby palm, but I was right behind him.

I snatched it away from him and scooped up the rest.

"Gods, Aurora. You're cold as ice!" He grasped after my hands to feel my skin again, but I lurched away, clutching the gold to my body.

His expression darkened to confusion and dread.

"Aurora, what is going on here? Where did you get that gold? Why aren't you eating?"

And then, before I could answer or move or act in any way, his eyes fell on the lumpy shape under my sheet. And with zero hesitation, he snatched it off.

"No!" I cried. But my hands were full of gold, and I couldn't stop him.

He whipped the sheet away, and the glass wheel shimmered in the morning sunlight streaming in through the window. The bobbin was already mostly full with shining thread.

Cael backed up two steps and stared at it, his mouth open. "What is going on here?"

I dropped the gold, and it clattered to the floor. I grabbed Cael by the shirt and pushed him toward the door.

"Aurora!"

"Get out, Cael. I don't need you to check up on me."

He pushed against my hands, but I clung on with determination, steering him out.

"What is that wheel? Where did you get it from?"

"Get out!"

"Aurora!"

I slammed the door in his face and locked it.

He pounded on it in protest. "Aurora! Talk to me!"

I leaned my head against the door jam, eyes closed, and begged him silently to go away.

"Aurora!"

Go away! I need to spin!

"Aurora, I'm sorry, okay?" he called through the door. "I'm sorry I pushed you away. I shouldn't have done that. Just talk to me!"

My heart thumped with that half-remembered longing from before. An old memory of Cael at the far side of the field of golden flax, his hat in his hand, staring at a rose-colored sunset. I used to daydream about him. What had that feeling been? I used to know.

"I'm all right, Cael," I said.

Silence met this statement, except for a single thump against the door. Maybe his head hitting it in defeat.

"I'll eat. I promise."

"What is that wheel, Aurora?"

"I know what I'm doing. Go home. Plant your field."

He growled in frustration, and his boots scraped across the porch as he spun away. I watched him from the window as he strode away down the lane. But when he reached the road, he turned right instead of left.

He was going to Mariah's. I'd bet my left shoe. They'd both be back tomorrow. Maybe even tonight. I glanced at the glass wheel, jealous that someone else knew about it now. It was mine. My own. The linen that came off it was a part of me.

I opened the wardrobe and sighed as the glow of the thread hit me. The aches in my body eased immediately. I had completed seventy-two hanks of linen thread. Seventy-two in five months. If I worked hard, I could finish another hundred before my year was up. The sight of it filling up my wardrobe would be glorious. I could see it in my mind's eye, and the image brought a little smile to my chapped lips.

I no longer cared about the gold. I just wanted to spin.

"You can't spin if the healer and the farmer interfere," said a familiar, melodious voice. It whispered up the back of my neck.

I whirled around to find the house empty. But I felt her. The warmth, the peace. I could feel her hand on my shoulder.

"Is that you, Weaver?" I asked in a tremulous whisper.

"It is I," the voice responded. "I have been keeping watch over you, my child. Haven't you felt me?"

As she said the words, they became true in my head. Yes, she had been there all along, just out of sight. She had been keeping me safe and focused on my task.

"What should I do?" I asked.

"Shut the house," The Weaver responded confidently. "We have work to do. They cannot interfere."

The smile melted into determination. Yes, I'd shut up the house. I was a grown woman. They couldn't come into my house if I didn't want them to.

So I went around to every window and pulled the shutters to, latching them securely. I only left my spinning window open, which I could shut the moment someone started down my lane. Then I barred the front door with an upright chair, just in case the lock failed.

Once that was done, I honored my promise to Cael and lit the stove. I took the time to cook up a real pork pie that would last me a few days at least.

I felt much better with a full stomach. When I turned back to the main room, The Weaver's long face melted out of the darkness in the far corner. She was lighter than I remembered, like mist in the morning sun. She'd faded to almost nothing in the months since I saw her last.

She smiled kindly at me, as if she'd been there the whole time and I simply hadn't noticed.

"Hello," I said with an excited smile.

"Hello, child," she responded.

"Do you like the thread?" I asked, gesturing to the wardrobe.

"It is perfect. Thank you," she said.

She held out her long hand to me, and I hurried to take it. The second her skin touched mine, all the ache and uncertainty faded to nothing. Blissful nothing. I knelt before her, holding her hand tightly in my own.

The Weaver smiled again and stroked my hair. "We have work to do."

"Yes," I said.

I returned to the glass wheel with fresh determination and a clean conscience. I placed the distaff in its socket, wet my fingers in the bowl, and began treadling. The fibers slid through my fingers as easily as ever, trailing golden magic onto the bobbin, and I sighed in relief.

The Weaver nodded her approval and settled back into her corner, almost disappearing in the shadows.

Cael did come back the next day, just like he said. I slammed the shutters closed the second he turned down my lane and ran to the door to wait for his knock.

"Let me in, Aurora," he said.

I glanced at The Weaver once, and though she said nothing, I understood what she wanted me to do. "No."

"Where did you get that wheel?"

"It doesn't matter! Go home, Cael!"

He came again the next day.

"I wish you'd let me in," he said, his deep voice muffled through the door. "I wish you'd let me help you."

"I don't need help," I said.

He came again the next day and the day after that. He didn't care that I never unlocked the door or that I refused to answer his questions.

After a while, he stopped asking about the wheel. "Are you eating properly?"

"Yes." That was a lie. I never made a second pork pie after I finished the first, but maybe it was time I did. I'd gone back to eating cold veg out of the can, with a couple of baked eggs. My joints were so stiff, not just in my arms and legs, but everywhere. Cael was right. I needed to eat. Why did I keep forgetting?

He let out a heavy sigh. "I'll come back tomorrow. I hope you'll let me in."

I never did. All I could think about was spinning on the glass wheel and the warm touch of The Weaver's hand on my shoulder.

Every day, The Weaver grew a little more tangible. Sometimes, I turned around to find her at the wardrobe, dwarfing the room with her incredible height. She ran her translucent fingers over the glowing thread and sighed with delight.

During the day, she disappeared altogether, as if the light made her truly invisible. But I could feel her nearby, and her presence kept me focused on the task at hand.

But I was grateful to Cael, though. He came to the door every single day, forcing me to get up out of the chair. And once he left, I'd usually cook something since I was up anyway.

But then I'd sit back down and pick up the flax once more.

One day, a trickle of sweat ran down my brow. I wiped it away and stared at the moisture in awe. Was I hot?

I looked out the window at the overgrown field. Summer had come without me noticing. That field should be a sea of pale blue flax flowers, but I never hired someone to plant it. Not that it mattered. I never needed to spin again after this year. I could sell the whole place and let someone else farm it. I'd go south to the real ocean, just like Father had always talked about. Maybe see how it compared to a flax field in summer.

A small smile crept up the corner of my mouth, and I kept spinning.

But the problem with my constant spinning wasn't my aching body, my lack of sleep, or my steadily degrading living situation. It was the fact that I ran out of flax far sooner than I could have anticipated. One day in high summer, I went to the storage closet to get a new strick but found only cobwebs. I reached into the dark corners and even got a stool to check the highest shelf in a panic, but nothing. It was all used up. I had spun every last fiber that we'd harvested the year before.

I leaned back against the wall, my chest heaving breath in and out, in and out.

Just breathe, Aurora!

But I couldn't. I had to spin. I needed flax.

I looked for The Weaver in the darkest corners of the house. "Are you there?" I asked the empty room, but only silence met me.

Of course she didn't answer. It was full daylight.

I had to get flax. And with The Weaver unable to help me, I had to help myself. My first thought was the market in Barano. It was the wrong season for it, but one could reliably find at least a few stricks for sale somewhere. I could be there and back in under two hours.

I ran to the pile in the corner and dug out my cleanest shirt and pants, changed as fast as I could, and hauled on my boots. But I only made it about halfway down the laneway before the panic set in. My heart pounded against my ribs, and I couldn't catch my breath. It was like drowning in molasses. I fell to my hands and knees, gaping and gasping. The gravel dug into my skin, but I barely felt it.

I crawled back toward the house, and with every agonizing inch, breath came a little easier. Soon I was able to scramble up to my feet and get back inside the comforting cave that my house had become. I went straight to the wardrobe and opened it.

The glow of more than a hundred hanks of linen thread hit me like the sun after a storm. I sucked in a deep breath and laid my face directly against the nearest stack, soaking in their warmth.

After a while, I settled down on the floor, staring up at my thread in despair. I was out of flax. I couldn't go buy more. Cael would never enable me by getting it for me. If he saw me now, there's no telling what he'd do.

I twirled my fingers through the end of my tattered braid, wearing a hot spot into my fingers where it traveled the same path over and over. What was I going to do?

Later, when the sun dipped low in the west, The Weaver reappeared. "What troubles you, child?"

I scrambled to my feet and ran to her, taking her hand frantically. I closed my eyes and sank to the floor in relief. "I ran out of flax," I admitted. "I can't spin anymore."

The Weaver stroked my tangled hair, and I leaned into her touch. "Do not fret."

"But I need to spin! I have to! I can't get into town. Why can't I leave the house?"

"You are connected to the thread," she said, drawing a hank near. She held it up to me, and I stroked it lovingly. "It is a part of you. You cannot divide yourself by leaving."

This made perfect sense, but fear threatened to come in at the corners. The thread was a part of me? I could never leave the house? What would happen when The Weaver took the thread away?

But I clung to her hand, and I banished the fear away. That was another problem for another day. The Weaver would never let me come to harm. I focused on the heavenly emptiness that her touch gave me, and I forgot to fear.

"What do I do?"

The Weaver stroked my hair, running my ratty braid through

her hand from root to tip. "It does not matter what you spin," she said, catching my eye meaningfully. "It only matters that you do not stop."

She held up my braid.

I stared at the braid in my hands, like dark, thin flax fibers. My father had always said my hair shone like flax. Maybe, just maybe, it would be close enough?

If *The Weaver* said so, it must be true.

With aching hands, I undid my braid and finger combed through the length of it, pulling out a good amount of loose strands. These I took to the wheel, and after a steadying breath, began treadling.

The hairs spun up together just like flax, and with a gasp of delight, they began to glow as they passed through my fingers. The smooth, perfect thread wound onto the bobbin, identical to real linen.

"It worked!" I said, and The Weaver smiled in response.

Then, without hesitation, I ran to my dresser, dug through the scattered contents on top, and found my comb in the debris. I combed my hair hastily, careful not to lose a single loose strand, and then took my sheers and cut it right off close to my scalp.

The heavy strands fell into my hands, shining despite the weeks of accumulated dirt. It felt like the silkiest flax I'd ever handled. I went straight to the table and dressed my distaff with it.

My hair spun up beautifully. Once I'd spun all three singles and plied them together, I compared the hair yarn to the linen in the closet. Identical.

But of course, that had only taken two days. I still had months to go before our deal was up, and I had no more hair left to spin.

"It doesn't matter what I spin?" I asked The Weaver.

"It does not matter," she confirmed, her voice a whisper in the dark.

My house was a treasure trove of fiber. Curtains, bedsheets, clothes, washrags. I cut it all into strips, which took a frustrating amount of time, but it was worth it. I attached it to the leader on the glass wheel, and as the fraying fabric strips passed through my fingers and onto the wheel, it became a perfect, glowing thread. Fine, shining filament—strong and beautiful as the best linen.

I relaxed into my chair, the wheel turning steadily on, and I spun every last scrap of fiber in my house.

Six

And so, the last of summer passed away in a blur of shredding, spinning, washing, and drying. I took to spending nights on the floor in front of my wardrobe, staring at my golden hoard between fleeting hours of fitful sleep. I ran out of canned food, and I'd never bothered to plant a new garden in the spring. I relied on the weekly baskets that Mariah still sat on my front porch and the steady supply of eggs that my chickens gave every afternoon.

But I didn't care so much. I didn't get hungry anymore. I only ate because Cael came by every day, sat on my porch with his back against my door, and talked to me through the wood. I sat on the other side, listening in silence as he told me about the progress in his new fields, about the good prices he expected at the market in a few weeks, about the pair of goats he'd bought from someone traveling through to the capital.

The more time I spent eating and sleeping, the less time I had for spinning. And so, I stopped eating and sleeping and just spun. My only company was The Weaver, and my only balm was her calming touch. My body ached and groaned, but I ignored it. It felt like it belonged to someone else now. It belonged to the thread in the wardrobe.

Then one fall night, as I sat spinning in the light of the thread, my leg cramped. Usually, I would just take a break, stretch my ankle, and get back to work in a few minutes, but this was unlike any cramp I'd ever had.

It started with an ache, which I ignored. But then came stabbing pains, like someone cut into my leg with a knife.

I yanked up my skirt, expecting to see a wound, blood, anything. But everything was as it should be. Smooth, fair skin from ankle to knee. It wasn't even red.

"Weaver!" I cried. "What's happening?"

"There is a sibyl in the village," The Weaver said, melting back into the darkness. "She is injured, but she will move on soon. You need not worry. But I cannot stay while she is nearby."

A sibyl, or a mindwalker, as we called them in this part of the world. A telepath and a mind reader. One heard of them from time to time, but I'd only ever seen them in passing. They mostly kept to themselves.

I rubbed my calf furiously, trying and failing to ease the phantom pain. "Help me!"

"I cannot."

"Weaver!"

But she had completely disappeared. I couldn't feel her at all. She'd abandoned me. All because of some mindwalker passing through the village.

The pain continued. Horrible, breath-stealing agony that radiated from my leg up into my trunk, like fire. I cried out in pain, scrabbling at my leg desperately. I snatched down a hank of glowing thread and pressed it against my calf, but it didn't help. I threw it aside and ran for the front door. I hopped to the well in the yard and hauled on the rope.

"Come on, come on!" I said through gritted teeth, but my

arms were weak, and it took every ounce of effort I had in me to get the half-full bucket up.

I splashed the cold water on my leg, desperate for relief, but nothing. The phantom pain continued. Nothing helped.

So I hobbled back inside, whimpering, clutching at my leg, to lie down in my nest of blankets in front of the wardrobe. I curled up, gripping my calf as tight as I could, and cried.

An hour later, the pain stopped as suddenly as it began. I sat up and examined my leg, but no mark marred the smooth skin. I looked around at the house. With The Weaver gone, my head cleared for the first time in a long time, and I saw the state of the place.

My bed was stripped and shredded, my clothes entirely ruined, my curtains all gone. Dirty dishes had been piled up for so long, even the flies had abandoned them. I'd dragged in a huge mound of straw when I'd run out of fabric to spin, and it skittered here and there with barn mice.

With the shutters closed and the lamps all cold, the place was a dismal cave. The only light came from the wardrobe and the magical thread stored inside.

What had happened? How had I let things get this bad? I should have stopped when I ran out of flax. I had long since spun enough to be wealthier than any queen. Why did I keep going? When was the last time I ate?

I hauled myself onto shaking legs, shocked at how thin I'd become. How long since I'd gathered eggs? I started to move toward the kitchen, determined to wash something finally, but fatigue hit me hard. How long since I'd slept? I couldn't recall.

I collapsed back onto the floor, dragging a torn blanket over myself, and passed out.

～

"Aurora, wake up."

Someone shook my shoulder.

I rolled away, grumbling, "Sleeping."

"It's time to get up." Mariah's voice. How had she gotten in?

She shook me again, and this time, I opened my eyes.

Her haggard face swam into view. Her usually tidy hair was askew this morning, with the gray streak spilling out in a wind-blown tangle, like she'd been running her hands through it obsessively.

"How did you get in here?" I asked, giving voice to the one thought that my foggy brain could hold onto.

"Your front door was open." She hooked a thumb at the door.

My muddy footprints from the night before led a direct path to where I lay sprawled out on the floor. I must have left it open after I'd gone to the well to ease the pain in my leg.

"And as surprising as that is," she continued in a deadpan tone, "I'm more shocked by the huge pile of glowing thread you've got in your wardrobe. And the weird glass spinning wheel you've got by the window. And the huge mound of straw you've filled the house up with. If I didn't know any better, I'd say there was something strange going on here. And what in god's name did you do to your hair?"

I glared in response to her sarcasm and flopped back down on the floor.

"I don't think so," she said, grabbing me by the arm. "You're going to get up, and we're going to have a chat. But not here. It stinks. The front porch."

She pulled me up and led me outside, and I didn't have the strength to stop her. She sat me down on the bench by the front door and pulled her usual milk crate of food closer. She passed me a pitcher of goat's milk and a crock of grits, and I proceeded to eat directly from the containers.

She raised an eyebrow at me. "Well, that's manners if ever I saw them," she said with a sniff.

I ignored her sarcasm and tipped the pitcher up to drink heavily.

Once I'd eaten, Mariah sat staring at me in silence, one eyebrow still raised in expectation. "Talk," she said.

And finally, the fight went out of me. I didn't have the energy or the desire to push back anymore. So I leaned back against the bench, and I talked.

I told her about the argument Cael and I had, about getting lost in the woods and meeting The Weaver. I told her about the deal we'd made and finding the glass wheel in my house when I got home. I told her about my growing obsession with the thread and about Cael coming every day to talk to me through the door when I wouldn't let him in.

"I didn't realize how bad it got," I said finally. "I was so excited when I found the wheel would spin anything and that I could keep going. I just couldn't stop."

I sucked in a heavy breath and fell silent, staring down at my grubby hands. Had I been spinning with dirt and grease all over my hands? My father would be horrified.

"So what are you going to do now?" she asked.

I shrugged. "Keep spinning."

"Aurora..."

"Why not?" I asked. "What difference does it make at this point? I've already come this far. Why not keep going?"

"Why not?" she repeated, incredulous. "Because you're going to kill yourself if you keep going like this. What if I hadn't been bringing you food all this time? I almost stopped, you know."

"No, you didn't," I said with a scowl.

"Don't sass me, girl!"

I crossed my arms and stared out over the overgrown field. We both fell into mutinous silence.

Finally, Mariah spoke low, troubled. Like she was scared to speak at all.

"Last night—" She hesitated, then tried again. "Last night, a man brought a teenage girl to my house with her leg all torn up."

I glanced at her, then averted my eyes to stare at the dead petunias in the pot by the porch rail. The memory of the phantom pain from the night before sent shivers down my spine. I remembered The Weaver's words from the night before.

There is a sibyl in town. She is injured.

"It was bad, all infected and swollen," Mariah continued. "He sent everyone else away and convinced me to clean it up. Said if I didn't, she'd die. He was right, of course. The girl had a bad fever already."

"He had to talk you into saving her?" I asked, confused. Mariah had been a local doctor for decades. She'd never turned anyone away in all the time I'd known her.

Mariah kicked her toe through the dead leaves that I'd never bothered to sweep off the porch. "She was one of them. A mindwalker."

I clenched the edge of the bench in sudden alarm. A mindwalker? That confirmed it. The Weaver had been afraid of Mariah's mindwalker. The pain hadn't been mine at all. It had been sent from her.

"I almost didn't do it," she said. "I almost turned her away, but when I looked at her, it made me think of you. Here alone, suffering. How I'd left you here so long. How I've been enabling...whatever this is." She waved vaguely at the house behind us. "Of course, I had no idea what was really going on here. I thought you were simply depressed."

"I was," I said. And with shuddering clarity, I realized that's exactly what had been going on the past year.

"Come home with me, Aurora," she said. "Right now. Lock up the house and let's go. We'll send Cael back for the chickens tomorrow. Come with me and don't look back."

I sighed heavily. Wouldn't that be nice? All this could be over. I'd already earned enough gold to last me a lifetime. I didn't have to spin another inch of thread for the rest of my life if I didn't want to.

For one shining instant, I thought maybe I could get up and leave all this behind. Never look at this damned house again.

But then I remembered why I had resorted to cutting off my own hair when I ran out of flax. The pounding heart, the loss of breath. The thread wouldn't let me leave. It was too late. I'd already poured so much of myself into it. There was no going back.

"I can't."

"Of course, you can," she said, turning toward me. "Just get up and start walking."

"It's time for you to go home, Mariah," I said, standing up and shaking out my skirt.

"Come with me!"

"I can't!"

"Well, I know better than to waste time trying to help someone who refuses to help themselves." She stood abruptly and marched down the steps, then turned back with a staid expression. "The offer stands. Come stay with me whenever you like. But I won't be bringing you any more food. Come or stay—it's up to you."

I clenched my teeth and watched her steady progress down my lane.

No more food. Only eggs left, and the hens would stop laying long before my year was up. I couldn't leave the house to buy supplies. I couldn't get help from Cael without letting him in. Mariah was cutting me off.

I watched Mariah until she reached the road, turned south, and disappeared behind a stand of elm trees

All this for a bit of gold. This wasn't what my father wanted.

Seven

I went back into the house and glared at the wheel shining dully in the light of the one open window. The thread on it glowed like the morning sun, spun out of old moldy straw from the barn.

"Why do you hover, Aurora?" The Weaver asked from her dark corner. She cradled several hanks of thread in her arms, as usual, illuminating her face from the underside and distorting her fair features into a grim mask.

"You're back," I said.

"The sibyl has moved on."

I nodded my understanding.

"There is work to be done," she said.

"Don't you think this is enough thread?" I asked, gesturing at the wardrobe.

"The more you spin, the more gold you will earn," she said. "Was that not your wish?"

"Yes, but..." I trailed off, looking around at my ruined house. "I think I've earned enough. And this is more than enough thread to make a cloak. It's enough to make three cloaks."

The Weaver unfolded herself from her corner and stood

hunched with her hair brushing the ceiling. "You wish to go home with the healer."

"I want this to be over."

"Our contract was for one year and one day," The Weaver reminded me gently.

She took my arm, and warmth spread through me. My joints eased. My shoulders relaxed. She guided me toward the wheel.

"We still have two months to go. You've come this far."

I sat down in the chair, my thoughts pleasantly vacant and warm. My sore hands reached for more straw, and my feet landed on the treadles like clubs.

Wait, no. This wasn't right. I had been saying something. Who had I been talking to before?

"Someone was here?" I asked, turning to look up at The Weaver.

"No one was here," she assured me, guiding my hands back to the straw. "Only you and I."

"Right," I breathed, but though I managed to pick up a handful of straw, I let it rest in my lap as confusion took over. What was that taste on my tongue? Heavy, creamy, smooth. Goat's milk. I didn't have goats. Where had I gotten milk?

Come home with me.

"Mariah was here," I said, rising up off the chair.

The Weaver put a hand on my shoulder and pushed me back down firmly. "The healer is gone now. It's time to work."

"But..." I began.

"But nothing, Aurora!" The Weaver said in a commanding tone.

I shrank away from her and turned obediently toward the wheel, clutching the straw in my lap. She was right. It was time to work. I had come this far and survived. The Weaver would help me, just like I was helping her.

Then I looked up and saw Cael coming down the road toward my lane. He was so small from this distance, so far away. He would come and sit on my porch and talk to me through the front door as usual. A few moments of happiness.

But I'd left the front door open after Mariah had left. He wouldn't sit outside. He'd come right in. He'd probably touch me, hold me. I ran my fingers over my own hand, remembering the way it had felt nearly a year ago, when he'd kissed me. Had it really been that long?

Maybe Mariah was right. It was time to stop all this. It was time to remember what it felt like to want him.

I almost glanced toward the open door, but forced myself to turn back to the wheel instead. If The Weaver realized I'd left it open, she'd remind me to shut it. She'd *make* me shut it. But she kept her focus solely on the wheel and the hanks of thread in her arms.

Cael reached my lane and turned toward the house, his eyes on his feet. Still so far away but getting closer with every step.

With a rush of excitement, I hauled myself to my feet. The straw tumbled out of my lap and onto the floor.

"Aurora!" The Weaver said in shock. She reached for my shoulder once more.

I stumbled away from her. By all the gods, what was I supposed to do now? I couldn't make her leave. I couldn't make her do anything. She had complete control. She was going to make me spin until I died. Mariah had been right about all of it. That gods damned glass wheel was going to be the death of me.

"No," I said.

She stepped closer, bent awkwardly to avoid hitting her head on the ceiling. "Aurora, my dear," she said in placating tones.

"No!" I repeated.

Cael was halfway up the lane now.

The Weaver followed my glance, then darted her ice-white eyes at the open door. "I see," she said. "You think the farmer will save you."

"I don't need saving," I said. I gripped the back of my chair, maneuvering to keep it between myself and her. "I've completed our bargain. When the time is up, you will purchase my thread at the cost of one gold ingot per fifty yards. But I'm done spinning, Weaver. I'm done."

Her face distorted into something altogether ugly. A snarl peeled up her lip, exposing blindingly white, elongated teeth. Her eyes shone in the darkness, throwing the sunlight back at me like a cat in the dark.

"You're not done until you've spun every last bit of life you have, child," she hissed. She reached for me again, lunging with innate speed and grace. Her fingers brushed my shoulder as I lurched to one side, sending a wisp of her blissful emptiness through me.

I stumbled, gasping, desperate to hold onto what was real.

Mariah. Cael. Father. A flax field in spring. A rosy sunset. Mariah. Cael. Father.

"Cael!" I cried out. I backed toward the window, away from The Weaver, dragging the chair with me. It scraped across the floor, catching on the pile of straw.

"Aurora?" he called from the yard.

Running footsteps clunked up the stairs and across the porch. Cael appeared, framed in the doorway, shocked at the display before him: the destroyed house, the moldy straw, the glowing thread. But the most imposing image by far was the impossibly tall Weaver in her sheer, barely there dress. He stared up in wonder at her, mouth ajar.

"By all the gods," he breathed.

A vicious smile spread across The Weaver's beautiful face. "Ah. The farmer," she said. "We meet at last."

It happened in slow motion. She extended her hand toward Cael, who was too shocked to move away. And though he'd seen how far I'd fallen over the past year, he couldn't know what her touch would do to him. I'd always welcomed the emptiness, the bliss of not caring. But Cael didn't deserve that.

The Weaver couldn't be allowed to touch him. Not ever. But there was nothing I could do to stop her. Nothing at all. Her long fingers stretched toward him, too fast. Too close.

In a burst of madness, I tried to lift my father's heavy chair. But I had grown too weak. I had given all my life to that damned thread, and I had become a ghost of myself.

The Weaver's fingers wrapped around Cael's arm, and he stared up at her, eyes blank, shoulders relaxed. Peaceful. Empty.

I stared in horror as The Weaver turned her beautiful face toward me. "I thought removing your father would be enough," she said, pulling Cael closer.

He stepped forward, bliss distorting his face. He shouldn't look so innocent, so helpless.

But then The Weaver's words locked into place in my mind. My father?

"What?" I asked, my voice barely a whisper.

"I needed you pliable," she said. "I needed you alone, you who loves your craft so much. The best spinster the world has seen in decades. But you have such an affinity for farmers. First your father, now this one." She turned back to Cael, and her expression melted back into sweetness and comfort.

He gazed up at her with worshipful eyes.

"You are clouding her focus, aren't you?"

Cael nodded and swallowed hard. "Yes. Forgive me."

"Stop it!" I croaked on a sob.

"You are forgiven," The Weaver said and raised her hand to his forehead. With one finger, she moved to touch him between the eyebrows.

I could see it in my mind. The Weaver crouching over my father's bed, dwarfing his room, touching him on the brow every night as he grew sicker and sicker. Planting the seed of disease in his mind until he wasted away to nothing.

And now she would do the same to Cael. Her finger drew closer and closer to his grime-streaked forehead, and I snapped.

"No!" I screamed, my voice paper thin. With a grunt of fury and frustration, I pushed the chair over, just hoping it was heavy enough to do the job on its own.

The chair tipped up on two legs, teetered for a second or two, then toppled over. Its back smashed into the glass wheel, shattering it into a million shining pieces. The bits of glass scattered across the floor, mixing with the straw and sparkling across the dingy floor. The distaff hit a second later, shattering likewise and sending glass shards everywhere.

"What have you done!" The Weaver cried, releasing Cael. Her hands hovered over the ruins of her wheel for a few seconds before she staggered, breathless, to the wardrobe.

All the light had gone out of the thread. Every single hank had reverted to mundane, ordinary linen, recycled fabric, hair, and straw. The Weaver clutched it to her chest, grasping and grabbing as much as she could. But it did nothing for her. All the magic was gone.

"What have you done?" she repeated on a sob.

I jumped when a warm hand grabbed my arm, but it was only Cael.

"Let's go, Aurora," he said under his breath.

I nodded, backing away from the sobbing Weaver. As we watched, she grew paler and thinner, until she was almost as transparent as her dress.

"What have you done?" she asked again.

I stepped in glass immediately, stumbling against Cael with a gasp of pain. He picked me up and marched me out of the house, his boots crunching through the remains of the glass wheel.

As he carried me out, I stole one last glance at The Weaver.

She met my eyes, tears pooling in the corners. She mouthed, *What have you done?* one last time, though I couldn't hear her properly. She faded to the barest outline, then disappeared. The hanks of plain thread fell to the floor in a heap.

She was gone.

EIGHT

A week later, Mariah, Cael, and I went to the graveyard to visit my father. I stood between them, my hand held firmly in Cael's, and breathed in the fresh air.

After a few days of good food and rest at Mariah's house, I felt more like myself than I had in a long, long time.

"I'm sure breaking that wheel didn't hurt either," Mariah said in a dry tone when I mentioned it.

I grimaced. "Yes, probably so."

I knelt down and brushed away some fallen leaves that had covered my father's stone.

"He'd be right proud of you, you know," Mariah said. "Not many could have scrapped with one of the Old Kind and lived to tell about it."

I stood up with a heavy sigh and slipped my hand back into Cael's. He kissed my fingers once and squeezed.

"So have you decided what you're going to do next?" Cael asked.

"Not yet," I said. "I can't go back to that house any time soon. Maybe I will sell it after all."

Mariah patted me on the arm. "You stay with me as long as you like. My house has been empty for far too long."

"Thank you." I looked between them, a small smile on my face.

It felt like going home, standing here with these two. Mariah, with her practical frown and dark hair, and Cael, with his broad shoulders and heavy eyes. These two had never given up on me, and it was time I made the most of that gift.

"Do you mind giving me a minute?" I asked.

"Of course, dear," Mariah said. "We'll be just down at the gate."

"Take as long as you need," Cael said.

Once alone, I sat down in the grass in front of my father's stone. I ran my fingers over his name, reveling in the ache that sat in the pit of my heart. I had gone so long without feeling anything at all. It was a relief to finally feel this pain.

What would he say now? Would he congratulate me for defeating The Weaver? Would he admonish me for getting caught in her trap in the first place? Would he say anything at all?

Yes, he would say something. He'd put one arm around me and squeeze me tight against his side. Then he'd kiss me on top of the head and say, "Time flies like the wheel, Aurora."

"Time flies like the wheel," I whispered back with a small smile, and a single tear slid down my cheek. I kissed my fingers and pressed them against his stone.

I sniffed hard, wiped under my eye, and started down the hill after Mariah and Cael.

"You done already, child?" Mariah asked as I approached.

I went straight to Cael's side and leaned into his warmth as he put his arm around my shoulders.

"Yes," I said, smiling up at him. "Let's go home."

BLUEWATER

PROLOGUE

Miles sat at the bar, twisting a bracelet around his wrist. It was a simple thing. Just a length of braided sinew with a shark-eye shell threaded on. He had chosen this bracelet specifically because of the shell. It was deep hazel brown, with traces of iridescent blue following the path of the spiral.

Miles spun the bracelet around, around, around, dragging a path through the grit and sweat on his wrist.

The brown-blue of the shell reminded him of *her* eyes. That's why he had chosen it. The woman by the shore, with the sad, endless eyes, had sold it to him for a saucepan.

One didn't see shells like this often, even in a seaside country. They required sharp eyes that spent many hours combing the white sand along the shore. And nobody was willing to risk *that* for a few trinkets.

"That's a fine bauble," the barman said. "Is it for trade?"

Miles jumped, startled. The public house was relatively quiet. Only half the tables were occupied, which didn't bode well for Miles's prospects. Small crowds meant small profits. One didn't get paid to sing to an empty room.

"I'm afraid not, my friend," Miles said, putting down his empty glass with a note of finality. "Just coin today."

"As you say." The barman accepted the copper piece Miles tossed onto the sticky bartop.

In fact, the lack of patronage had Miles considering moving on without singing at all. He was tired and sore from travel, and the food at the pub had been so unappealing he had left most of it in his bowl. If he got out quickly, maybe nobody would notice the bag on his back was vaguely lute-shaped and then insist that he play. Maybe he could find a piemaker stall still open, where he could buy some decent dinner.

"I know you," said a melodic, male voice from behind. "You're that bard, ain't ya? Geof, it's that bard who sings about the merfolk. I heard him sing in Glenfall Cove last month."

Miles closed his eyes slowly, mentally cursing himself for not getting out sooner. Maybe if he didn't turn around, if he pretended he didn't hear, he could just walk out.

"It *is* you! I'm sure of it." The drunk slapped his knee and guffawed, delighted with his own well of knowledge.

Miles suspected that well was more like a puddle than anything.

"Are you going to play, then?"

Heads began to turn all around the dim room, and eyes lit up.

Shit, Miles thought to himself. There went his prospects for dinner.

"We haven't had a bard through here the last two months together!" A middle-aged woman called from the back.

"Are you going to play, then, bard?" someone else asked eagerly.

"The one about the merfolk, yeah?" added the man who had first recognized him.

Well, small profits were better than no profits at all. And besides, he had made a promise to the woman on the beach. He could still hear her voice in his memory.

Tell them about me, Miles. And maybe then, all that happened will mean something.

Miles turned to face the room at large, a wide, knowing grin pulling a dimple into his left cheek. Handsome smiles meant better tips.

"The merfolk?" he asked in a loud voice designed to draw people in. "Are you sure? What about the 'Princes of Authe Ida'? Or 'The Blue Bannock'?"

Their response was predictable. "No! No!" The disappointed group of afternoon drunks booed him until he shook his hands, placating. "'The Mergirl of Bluewater'!"

"All right! Okay!" Miles said to the gathered crowd, pulling his lute out of its bag. He plucked at the strings and turned the pegs until the notes sang clear. The shark-eye bracelet slipped sideways on his wrist.

Again, he thought of the woman. Her eyes were just this color, there on the beach in the evening sun, while she braided bracelets and laughed like a woman only pretending to be alive.

"'The Mergirl of Bluewater'," he said in a lower voice, as if to himself.

The meager crowd leaned in, clutching steins and glasses. Even the barman stopped his cleaning to lean on the bar and listen.

Miles's fingers flew across the strings, plucking out a melancholy tune with effortless ease. Not strumming, but singsong and wistful, each note leading to the next like waves driven by the tide.

The crowd held its breath, entranced by the song even before it began.

Miles closed his eyes, and his fingers continued their rhythmic plucking without conscious thought. He drew deep on the longing in his chest, recalling the fear and hope in the woman's eye when she had first spotted him walking down the beach.

And when he had achieved just the right frame of mind, he began to sing.

~

Stay away, they said.
Go home, they said. Flee.
Turn your back.
Close your eyes.
Look not upon the sea.

But little girls who wander
And live relentlessly,
Who disobey,
Who run away,
They're the ones who see.

ONE

They say you shouldn't stare too long into the water.

But if the water is so dangerous, then why did they build a whole city right on the shore?

I was born in Bluewater, and I'd been staring at the sea my whole life. Not out over the horizon or at the beautiful cloud formations or sunrises, but right down into the water.

When I was little, Mama used to take me down to the rock that jutted out from the sandy shore just below our house. There, we could lie down at high tide with the sun warming our backs. We looked deep into the wicked blue for as long as we liked, and no one would ever know.

The water was restless and old, endless and wild. It changed color every second, from cobalt blue to gray, azure to turquoise.

Closer to the shore, she pointed out the creatures living in the tide pools: fish and crustaceans of every size and color. But the ocean didn't care about them any more than the air cared about us.

"The ocean just is," Mama said with a wistful expression.

"And it always will be," I added with the confidence of a child who still saw the world as a mysterious, ancient place.

Mama got up after a while and went down the beach until she was just a pink and white smudge on the shoreline. Her skirt blew up in the wind, turning her into a billowing cloud. Air, sand, sea— all that was missing was fire.

The ocean made the people of Bluewater nervous, but they still craved its gifts: shells, pearls, and the fine, white sand. Because of that, Mama and I usually had the shoreline to ourselves. The people of Bluewater would stay behind their cement walls and let us brave the tricksy water for them.

Even at ten years old, I knew there was something wrong about this arrangement. The ocean's gifts were free. To purchase them with coin turned them into trinkets, when they should have been talismans.

But when The Great Hunger swept across the land—a devastating famine lasting four years when Mama was a girl—people grasped at any excuse to assign blame. It was decided that the gods had grown jealous of the Old Kind: the merfolk, faeries, witches, and mindwalkers.

And so, the wall was built.

A heavy, lumbering thing of white masonry and cement hid the view of the shore. Anyone who could hear the hidden thoughts of their neighbors was called possessed. And before long, Bluewater forgot the Old Way, and they only pretended to be people of the tides. All that was left was the name of their city and the trinkets they wore on their wrists like jewelry.

"So long as you and I don't forget, Ayana," Mama liked to say, "then the magic isn't lost."

Maybe that's why I wasn't so surprised to see a face in the water that day by the shore, when Mama was just a cloud on the horizon. To me, the magic had always been real.

Two huge eyes, black as the dried ink around the rim of our inkpot. Creamy gray, iridescent skin. A wide, flat nose and pert mouth. She was just a girl, like me, with hair resembling slippery black seaweed pasted to her delicate shoulders.

One of the merfolk. She had to be. Why else would there be a gray-skinned girl with no clothes in the water?

I froze. She was so pretty. I just wanted to stare at her, wanted to *be* her. Was she even real? I blinked hard, but my eyes were clear.

If I moved too fast, she would spook and disappear beneath the gentle, rolling waves. She'd turn into salt and dissolve or simply break apart into flotsam.

I took a tentative step forward, my bare toes barely shifting the sand.

The face in the water didn't disappear. The swell of the waves rolled her slippery hair over her shoulders and sent it undulating in the water behind her. Was she real, then? Flesh and bone and blood?

If I touched her, would she stay? Would her skin feel rubbery, like a shark? And what about her tail? I had heard so many conflicting stories about the merfolk. That they had twin tails like two legs. That they only had one muscular tail, like a seabass. That their lower bodies were long and sinuous, like an eel. That their tails were full of poison spines, their teeth were sharp like needles, and their fingers were webbed and taloned, with razor claws.

But she had no talons. No spines. I couldn't see this girl's teeth, but judging by the shape of her mouth, they weren't any more dangerous than mine.

I squatted down while the water licked at my toes. "Hello."

The face dipped a little lower in the water, and my heart skipped. But she didn't disappear. Not yet.

"Don't go," I said. I kept my hands clutched around my knees for fear she would see any reaching gesture as a threat. "What's your name?"

The girl in the water glanced up the shoreline to where Mama stood, picking through her basket. She was too far away to hear us and too far to see a little face in the water.

"Eden," the girl said.

A smile born of wonder spread across my face. Her voice was

like music. Like the morning sun reflecting off the waves. Like Mama singing as she cracked eggs into a bowl for breakfast.

"I'm Ayana," I said, creeping a little closer.

"Is this Eventide, Ayana? This shore?"

I shook my head. "No, this is the city of Bluewater. Where's Eventide? I've never heard of it."

Eden cast her too-large eyes at the heavy wall behind me. Despair clouded her brow. "I don't know."

A girl this young shouldn't be so afraid. I wanted to fix it, to make her smile, so I crept a little closer. Eden's attention darted back to me in alarm. I stopped and sat down gingerly in the shallow water.

Eden tucked her chin down and to the side, unsure of what to do. "You've never heard of Eventide? It's an island."

I shook my head. "There are many islands along this coast. That's Mona Island just there." I pointed to a distant shape on the horizon. "But I've never heard of Eventide. Is it a merfolk name? Maybe you have a different name for it than we do."

Eden shook her head. "No, there are people there too. They're nicer there. A couple of boys threw rocks at me this morning. By the pier..." She rubbed her cheek, which was a little pinker than the rest of her skin, now that I looked closer.

"What?" A spark of indignation started up in my chest. "Who did it? Where? Did they have red hair? I'll bet it was the Clark twins. Their uncle is a merchant, so they're always running about the pier, making pests of themselves."

Eden tucked away into the water, startled by my outburst. I checked my anger and tried again.

"They shouldn't have done that," I said. "Why are you looking for Eventide? Is that where you're from?"

Eden nodded and changed position in the water. Her tail broke the surface and flashed briefly into view. All the stories were wrong. It was longer than I expected but not slimy and curling, like an eel. Strong, powerful, muscular, and covered in beautiful scales that shone blue, green, iridescent pink, and blushing lavender. Her scales were like gemstones, and transparent blue fins rippled through the water when she moved.

"How did you get here?" I asked, transfixed.

Eden hunkered down in the water, low enough that her bottom lip went under. "The storm...I got lost."

"Oh," I breathed.

Yes, there had been a storm. About two weeks before, the winds had howled fiercely for an entire day, and the sea had risen several feet, almost to the steps of our house, which was one of the few buildings outside the wall.

Mama and I had stayed inside, playing games and making shell curtains by lamplight. When we came out the next day, palm fronds, tree branches, and debris clogged the road, and the southern wicket gate was completely blocked by a fallen palm. It took us a full day to get back into the city.

Some people had lost their houses to the fierce winds, but we were fortunate. We only lost one chicken and one of the lemon trees that flanked our front door.

"So, you can't find your way back to your family?" I glanced up at Mama in the distance, not knowing what I'd do if I couldn't find her. And Eden was little, like me. Just a child. "I'll be your friend, for as long as you stay in Bluewater. That's our house just up there."

I pointed to where the peak of our roof was only just visible over the cliff's edge.

"If you want to talk or anything, I'm here most mornings. And nobody comes here but me and Mama, so no one will be mean to you. And if they are, I'll stop them. Those Clark twins aren't as tough as they like to think."

Eden followed my pointing finger, an expression of hope on her strange, beautiful face.

"You can tell me what it's like to be merfolk. And I can tell you all about people," I said.

"I know about people." Eden perked up a little. "I have lots of human friends on Eventide. The people there like to swim with us."

"Really?" I asked. "They're not afraid of the sea?"

"No. Why would they be?"

"They say it's bad luck to stare into the water. No one swims here."

"That's so sad," Eden said. "Do you swim?"

"Ayana!" Mama's voice floated down the beach on the wind. "Ayana! It's getting late! Are you ready to go?"

Eden slipped down into the water until only her eyes were visible.

"I'll come back later!" I whispered, and she nodded once before disappearing completely.

I scrambled out of the water and fetched my basket from the sand where I had left it. The basket was half full of shells and sea stones worn smooth with the tumbling crash of the waves. I ran down the beach toward Mama, scattering wet sand as I went.

What happened by the water?
To make them so afraid?
They had forgot
And never thought
Of how much fear could weigh.

But when they turned to fire,
To terror and to blade,
The girl, she knew
What she must do.
The choice already made.

Two

"Why do we have to leave so soon, Mama?" I asked as soon as I was close enough to be heard over the wind and the crashing waves.

Mama wiped her dark, wild hair away from her grim expression. She had rolled up her white, linen sleeves, and her skirt still blew in the relentless wind. "There's a burning today, sweetheart."

I stopped short. My brows drew together in consternation. I had only ever been to one burning before. They didn't happen often. I had been very little, and I couldn't remember much. But the smell was something you never forget.

"Do we *have* to go?"

Mama shifted her basket to her other arm and gripped my shoulder in a firm, comforting hand. "Yes, Ayana. We have to. It's the law."

I wanted to argue, but I didn't know how. So when Mama turned me back toward the house, just barely visible on the cliff way down the beach, I didn't pull away.

I didn't know when the burnings started. Long before I was born, certainly. Mama always said it began when Eustis Metaxis came into power, but everyone else claimed we had been doing it forever. Ever since The Great Hunger. So that the gods would see our purity and be kind.

But I knew one thing for sure and certain: Nobody else in Authe Ida burned their mindwalkers. Just us. Only Bluewater.

Mama and I entered the city through the southern wicket gate and joined the crowd gathered around the pyre in the district square. Tall buildings rose around us in swaths of brightly painted cement, and eucalyptus trees in tidy squares of gravel protected us from the afternoon sun.

I clung to Mama's side as the people elbowed us along. Mama caught sight of a friend nearer the front, and she pulled me through the crowd.

"Hello, Marta," Mama said.

The two women greeted each other with a quick hug and a kiss on the cheek. Marta had a baby boy, Nikolas, who was busy drooling on her shoulder. He wasn't big enough to stand yet, but he watched me over his mother's shoulder and babbled a happy greeting to me as well.

"Hi, Nik!" I said. For a moment, I forgot where we were and our reason for coming. There was only this happy baby with a poof of black hair on his head. And when I hid my face with my hands and uncovered it again, he squealed with delight.

Since the entire district was required to attend a burning, Marta and baby Nikolas weren't the only familiar faces in the crowd. A flash of orange hair caught my eyes, and I flushed red with sudden anger. It was the Clark twins, Kris and Andrei. They were nearly two years older than me and loved to push their weight around. Even now, they were throwing pumpkin seeds at the back of a younger boy's head, delighting in his confused agitation.

"Ow!" cried Marta. "Don't pull my hair, Nik!"

Marta moved Nikolas from one shoulder to the other, effectively ending the game I had been playing with him. But that was okay. The sight of the twins had fired my blood so much that I didn't want to play anymore anyway. These were the two who had thrown rocks at my new friend, Eden, and for what? Just because she was a little different? Just because they could?

I was halfway toward the Clarks when I spotted yet another familiar face in the crowd—my best friend, Hollis. Hollis lived in town near the gate by our house. He was the oldest of seven children, all of them golden as the midday sun. He shoved through the crowd toward me, and a patch of afternoon light set his blond hair glowing. Hollis slipped behind Andrei Clark, and a flash of silver at his waist made me wince.

I grinned. Hollis had swiped the blade of a sharp little knife across the bag of pumpkin seeds, spilling its contents over the cobbles. He was there and gone before either of the twins noticed him. Their ammunition was all over the ground, damning them, and they were caught. Their victim's father rounded on them, yelling.

Hollis sidled up to me and smiled pleasantly.

"Those two are the worst," I said.

"I'm sure they wouldn't agree with you on that." Hollis crossed his arms, looking satisfied with himself. His brothers and sisters appeared around him, like baby chicks trailing after their mother through the crowded courtyard.

I greeted them all. We fell into laughing and chasing each other, shoving people aside for our play. Nikolas squealed and laughed, kicking with delight in his mother's arms.

We were so wrapped up in our game that we didn't notice when the courtyard fell silent. It took Mama grabbing my arm and hissing at me to stand quiet for me to remember why we had gathered there.

We were near enough to the front of the crowd that I could just peek over Grady Larson's shoulder and see what was going on. In the center of the square stood a great pyre taller than a man. A ladder had been laid against one side to reach a crude, narrow platform on top. Through the center of the platform thrust the straight trunk of a palm tree, still green from felling.

That they would sacrifice an entire palm tree for this showed just how serious the burnings were.

"Do you know his name?" I asked Hollis.

"Who?"

"The mindwalker they caught?"

"No."

"Kealan," a stranger said next to me. "He's my neighbor's cousin. A fisherman."

I stared up at the man who had spoken. My heart broke a little. "I'm sorry, mister."

The man harrumphed. "Don't be sorry, girl. Be glad we caught him. These mindwalkers look just like us. You'd never know they were in your head, would you? It's terrifying."

I edged away from the angry man and tightened my grip on Mama's hand. She kept her eyes straight ahead and expressionless. Only her firm grip belied her feelings.

A swell of chatter arose from the front of the crowd, signaling to the rest of us that it had begun. Two soldiers led a swaying man up the ladder to the platform.

That must be Kealan.

He grinned maniacally, his eyes unfocused, while he was positioned against the wooden post.

"Why is he smiling?" I asked Mama, feeling a little sick.

"They gave him medicine to make him calm." Mama squeezed my hand once, commanding me to be quiet.

"It's a mercy." Marta stood next to her, her voice grim. "It's a kindness so he won't suffer while the magic is burned out of him."

But as I watched Kealan stumble up the ladder, it didn't seem like a kindness. This man was about to die, and he wasn't even allowed to be afraid.

I searched Hollis's face, then Mama's, looking for answers. This wasn't right, but everyone was just standing around, watching.

One of the soldiers tied Kealan's hands behind him and

around the palm trunk. The mindwalker let him do it without fighting. He leaned back against the palm, grinning at the sky.

The entire square went quiet. The only sounds were Kealan's stuttering giggles and muttering. It was an eerie feeling, knowing he went happily to his death.

Then a crier stood on the pyre to be easily seen over the heads of the crowd. Kealan stared at the back of his head, fascinated by something that probably wasn't there.

"Hear now, all gathered." The crier rang a large brass bell twice to get our attention. "Here stands Kealan Muscor, who has confessed of his own volition to be a mindwalker. He possesses vile magic that must be purged from our lawful society. Alderman Petritis, acting as the representative of Eustis Metaxis, our lord of Bluewater, sentences Kealan Muscor to death by burning. This we do in remembrance of The Great Hunger, which was a punishment from the gods for harboring evil in our midst."

There followed a haunting call and answer. The crier spoke a phrase, and everyone in the crowd repeated it in a rumble of many voices.

"This we do to remember The Great Hunger, that we may never want again."

"This we do to protect ourselves from demons, wickedness, and spirits, lest they contaminate us all."

"This we do with courage, not fear."

"This we do with justice, not vengeance."

He rang the bell once more. The chime bounced off the cement buildings surrounding the square, startling a bevy of pigeons to take off in alarm.

Silence met this perfunctory speech, except the accused. Kealan whooped, as if cheering for a friend who had dared to jump off the end of the city's main dock, where the water was deep enough for a frigate. His giggles filtered between us, putting every person in the crowd on edge. I cringed and clung closer to Mama.

The crier was wrong. This wasn't courage or justice. It was

fear, pure and simple. And what justice? What crime had been done? Kealan had been a fisherman, a cousin. He was someone's son. Maybe someone's father or husband.

Did anyone cry for him in the crowd? I couldn't tell. Too many bodies pressed close.

I thought again of the little girl in the water. The mergirl named Eden, with wide eyes and beautiful skin. If anyone knew about her, she would be burned too. My feet began moving on their own. My vision narrowed to the ladder, which was being lifted away.

It didn't matter. I could climb.

I pushed through the few people in front of us, not hearing Mama's cry of alarm, and scrambled up the pyre toward Kealan.

The branches were coated in some slippery, oily substance that shone greenish on my hands and stained my shirt. I pulled myself up, hand over hand, using the piled branches to lever my body up until I stood on the platform, panting with urgency.

Kealan grinned at me, his eyes wide. He made faces in a horrible mockery of the game I had been playing with Nikolas a few minutes before.

Peek-a-boo!

I shuddered. What now? I didn't have a knife to cut his ropes, and I couldn't get him away from the guards or away from the surging crowd, who stood around and did nothing to help.

But there was no time to think. The soldiers had already lunged forward to fetch me down. Panicked, I reached for the rope holding Kealan's wrists securely behind the palm trunk. I yanked at the knots even when the ladder was thrown back against the pyre and two soldiers climbed up.

"No! No!" I said under my breath, hopping with agitation.

One knot came free just when big hands wrapped around my waist. My fingers immediately moved to pry on the next knot, but it was too late. The soldier lifted me off the platform, and the ropes ripped out of my little hands.

"No!" I screamed, my voice pitched high in childish fury. "No! It's not right! Let me go!"

I kicked and struggled, but I was just a kid. The soldiers passed me down from the pyre, ignoring my flailing fists.

"It's not right! It's not right!" I squealed, screamed, kicked, and raged. But I might have been a hermit crab in the beak of a seagull for all the good it did.

"Ayana!" Mama's terrified voice cut through my screams.

"Is she yours?" one soldier asked.

"If you can't keep her under control, we'll do it for you!" barked the man who carried me.

I was passed off to Mama, who picked me up and hauled me away from the pyre and back through the crowd. Marta trailed after, clutching a wailing Nikolas to her chest.

I continued screaming, prying at Mama's grip on me. I couldn't hit her—not like I could the soldiers—but I pushed, pulled, and tried to squirm out of her arms. She was like me, though: fierce, determined, and strong. There was nothing I could do.

The crowd jeered and hissed at us while we moved through them. "He's a demon, girl!" "Teach your daughter better!" "Witch lover!" "Go home!" "This is what comes of living outside the wall!" They parted like water before Mama, with Marta following closely behind. Nikolas squirmed and screamed in her arms in a little mimic of my anger.

"It's not right!" I cried through furious tears. "It's not right!"

If anyone heard me over the shouting crowd, they didn't care. To them, Kealan was a monster, and killing him was the right thing to do.

Hollis's golden head popped into view in the jostling crowd. He watched me borne away, holding his youngest sisters by the hand. And for a second, I thought there might be a little hope.

"Hollis!" I screamed. "Hollis, help him! It's not right!"

But Hollis didn't move. He pulled his sisters closer and just watched us go. My heart sank. Hollis had been my last hope. The one who always knew what to do and how to do it right. But he only stood there.

Hollis didn't do anything at all.

Two familiar, laughing voices wove through the throng, and I turned. The Clark twins were leering at me. Mocking me. In a haze of petulant rage, I ducked my hand into Mama's basket of shells and hurled as many as I could in their direction as we passed. They shielded their faces from the sharp little things, scowling at me.

"How does it feel?" I screeched at them, referring to how they had thrown rocks at Eden.

But they must have assumed I meant the pumpkin seeds, because they threw the last few they had at Mama's retreating back, shouting bile at us both, just like their parents.

And far behind, a fire burst into existence.

Finally, my furious screaming halted in my throat. The oiled logs caught eagerly, and I watched in mute horror while Kealan disappeared, laughing, into the flames.

~

The years cannot be halted.
There is no time to wait.
Stuck between
The land and sea
The girl must face her fate.

THREE

THIRTEEN YEARS LATER.

"What's that one called?" Nikolas asked, pointing at a shell in the shallow water.

I had brought the boy with me today, promising he could wait for Eden to return with news. He had been in and out of the water all morning long, and it shed off his high, black curls in energetic droplets.

Nikolas had grown a good two inches that summer alone, all elbows and knees. Gone was the baby fat and round cheeks. When had he grown up? I had missed it somehow. Soon he'd be taller than me, and I would never hear the end of it.

I had grown as well, though from his perspective, I had always been an adult. It didn't help that I had latched onto him like the aunt he never had: protective, watchful, friendly.

Nikolas slipped off the rock and into the water up to his knees. A moment later, he had the shell in question in his hands. He rinsed the sand away and held it up for me to see.

I rested my head on my arm. "You should know this one, Nik."

"Scotch bonnet?"

"Close. It's a whelk. See the elongated end?"

"Whelk," he said, examining the shell more closely. "Do they have seashells in the north?"

I chewed on my lip. Was this sadness in his voice? Or longing? "Well, they don't have a sea, so probably not. But they have snow."

He looked up, a new light in his eyes. "I can't wait to see snow! Mother says it gets higher than your head in some places."

I grinned at the happiness in his voice. "I've heard that too."

"You should come with us," Nikolas said, his attention already back on the seashells in the sand. "Don't you want to see snow? And they have different fruit there. Apples and peaches. Have you ever had one of those?"

"No. Have you?"

"Of course not," he said. "But I will. I'll plant a tree in our garden when we find a place to live. And pears and...and what was that other one you told me about?"

"Plums?"

"Yeah, plums!" He pulled back his arm and threw a broken shell out into the deeper water. "You could come visit us and try some of everything."

"Maybe," I said, but in my heart of hearts, I knew I never would. I looked out over the water, and my heart beat in time with the waves. My skin glowed with the heat of the sun. How could I ever leave this? How could I ever go somewhere Eden couldn't follow?

Nikolas's expression stilled. "I understand. It's hard to leave your home. I'm excited to meet Eden, though."

I reached out and squeezed his hand. "Soon. You'll meet her soon. But Nik, you have to be more careful than that. I know you feel safe with me, but you need to practice responding to what I say, not what I'm thinking."

Nikolas threw another broken shell out to sea, this time with a little more force and a stiffness to his shoulders. "Not in the north. I won't have to pretend there."

"I bet you will. At least a little bit. Everybody pretends about something most of the time."

When he didn't turn around and his shoulders didn't relax, I splashed some water at him. I got him good. The water hit his full body from waist to head. He cowered and turned to face me with an incredulous expression.

"What was that for?"

"To make you smile," I said.

A devilish grin spread across his face. He bent down and thrashed his arms through the water, sending huge splashes in my general direction. I cringed away, laughing, protecting my face. While I didn't get terribly wet—he had no technique—every chilly drop sent a shiver down my body.

"I should have known I'd find you two here." The familiar voice worked its way to me through the noise of the crashing waves and the crying gulls.

Hollis made his way toward us down the sandy path from my house. His wavy blond hair reflected the morning light, turning it to bright gold. He smirked when he noticed me lying on my rock, staring at the sea when I should have been working.

"I've been looking for you two everywhere. Hi, Nik."

"Hiya, Hollis!" Nikolas waved.

I lay back down, exposing my bare back to the sun once more, tossing my messy black braid over my shoulder. The warmth spread through me, contrasting beautifully with the icy droplets of seawater kissing my skin. I dipped my arm into the water and dragged my fingers through the sand.

"We're hunting for shells."

"No, you're not," Hollis said with the long-suffering tone of someone who had heard that excuse a thousand times. He sat cross-legged on the rock next to me.

"Yes, we were!" Nikolas sloshed over to my rock to hold up a basket half full of Scotch bonnets, king's crowns, Naticas, shark eyes, and a dozen others. They rattled against each other in happy *click clacks*.

These shells would become curtains, necklaces, wall hangings, and talismans. Simple things. Pretty things. That's what Mama and I had always done. I'd been helping her hunt for shells since I was old enough to pick them up without putting them directly into my mouth, sand and all.

But it had been just me the past few years. Mama had married a gentle man and moved inland. As for me? I couldn't bear to leave the sea.

"Any pearls today?" Hollis asked. He picked up Nikolas's whelk and inspected it.

I sighed and rested my chin on my arm. "Not today."

"So, no visits from the mysterious Eden, then? This diver you're always talking about?" His voice carried a hint of teasing.

I flicked my hand through the water, sending droplets scattering. "Nope. She usually comes in the evenings."

"Why haven't I met her yet?" Hollis asked, then pointed at Nikolas. "Have you met her?"

Nikolas shook his head. Silently, I begged him not to say anything about Eden at all. Nothing. Don't even mention we were here waiting for her. I had no way to know if he heard me, so I had to simply trust that the message got through.

"Why are you the only one she sells her pearls to?" Hollis asked.

I half shrugged. This was a question I had been asked a dozen times, and I had never been any good at lying. So the smartest answer was no answer at all. Let them think what they wanted about the pearl diver no one had met.

Hollis continued. "If she would just sell to more people, she'd make a fortune. Divers are few and far between these days."

Nikolas chipped in. "Ayana's the only one I know who has pearls always."

Hollis nodded sagely, as if this thirteen-year-old boy was the highest and best authority on the subject of the pearl market. The knowing grin stretching across his face was almost audible. "Or is there some other reason why you keep so quiet about her?"

"Stop it, Hollis," I said, but there was no fight in my voice.

"You like her," he said with a confident nod. "I knew it. That's dangerous, you know."

Nikolas's devilish grin returned, then instantly faded. He didn't know how to take this statement, and neither did I.

My heart skipped. "What? What do you mean?"

Hollis glanced down at me, still teasing. "Mixing business with romance. Nik's right. You're the only artist in town with a steady supply of pearl. You're doing well. But what if you mess things up with this Eden person? Then where will you be? There are no other divers around to trade with. Haven't been for a while."

My heart slowed, and I settled back down on my arm. "Some things are worth the risk." In my mind, I pictured her dark hair flowing through the water, her slow smile, the way her hand felt like silk on mine. I thought of her laugh while we sat out the sunset together.

But this morning, I had been waiting for Eden for an entirely different reason. She had promised me news as soon as she got back, news that could save Nikolas's life. News of passage to the north, where a mindwalker could live without fear.

"Which brings me back around to the big question..." Hollis said, unaware of my worries. "Why haven't I met her yet?"

I chewed my lip. "You will someday."

He laughed. "I'll bet. *Someday*. Do you know what you really need, though?"

Oh, this should be good. "What's that?" I asked.

"You need some handsome stranger to come walking down the beach, fall in love with you, and finally convince you to leave the water for good. It worked for your mother. It'll work for you."

I laughed out loud. "They'd have to be very handsome indeed!"

"As handsome as me, at least," Hollis said.

"No one's as handsome as you." I flicked water at him. "And you'd be the first to say so, you vain prick. And if you could never get me to fall in love, then I doubt any man ever could."

"A woman, then," he amended, still determined to outwit me.

"The only woman I ever loved was the sea herself." I gestured out over the water, at the roiling waves, green as glass in the sunshine. "How could I not?"

Nikolas laughed.

"No!" Hollis cried in mock defeat. He clutched at his heart in dramatic fashion. "Anyone but the sea! She'll fool you. Mark my words. She'll pull you under and never let you out again."

I thought of Eden and of the warnings I had been told all my life. *Don't stare into the water. Stay away. Go home.*

I hadn't heeded any of them. Not one.

"Stuck, you are," Hollis continued, squinting his eyes against the sun.

"I'm not stuck."

"Yes, you are. Stuck between the land and the sea." He leveled his blue eyes at me. "You always have been. It's not healthy. Your mother knew it. She got out. When are you going to do the same?"

"Why did you come looking for me?" I asked, changing the subject. But when his mood shifted, the way his shoulders slumped and his expression turned grim, I instantly regretted it. "No. Never mind. Forget I asked."

"You have to come to the burning today, Ayana," Hollis said.

Nikolas turned his back to us

I refused to face him. "I don't want to."

"Me either," Nikolas said, still facing out toward the open ocean. He squatted down in the water and pretended to search for more shells in the sand.

"You missed the last one in our district," Hollis said to me in an undertone. "People noticed. If you miss another one, they will start talking. And with you living so close to the water..."

He trailed off. We all knew what he was insinuating. Mama and I had always lived on the edge of Bluewater, both metaphorically and literally. And now that it was just me, the little girl who had once tried to save a mindwalker, everything had gotten worse.

They saw me as a necessary evil, the only reliable source of seashells, pearls, and sand. Even the other jewelry makers bought their shells from me, unwilling as they were to come to the shore themselves.

But only my oldest friends acknowledged me outside of market days: Hollis, Marta, and Nikolas. That was just fine by me. The rest of them thought it was a good idea to burn people alive.

"It's grotesque." My upper lip curled in disgust.

"All the same," he said, exhausted.

I stared down into the water. Eden hadn't come this morning, but that wasn't unusual. She came when she could, and I savored every stolen moment we had. And this time, she had gone on such a long journey, it might be another day before she got back.

I dipped my fingers into the water. The light filtering through the surface gave my golden skin a bluish tint. "They just want to scare us. It's all a big show so we'll betray our neighbors to save ourselves."

"I know," Hollis said.

"If they have to work so hard to make us afraid of the mindwalkers, then maybe they're not as bad as they want us to think."

Nokolas's back was taut with tension, no matter how well he tried to hide it. He kept his eyes on the seafloor under his knees.

"We've been over this so many times, Ayana," Hollis said. "It doesn't bear repeating again."

I stood abruptly and glared at him, then remembered Hollis wasn't the one burning people alive. Though I softened my voice, I kept the determination in it.

"It *always* bears repeating, Hollis. Always." I turned back to the water. "I'm not going. Never again."

"Ayana—"

"I'm not going."

"You can't sit on the beach forever, Ayana."

"Watch me!"

Hollis sighed, but he didn't push me further. "Nik, your mother's waiting for you."

Nikolas threw a pebble into the deep with frustration. But he trudged out of the water obediently and followed Hollis away from the beach.

~

What was built in decades
Could never stand on lies.
A secret love,
A little shove,
Will herald her demise.

FOUR

Alone once more, I settled down on my rock to wait, forcing myself not to look around when a whiff of smoke laced through the air. I didn't want to see the column of black billowing into the sky over the wall behind me.

Instead, I turned my attention to my craft. I had brought my tools down to the rock, like I often did, and continued working on a few bracelets. Even if I didn't open my market booth today, at least I could be productive. I drilled careful holes in the shells with my auger and braided them into sinew cords, finishing them off with clever knots for luck.

While I tied off the fifth one, a splashing sound worked its way into my brain. A sound like that at the seaside was nothing to take notice of, but this one didn't fit the regular pattern of low waves sloshing against the rocks.

I glanced up, hardly aware I had heard anything at all, and my heart leapt. A pair of large black eyes watched me from just above the water's surface. Human eyes at first glance, set in creamy pale skin, unblinking. But if you looked closely, the skin had a grayish cast to it, the onyx hair was almost iridescent, and the eyes weren't just large. They were *too* large. The inky irises blended so perfectly with the pupil that I couldn't distinguish one from the other.

And when I noticed them, they squinted into an unmistakable smile.

"Eden," I gasped, dumping my half-finished bracelet and my tools into the box next to me and scrambling for the edge of the rock.

When I slipped into the water, Eden rose a bit higher above the surface, exposing her small nose and elongated face. I pushed my way through the water toward her.

But Eden was one of the merfolk, and the sea was her home. With one flick of her powerful tail, she closed the distance between us. I wrapped my arms around her, burying my face in her cool neck. She laughed a little as we sagged back down into the water. Eden couldn't stand, so I sank onto my knees, submerging us both up to our shoulders.

"It's been *three* days," I said.

"I know. I'm so sorry."

"I was so worried!" I pulled back, framing her face in my hands and brushing away her slippery hair.

"It was a long journey," Eden said, drawing her eyebrows together. Her shoulders drooped, and the way she gripped my arms spoke of pure exhaustion.

Of course she was tired. She had been swimming for three days straight.

"I know, I know. Thank you for going." I pulled her to me and kissed her. I lingered against her mouth as her lips curled into another smile.

Every time it was like the first time. Not just the spark of heat swelling under my skin, but the comfort, the assuredness. With Eden I was home.

"I'm here now," she said.

I settled more comfortably in the water and readied myself for bad news. "Did you find her? The old woman that Nik dreamt about? You didn't find her, did you?"

"I did," Eden said. "I found her! I told you I would."

I sat up a little straighter, my hands up in an abortive gesture of triumph.

"She was right where he said. In that little fishing town with the broken pier."

"Glenfall Cove?" I asked, and Eden nodded.

"She was waiting for me on the beach," Eden said, and a ghost of discomfort passed over her large eyes. "She was expecting me, Ayana."

I tucked my chin down. "Do you not trust her? Will she help us?"

"She says she will." Eden shrugged one slim shoulder. "She says she'll meet us here tonight at sunset. I swam as fast as I could to get here in time. But Ayana, how did she know I'd be there looking for her?"

I shook my head and swiped my wild hair away with a wet hand. "She's supposed to be a mindwalker like Nikolas. Maybe she saw a vision of you. But how can she get here by tonight? It would take twice as long to walk here as it did for you to swim."

"I don't know," Eden said. "But I wouldn't doubt her. She was old, but her eyes were sharp. Why do we even need her? Can't your friends just walk north?"

I shook my head. "There's no way. Not without drawing suspicion. There's nothing north of Bluewater but the border. No one goes through the northern gate unless they're on a diplomatic mission. And even if they went the long way, taking the eastern gate and cutting through the salt flats, there are sentinel stations all along the border for miles. They'd never get through. Too many people have tried and failed."

"If that's the case, I wonder how the old woman could make any difference. The elderly are slower, right? They aren't as able."

"I don't know," I said. "But Nik says she's their way out of

Bluewater. She's been coming to him in dreams for weeks, and always, she leads him to safety. We have to trust that. We have to trust him."

"I hope it's enough."

"I'm just glad you're back." I pulled her into another embrace.

But Eden stiffened in my arms.

"What is it?" I asked.

She didn't answer. Instead, she slipped soundlessly under the water and propelled herself far enough away that the reflection of the sun and sky hid her presence.

I spun around in the water, my heart thumping. We weren't alone. My worst nightmare had finally come to pass. After years of meeting Eden in secret at the water's edge, someone had found my little protected cove.

But it wasn't just anybody. A wash of relief blew through me.

"Hollis!" I said, taking in the lean build and golden curls of my oldest friend.

Then I noticed the expression on his face, and the relief turned to ice in my chest.

"Hollis?" I said again, less sure of myself.

"One of the seafolk, Ayana?" he asked in a voice so low I almost didn't hear it over the swell of the ocean.

I glanced behind me. Eden popped the top half of her face above the surface. Just enough to clearly see what was going on.

"Hollis, it's not that bad," I said.

"Is this Eden, then? Your *diver* who brings you pearls? Are you insane?"

"I know it's dangerous, but–"

He spoke over me. "Dangerous? Yes, Ayana. It's *dangerous*. Completely aside from the fact that *it's not human!*"

I cringed and glanced back at the huge black eyes visible above the water. Eden's hair floated beneath the surface, creating an inky cloud.

Hollis barreled on. "If anyone saw this, you'd be burned at the stake. Just like that woman today. What would your mother say if she could see you now? To see her daughter consorting with one of the Old Kind?"

I glowered at him. "*Consorting*? Don't talk about my mother like that. You don't speak for her!"

He took an angry step forward and jabbed a finger at me. "Well, somebody has to look out for you. You were kissing it!"

"Her! I was kissing *her*!" I shouted. "Were you spying on us?"

"Of course, I was spying! Did you think I didn't notice how strange you were acting this morning? You *and* Nikolas? And then you didn't open your booth today? To come sit by the ocean? I wanted to know why!"

I couldn't find an answer to this.

Hollis's shoulders dropped, and he cast about as if he might see a signpost planted in the sand somewhere. Ayana's sanity—Five miles east.

"Why didn't you tell me about this, Ayana?" he asked. "How could you keep this from me?"

The victimized tone in his voice set my chest ablaze.

"Are you kidding?" I seethed. "Because I knew how you would react, Hollis! I knew that you would call Eden an 'it!' This was one conversation I *never* wanted to have with you! Best friend or not!"

His mouth curled into an angry snarl. "Don't you understand that your choices affect other people? What about me? What about my brothers and sisters? What do you think will happen to them if the city believes I knew about this? If they think I kept this secret for you? They need me, Ayana!"

"Well, which way would you rather it be, Hollis? Should I have told you or not? Because either way, I'm to blame, aren't I?"

"You shouldn't have consorted with it at all!" he bellowed.

"Her!"

Hollis snapped his mouth shut. He spun on his heel, slipping a bit in the loose sand, then stalked off around the outcropping of stone concealing us.

I let him go and slid down into the water. My entire body shook with rage. How could he dare? I had expected some negative reaction, but to play the victim? My best friend, a man who had been as good as a brother my whole life, could only see his own hurt in this situation. It didn't have anything to do with him!

Eden's cool hand slipped around my arm. She wrapped me in a calming embrace from behind. Her tail came to rest against my leg, and I pulled her a little closer for comfort. Her bright scales were like nacre, shimmering blue, green, and even a little pink when the light hit them just right through the rippling water. As beautiful as the day I had first seen her.

"You should go after him," she said in a low voice.

I glowered at the water. "He doesn't deserve it."

"He's your best friend."

I turned around in her embrace, incredulous. "Didn't you hear what he said? He called you an 'it!' And then to—to—"

"He cares about you," she said. "He's worried."

"Let him worry."

We sat in the water together for a few quiet minutes, and my heart slowed back down to its usual rhythm in time with the waves.

"Ayana, he heard our conversation."

"I know!" Apparently, I still had a little fight left in me after all. "Doesn't he have anything better to do than sit around and spy on me? I've never known him to be such a sneak. It's disgusting behavior."

"No, I mean...he heard our conversation about Nikolas and the old woman. About our plan to get your friends out of Bluewater."

The anger turned to slime in my chest, sinking low into my gut like a pit of tar. "He won't—" I swallowed hard. "He wouldn't betray us. He won't tell anyone."

"You're sure?"

No, I wasn't. I wasn't sure about anything anymore.

"Yes. I'm sure," I said instead. "He won't say anything."

Eden nodded, squeezing my hand. "If that's true, then maybe he does deserve to have you go after him."

I chewed my lip. "I have to go tell Nik and Marta about our meeting tonight. Will you wait here for me? I'll come right back."

"I'll be here," Eden promised.

I pressed my mouth to hers, to steady myself as much as to say goodbye. I savored the salty taste of her lips and lingered for just a second longer than I normally would have. When I pulled away, a wry smile teased her lips.

I went straight to the leatherworks booth Marta and Nikolas ran at the market and made small talk with them, admiring the orderly row of shoes on display. Silently, I relayed the information about the meeting planned for that night. Nikolas gave me a nod and an anxious smile to confirm he had gotten the message.

"Have you seen Hollis since the burning?" I asked Marta.

She shook her head, her eyebrows drawn. "No. Why?"

"He and I—" I paused, unsure how to tell her what happened without the risk of being overheard by Julet, who sold produce in the neighboring stand. After all, I couldn't just say that Hollis had caught me with my merfolk lover, could I? I settled with, "We had an argument. I need to apologize."

"I expect he's at work this time of day." Marta shrugged. "Go ask Fathima.

So, I said goodbye and went next to the palace, where Hollis worked as a server. I didn't really think I would find him at work, considering he had spent the last hour spying on me. But it was worth checking.

I entered the palace by the kitchen door, as usual, and pushed my way through the scullery maids and cooks toward the butler's office.

"Hollis didn't come to work today," said Fathima, the under-butler. "He sent along a message that he had some personal things to take care of."

"Oh yes, of course," I lied, not wanting to alert her that something might be wrong. "I think I know where to find him. Thank you, Fathima!"

"Any time, dear."

I left the same way I had entered. The tar pit in my stomach was solidifying into actual fear. What if I had been wrong? What if Hollis did betray us? There was no way to change the meeting with the old woman. If we missed our chance tonight, that was it. There would be no second attempt.

And as much as I didn't want to entertain the thought, a pang of guilt gnawed at my ribs. Hollis had not been right to react the way he did, but he was right about one thing: I had lied to him. I hadn't trusted my best friend with a secret so close to my heart that it had become a part of me. I should have told him about Eden years ago. I should have faced the inevitable bad reaction, which anyone in Bluewater would have had, and given him time to adjust. I should have trusted him like the brother he had always been to me.

There was nothing left to do but go back to Eden at the cove. We could only wait and hope.

Eden and I waited in companionable silence. She sunned herself on the rock next to me while I continued working on my bracelets. After a while, she slipped back into the water and began picking through the sand in much the same way Nikolas had done that morning. She sucked snails out of their shells and passed them to me to use in my craft, laughing at the disgust on my face when she offered me a bite.

When the sun moved toward the western horizon, I set aside my auger and lay back down on the rock in my favorite position. I watched Eden foraging, mesmerized by her grace, the way she moved through the water like it was a part of her. Her black hair rippled around her bare shoulders, curving around her arms like the silkiest oil. And her tail—that stunning, muscular limb shone like gemstones while the fins fluttered through the water in delicate ripples.

"She's quite beautiful, isn't she?" said a high, rasping voice over my head.

I jerked up and choked on my own gasp of shock. An old woman stood before me. I scrambled to my feet and swallowed hard.

Old was an understatement. Her skin looked like vellum handled carelessly for too many years. A cloud of white hair haloed her face, the frizzled locks breaking free of a ratty braid that fell over her hunched shoulder. Her gnarled fingers grasped a staff taller than she was. Feathers, bones, and beads had been strung along it, obscuring a worn carving at the top.

"You—Are you—"

The old woman thumped her staff on the ground impatiently and shifted her weight. "I'm Theo," she said in her hissing voice. "Your merfolk friend here said there was a mindwalker in need of assistance."

I glanced around, but Eden didn't seem to notice that Theo had arrived. Her full attention was on the seafloor about ten feet away. She ran her fingers through the sand, picking over stones, looking for another tasty bite.

"Well?" asked the old woman.

"How did you get here so fast?" I asked warily.

Theo shrugged, unconcerned. "What is time?" she asked, as if that was any kind of an answer. "What about the mindwalker? A boy, was it?" She looked around, as if Nikolas would simply be there.

"They're on their way. I expect them any moment."

"'They,' eh?" Theo's dark eyes landed on me and stayed there.

I squirmed under her intense stare. "Yes, Nikolas and his mother, Marta."

"And which one is the mindwalker?"

"Nikolas. He's thirteen."

Theo chewed on her lip and ambled away. "Well, that's something, at least." She eased herself down onto a low rock with a groan, holding onto her stick for dear life.

I darted forward to help her. Theo waved me away with an annoyed expression.

I settled down on my usual rock right at the water's edge. With a splash, Eden emerged, still chewing the contents of the shells she had found.

"Here's two more. This one's got a little pink in it." She froze when she caught sight of Theo and hunkered back down until only her eyes were visible above the rock. Eden stared at the old woman.

I shifted closer to give Eden something a little more tangible to hide behind. "This is Theo," I said. "Theo, you remember Eden?"

Theo nodded deeply. "Yes, Eden. Good to see you again."

"Thank you for coming," Eden said from her hiding place behind the rock.

Her voice was so quiet, and I barely heard her over the sound of the rushing water. How well could Theo hear at her advanced age?

"You asked, so I came," Theo said, proving her hearing to be quite good after all.

We all sat in silence, Eden and I nervous, Theo apparently bored. After a few minutes of awkward staring at each of us in turn, Theo tipped her staff in my direction. The bones rattled against each other.

"You. Why are you sad?"

"I, um—" I stared around, unwilling to talk about such personal things with a stranger.

"Ayana's friend, Hollis, doesn't approve of me," Eden said with uncharacteristic boldness.

"Eden!"

"They had a fight this afternoon," she continued, undaunted.

I covered my face with my hand.

"Who is Ayana?" Theo asked, sounding annoyed again. Like she shouldn't have to keep track of so many names.

"I am," I said.

"This Hollis person? Blond hair? Quite tall?"

I stared at her. Mindwalkers could be so unnerving. Would Nikolas grow up to talk like this old woman? Would he blurt out things he shouldn't know when he got old enough to stop caring what people thought of him? Or had this Theo woman always been this way?

"Ye-yes," I stammered.

"Yelled at him, did you? Say something you regret?"

I scowled. "He said just as much that *he* should be regretting!"

Theo cocked her head to one side, like an owl watching me from a low branch in the dark. "And what makes you think he doesn't regret it?"

My mouth snapped open, then shut again. "I-I don't—"

Theo blew past my stammers and leaned her stick toward Eden. "Your turn," she said. "Why are you sad?"

"Eden isn't sad!" I glanced down at her for validation of this statement.

But Eden's eyes went wide, and she ducked a little lower in the water.

"Eden?" I asked, my voice much softer. "Are you sad?"

I wracked my brain for any hint that Eden wasn't perfectly happy. Had there been a frown or a downward cast to her eyes, or had she looked away? But no. The entire afternoon, she had been the picture of contentment, just like always.

"Everyone's a little sad about something all the time," Theo said, sounding bored again.

"Oh?" I rounded on her. "Then why are *you* sad, old woman?"

"Ayana." Eden's voice was gentle.

She didn't need to say anything further. I knew what worried her. We needed Theo to save Nikolas. I couldn't afford to drive her away. But I couldn't help it. The indifferent expression on the old woman's face drove me to distraction.

"Instead of going around, picking at other people, why don't you answer your own question?"

"I *am* sad," Theo said on a deep breath. She shifted her weight before thoughtfully continuing. "I am sad because I am going to die soon."

That shut me up. I eyed her, unsure of how to respond.

But Theo didn't seem to need a response. "I always thought I'd be glad when the moment came. I've been walking this earth for so long, far longer than any person should several times over. But now that the time has come, I find myself growing nostalgic for my younger years. For the people I knew back then. I find myself visiting them more often than I should. I can't help it."

Her sharp eyes fell on our flabbergasted expressions, and she came back to herself.

"Perhaps that is why I decided to meet you now. To put off the inevitable just a little longer. To do one more good thing before the end."

"You speak in riddles," I said.

One side of her mouth turned upward. "Yes, I suppose I do. Your friends are coming, by the way. I thought you said there were only two? A boy and his mother?"

A pang of fear stopped my heart, and Eden slipped under the water. "There should be only two: Nikolas and Marta. How many are coming?"

Theo shook her head and waved her staff as if to say, *It doesn't matter.*

"How many are coming?" I asked again in a stronger voice. I stood over her, as if just by making her look up at me she would have to answer.

But before she could reply or even react to my disrespectful tone, Nikolas came bounding around the outcropping of stone hiding my little cove from view. Behind him walked Marta at a more careful pace. And after her appeared…

"Hollis!" I said breathlessly.

My friend's bright hair caught the sun, as usual, and I was struck once again with how beautiful he really was. His brown-eyed gaze broke my dominant stance. Even now, with his angular jaw clenched tightly and his hands balled into fists at his sides, his bearing was of pride and restraint.

He had come to listen.

I opened my mouth to speak, but Nikolas attached himself to my side, his eyes on Theo and her staff of bone and feathers.

"Hello, Granny," Nikolas said politely, his fists tight on my arm.

"Ho, boy."

"I dreamed of you. Have you come to lead us out of Bluewater?"

"That depends," she said, gesturing with her staff. "Let's have a look at you."

Nikolas shifted his weight from foot to foot while Marta made her way to us. They were both loaded down with heavy packs clanking with cooking pots and the leatherworking tools they would need to make a trade for themselves. The two of them were ready to go now. Just up and leave the only home they had ever known. Anything to save Nikolas from the fire.

Marta eyed Theo warily, but the older woman didn't seem to notice or care.

The two mindwalkers stood in silence, measuring each other up. Then Nikolas's face broke out into a mischievous grin, and he laughed at a joke only he could hear.

Theo gave a perfunctory nod, her own smile the twin of his. "Yes, I'll take him. We can leave straight away. Say goodbye to your mother, boy."

The burst of relief in my chest fizzled as Theo's words worked their way into my brain. "What?"

"What?" Marta asked at the same time. Her hand closed around Nikolas's shoulder in a tight, possessive grip.

Eden rose out of the water with a splash. "What did she say?"

Hollis remained on the outskirts of our little group and said nothing. His gaze remained fixed on Theo, as if she might burst into flame at any second and consume us all.

Theo eased herself to her feet with a grim expression. "I said, let's go."

"I'm going too," Marta said flatly. "He's not going without me. I'm his mother."

"Fine," Theo said. "Best of luck to you. Not sure why you called me here if you're just going to reject my help."

"Take them both out of the city," I demanded. "*Both* of them. That was the deal."

"There was no deal."

"Why can't I go with you?" Marta asked. "What difference does one more person make? I won't be a burden. I'm capable and strong. You need me."

"Wrong," Theo said. "*You're* the one that needs me. Without me, your only path is through eastern gate and attempt to go north through the salt flats. It will take you nearly a day to cross it in blistering sun, with no water save what you bring with you. Beyond that is the Brakish Lands. Salt swamps up to your waists. It's not as wide as the salt flats, but it'll take twice as long to cross. Still no fresh water. Only rot. Nothing grows there but red algae and stink. If you survive that, then maybe you get to habitable land and can cross the border into the Sacred Wood. If you're good of heart, the wood witch that lives there will let you pass. But don't dawdle. Again, best of luck to you."

"And with you?" Marta asked. "If that's the path on our own, then what path would you take us on?"

"Him," Theo said. "I would take *him* on a faster path through the void between worlds. It is instant and safe. But it is a journey only a mindwalker can survive. Your mind cannot leave this world.

If I took your body, your mind would be left behind, and you would be dead before we arrived. Him, on the other hand...” She jerked her staff at Nikolas, whose expression had lost all hint of levity. “He can be in another land in an instant. Gone before you can blink. Safe and sound.”

Theo turned her attention to Nikolas.

“It's your choice boy. Not your mother's, not mine. *Your* choice.”

Nikolas shied away from Theo and gripped his mother's hand. “I'm going with Mother. We'll go through the salt flats.”

Theo nodded and turned away. “Makes no difference to me.”

“Wait.” Marta's voice was barely a squeak, but it stopped us all in our tracks.

“Mother, no,” Nikolas said. “I'm going with you.”

Marta gripped him by his shoulders and set her jaw. “You're going with Granny. I will go the long way, and I'll meet you there.”

“No, Mama!” Nikolas said.

“Nik, you dreamed of Granny, right? You said yourself that she was the way out. Here she is. Things aren't exactly how we imagined, but you said this was the way.”

“What if I was wrong?” Nikolas asked.

“You're not wrong,” Theo said.

We all turned to the old woman.

“Prove it,” Hollis said.

All heads turned toward him next, but no one knew what to say.

“Excuse me?” Theo asked.

“I said to prove it. Prove to this woman that her son is safe in your hands. It's the least you can do.”

“The least I can do is go right now and leave you all to your fates. You all asked me here, not the other way around.” Theo sniffed and thumped her staff on the sand.

“Then leave!” Hollis said, unflinching.

Theo took five unsteady steps toward him and stared up into

his brown eyes. He held his ground, his expression daring her to make a move.

"Hollis, eh?" Theo asked. "Did you know, Hollis, that one day you will save the world?"

That got his attention. "What?"

"It's true. Oh, don't get all up in arms. It won't be some big heroic battle or desperate fight to the death. But one day, you will tell the truth to the right person, and that little act of integrity will change the fates of every human living on this continent and beyond. Hundreds of thousands of lives will be saved."

Hollis lowered his eyebrows. "Why are you telling me this?"

"Because if I didn't, you would never know. You would go home thinking, 'My, what a strange person that was.' And the world would keep on turning for you. Every day like the one before. But now you know. Your honesty is greatly appreciated."

"You're talking in riddles again," I said, drawing Theo's attention away from Hollis. "What a clever story that is. It can never be proven one way or the other, can it? But you can prove that Nik will be safe with you, like Hollis asked in the first place. If Marta is to travel all that way alone, at least give her some hope that Nik will be there, waiting for her on the other side."

Theo rolled her eyes like an indolent teenager. "This is what I get for coming among people again," she said. "I could be dead by now, you know! I could be done with all this!"

"No more talking! It's time to do it or not. The longer we stay on the beach like this in a group, the greater the chance we're discovered."

Hollis glanced reflexively along the wall. My house perched on the low cliff just below it, the peak of the roof only just visible. I followed his gaze on instinct, certain for a second that he had seen people up there, but the outcropping was as empty as ever. Even so, we needed to finish this.

Eden wrapped a comforting hand around my ankle, as high as she could reach from the water.

"Fine!" Theo said, then disappeared.

"What the—" Hollis gasped and threw out his hands in shock.

"Is that proof enough for you?" Theo's voice came from a long way off, and we all whirled around. She stood about fifty yards down the beach, just a black smudge on the pale landscape, her white hair whipping about in the wind.

"How did you—" I began, then stopped when Theo reappeared in front of us, as if she hadn't moved at all.

I had never...*No one* had ever heard of such a gift before. To disappear and reappear instantly somewhere else? This woman was like no mindwalker on earth, surely.

"Instantaneous travel." Theo sounded bored again. "An incredibly rare skill among mindwalkers. And one that I am happy to use in order to help this boy get to safety." She gestured her staff at Nikolas to emphasize her point. "But I am a very busy person, and I don't have time to stand around, bleating at each other like a bunch of old goats!"

"Nik, you have to go," Marta said, turning him to face her. "You go with Granny, and I'll meet you in the north. Nobody cares about me, so even if the border guard stops us, they won't prevent us from passing. But if they find out what *you* are, it's over! And I can't bear that! So, you have to go!"

"Mama, no!" Tears started in Nikolas's eyes. "I want to stay with you."

Marta hugged him tightly, then pushed him toward Theo with a determined shove. "Go before I change my mind!" she said in a cracking voice.

And that was it.

Theo wrapped her hand around the boy's arm, and they were gone. Where Theo and Nikolas had stood in the fine white sand, all that was left of them were their footprints.

Marta let out one heart-wrenching sob and covered her face with her hands. I put my arms around her, shushing uselessly.

How could a person comfort a woman who had just said goodbye to her teenage son? Possibly forever?

"Oh, stop your sniveling!"

Theo's voice jerked us all back to attention with a cry of alarm. She stood in her own footprints once more, but Nikolas was nowhere to be seen.

"Where is my son? Where is Nik?" Marta shrilled.

"Will you calm down? I took him three weeks into the future and left him with you on the southern border of Mauland, which is the first small town you should come to after the Sacred Wood."

"The future?" Marta asked breathlessly.

"But I don't advise that you stay in Mauland for long," Theo continued, waving her hand as if this were an afterthought. "As soon as you're stable, move a bit more north to settle down. You don't want to be there when...well, never mind. Don't stay in Mauland."

We all stared at her, our mouths hanging open in shock

"Well, don't stand there, gaping like a bunch of fish heads! You have a long way to go, woman! Find someone to go with you. Someone who travels for a living. Go now."

When Marta remained frozen in my arms, Theo shooed her away with her rattling staff.

"Go!"

Marta jumped out of her skin. "Okay. Thank you, Ayana. And Eden. I have to..." But she couldn't finish her sentence. The last twenty minutes had just been too much. She squeezed my hand and fled up the path, out of sight.

"Oh, no...Don't thank me..." Theo retreated with a sour expression.

She turned to Hollis, Eden, and me, working her mouth like a cow chewing cud. Then, like a storm cloud throwing lightning bolts at random, she pointed her staff at each of us and destroyed everything in her path with just a few well-chosen words.

"She plans to leave forever," she said, pointing at Eden. "He already betrayed her," Theo said at Hollis, then turned to me. "And this one would have carried the secret of her merfolk lover to the grave without ever thinking twice. So, I think you all have a lot of talking to do. And maybe some running."

Theo disappeared once more. Something about the tone in her voice convinced me she wasn't coming back this time.

The three of us were left gawking at each other. I couldn't fathom what was going on in their heads. Hollis had betrayed me after all? My oldest friend, who I had known even longer than Eden...How far had he gone? Had he told the authorities about Eden? Had he simply told them where they could catch me in my protected little cove? Had he come here just to lead the way? Were they advancing even now?

But though all these questions were vital and immediate, I could only think about what Theo had said about Eden.

"You're leaving me?" I choked out. I slipped down into the water so I was eye level with her.

"I-I don't..." she stammered.

"When? Where will you go? You're leaving?" My voice rose to a panicked squeak and broke off.

"I don't know! Maybe!" Her cool hands gathered up my fingers, and I held on for dear life. If I didn't let her go, she couldn't leave.

"Why now? Where will you go?"

"I met an old friend when I went to Glenfall Cove to find Theo. He told me the way to Eventide. I can go home, Ayana! My family is still there! I can see them again!"

I gripped her hands close. "You're leaving me?" I said again in a whisper.

"I'm so sorry, Ayana." She pulled me nearer, and I wrapped my arms around her. Eden fit so perfectly against me. How could this be wrong? How could we be apart when we were made for each other?

"Let her go, Ayana," Hollis said. "Let her go home. She doesn't belong here."

Something snapped inside me at the sound of his voice.

"What do you know about it?" I hissed. I clambered out of the water, ignoring Eden's protests, and advanced on the man who had been my best friend for as long as I could remember. But not anymore. "You've known about her for one day. *One* fucking day, Hollis! You don't know her! You don't know *us!* All you know is what you've been told by a city made of cement, stone, and stucco. We're supposed to be one with the sea!"

"And what do *you* know?" Hollis shot back. "You're just a silly girl with a crush! You don't know anything about being responsible for people you care about! All you can think about is your girlfriend! Where do you think this will end, Ayana? You can't live with her in the water, and she can't join you on the land. There is no future here!"

"How dare you!" In a flash of blind rage, I lashed out. I was not sure what happened, but there was a pressure on my hands and a surge in my shoulders and arms. The next thing I knew, Hollis was sprawled out on the sand.

"Ayana! Don't!" Eden cried out in alarm.

But it was too late for warnings. I had shoved him down. I'd pushed him like a child in the school yard, arguing over a toy. And I stood before him, shaking.

I should back down. I should apologize and help him up.

But his words kept cycling through my mind. *There's no future here. You're just a girl with a crush. Just a girl with a crush. Just a crush.*

"You don't know anything about me," I spat.

"I know you better than you know yourself." Hollis propped himself up on his elbows and glared back. "I know when you found out I had betrayed you just now, all you cared about was your girlfriend leaving."

"Is that it, then? You're jealous? You think I care about her more than I care about you?"

Hollis picked himself up and made a few half-hearted swipes at the sand sticking to his skin and clothes. "First of all, yes. I do think that. And don't you try to deny it. You've proven that already several times over."

"I don't—"

He cut me off before I could get in a retort. "But if you would just listen to me for once in your damned life, maybe you'd hear something beside the voice in your own head! I betrayed you, Ayana! I told them about Eden! I told them you would be here. I'm surprised they're not here already!"

"I know, you asshole!" I screeched, trying to shove him again.

But he caught my hands in midair and held on like a vise.

"Shut up and listen!" he said over my grunts of effort as I struggled to pull out of his grasp. "I was scared and angry. I was afraid for my brothers and sisters, and I did the only thing I could think of to keep them safe. I shouldn't have told the guard, but I did. And I'm sorry."

I stopped and scowled at him. "You think that makes it better?"

"No, you idiot," he said. "But I needed to say it. Now you need to stop fighting me and run."

Eden cried out in alarm, and with a splash, she disappeared under the water.

"Eden?" I peered into the deep, but she was nowhere to be found.

A blur went by my head, only a couple of feet away, and an arrow sliced through the surface, right where Eden had been a second before.

"Eden!" I screamed.

There was no blood in the water. She hadn't been hit. Oh, please, don't let her be hit.

Hollis grabbed me from behind and hauled me away from the water. "Here! She's here!" he cried as loudly as his voice would go.

"Hollis! Stop!"

But it was too late. The soldiers had spotted us on the beach and were already halfway down the path. There were only six, but that was more than enough to subdue me, especially with Hollis handing me over like a sack of grain at tax time. They were fully armed with daggers and clubs, with one bowman and one captain with a double-headed axe.

Among them were Kris and Andrei Clark, the hateful red-headed twins who had once thrown rocks at Eden. Andrei was the bowman, and Kris carried a vicious dagger in one strong fist.

"Hold her!" Kris Clark shouted.

Andrei raised his bow. He didn't draw the string yet, but he aimed the arrow directly at my face. I stared down the quivering shaft.

"I should have known it would be you two," I hissed at them.

"Come quietly, water witch!" said another soldier whose name I didn't know.

"We don't want to hurt you!" Andrei added from behind his bow.

That lie sent chills down my spine. I recognized it in their manic eyes, in their self-righteous smiles. They couldn't wait to drug me and lead me up to the pyre.

But I wouldn't go happily to my death. Not ever. It was my right to be afraid.

Hollis's arms were like a vise around my body. I beat and pried at his hands, scratched at his skin, but I couldn't get him off me. The seconds stretched into hours and one horrible certainty became clear in my mind. Hollis was giving me up. I wasn't safe with him.

And the soldiers edged closer with every stuttering effort to breathe. Their leather armor squeaked, and their weapons clanked against each other. Their boots were like thunder rolling in over the tides.

I was going to die. This was the end.

If they didn't kill me right here and now, they would burn me in the morning, just like Kealan. They would feed me the tonic and I'd laugh my way up the pyre, just like all the rest. Whether I wanted to or not.

"Throw me to the ground, and then run," Hollis said in my ear. "Do it now! And don't stop!"

Still half panicked, I latched onto his instructions and obeyed. I heaved Hollis to the side, and with his cooperation, I threw him to the ground, stumbling a bit in the sand. When I scrambled to my feet, the soldiers were not far behind.

But I wasn't fast enough.

One heavy hand slammed onto my shoulder, causing me to lose my footing. It was Kris Clark. He scrabbled at my shirt, trying to get a good hold of me through his heavy gloves.

"No!" I screamed, just as panicked as I had once been while trying to save a man called Kealan. I hadn't been able to fight off the soldiers then, but I was bigger now.

So, I swiped my hand through the sand, grabbing as much as I could in my fist, and flung it at Kris's eyes. He shrieked and spat, letting go long enough to scrape at his face. I hoped he went blind. What justice that would be.

"Stop!" Andrei yelled, pulling his bow.

The arrow whistled through the air, but his aim was wide. The arrow caught at the skin of my shoulder, leaving a stinging cut. But it wasn't enough to stop me. I scrambled to my feet and ran as fast as I could down the beach.

My wet clothes clung to my legs. The sand chafed at my skin. The wind in my ears drove out all sound, and the thunder of the soldiers' chase faded to nothing. My lungs burned with the effort of breathing, in and out, in and out, as my feet pounded along the compacted, wet sand.

Run. Just keep running.
Don't look back.
Run.

~

All is done and ended.
The boy was finally free.
But she was left,
A deep unrest,
Alone, by the sea.

FIVE

How far did I run before I collapsed? I couldn't guess. The endless beach and crashing waves blended into a continuous stream of blue, beige, and white. I passed all landmarks I knew, went further than I ever had before. And finally, when my shaking legs threatened to give out, I stumbled toward a clump of gorse bushes and crumpled to the sand in their shade.

I peeked down the beach between the yellow flowers, but there was only a single line of footprints in the sand. No one had followed me this far. Likely, they never would. It wasn't safe to stay close to the water for too long, after all.

I collapsed flat on my back, my chest heaving and my breath loud in my ears. Now the danger had passed, the reality of my situation slammed into focus. Nikolas and Marta had gotten out safely, and I was grateful for that. But it had cost me everything.

The life I had known was over. I could never go back to Bluewater. Not ever. They would remember the girl who had consorted with the merfolk. They would arrest me at first sight, no questions asked.

I'd never see my mother again. I had planned to travel inland at the solstice, to visit her and her new family for the holidays, that would never happen now. How long before news of my blasphemy reached her? What would she think of me?

I'd never know.

And Hollis...

Dear Hollis had faltered, but in the end, he had been my friend. At least, he had tried to be. I couldn't imagine how hard it had been, knowing his brothers and sisters were in danger if he were complicit. Hollis had done the only thing he could think of to keep his own name clean and get me out at the same time.

And now, just like my mother, like my stall at the market square, like my house with the lacy curtains and the stove where Mama had taught me to cook—it was all lost to me. Forever.

And Eden was gone. Even if she tried to find me, I wouldn't be in my little cove. She wouldn't know where to look.

It didn't make a difference, though. She should be halfway home to Eventide by now. If she were smart, she would never look back. Eden should stay with her family, where she was safe.

So, what else was there to do but lie there in the sand on an unfamiliar beach, listen to the crash of uncaring waves, and cry?

Time passes slowly when you're alone. I should have moved on, should have kept going until I found a town where I could start over. What was keeping me at the water's edge?

Nothing.

But I couldn't leave the shore. I found myself staring out over the water for hours on end, chasing the shade of the palms as the sun moved overhead. I didn't think Eden would come looking for me. Really, I didn't.

But what if she did?

So, I stayed. After a while, I had to get up and do practical things. I needed food, water, and shelter from the sun and the unpredictable rain.

These things were all easy to obtain. Some driftwood and palm fronds made an acceptable shelter, and banana leaves set up over coconut husks provided plenty of rain collection. I had run off without my box of tools, but I was able to make a rudimentary fishing net by spinning coconut fibers between my fingers and knotting the threads together.

My days were spent on menial tasks: spinning, crafting, basket weaving. These could be done with one eye on my work and the other on the sea.

What if?

One day, a young man with dark hair and a large pack came walking down the beach. At first, I hid, but the absurdity of it nearly got a laugh out of me. How could I hide with my shelter and all my half-finished projects lying about?

"Ho, there!" the man said with a wave. "It's bad luck to stay too long by the water, you know."

I forced friendly confidence into my voice. "I could say the same to you."

The man laughed, putting his dimples on display. "Fair enough! I'm Miles. What's your name?"

"Ayana."

"Good to meet you, Ayana. What are you making there?"

I held up the shark-eye shell I was braiding into a sinew bracelet.

He knelt to examine my work. "You don't see shells like this very often. Is it for trade?"

"It's not finished," I said.

"But it's close, right? Then I'll sit with you a while, if you like."

"What will you trade for it?"

"Would you take a song?" he asked, patting his bag.

I looked closer. The shape indicated it probably held some kind of stringed instrument. A bard, then.

"I have no use for songs," I said.

"Everyone has a use for songs. But I won't insist. What will you take for it?"

"A saucepan."

Miles's eyebrows shot up. "A saucepan?"

I gestured at my cook fire. "I'm tired of roasting things. There are some good clams down the way, and I need a pan to cook them right."

He spread his arms wide and gave me a disarming smile. "I don't have a saucepan."

"Then you don't have a bracelet either."

"What about some bread and honey?"

My hands froze on the bracelet, and I narrowed my gaze on his face. I really needed a saucepan, but my mouth watered at the thought of real bread. Of anything sweet.

Miles arched his eyebrows, enticing. He'd caught me, and he knew it. "Eh? What do you say?"

"Let's see it, then."

He fished out a loaf of hard, crusty bread wrapped in an oil cloth and a crock of honey with a tight-fitting lid. His lunch for the day, no doubt. Its smell wafted into my nostrils even over the briny sea.

"You have yourself a deal," I said.

We spent the afternoon eating honey bread and talking companionably about nothing of consequence. By the afternoon, he had a bracelet, and I had a full belly.

Two days later, Miles came back. This time, he brought his sister, Annaliese. She *oohed* and *aahed* over the baskets and bracelets I had busied myself making over the last few weeks and traded a linen handkerchief for one.

"And this is for you." Miles tugged a small saucepan out of his pack.

"You already paid for your bracelet," I said, eyeing the shark's eye glinting dully on his wrist. It looked good on him.

"Consider it a gift."

And as much as I wanted to refuse, the thought of doing without a saucepan for even one more meal was intolerable. What harm would it do to accept a small gift?

"Thank you."

Annaliese was a flighty thing, running here and there along the beach and loving everything she saw. Her blonde hair reflected the sun, just like Hollis's used to.

I turned my eyes away from her and back to the shells in my hands.

Where Annaliese ran wild in the surf, Miles sat with me. He helped me improve my shelter by adding supports to the walls and extra thatch to the roof. Sometimes, he pulled out his lute and practiced his music. He was in the middle of writing a song about a blue bannock that rolled out of a baker's basket and made it all the way to the sea.

It was a silly, nonsensical song, and I found myself laughing more than once. A strange feeling. I hadn't laughed in weeks.

"Come into town with me," he said, his dimples on full display. "I'm playing tonight in the square. We can have a drink. Make a night of it."

The laughter died in my throat, and I shrank into myself. The thought of going into town—of leaving the water to go anywhere—it felt like dying.

Miles's smile faded. "Or I can bring you a drink next time I come. How's that sound? You're getting a private concert now anyway. Why would you want to hear me play again?" He plucked at his lute and flexed his hand on the frets, pulling a mischievous twang out of it.

I wrapped my arms around my knees and smiled again, but it was just a mask now.

Miles didn't ask why I stayed by the water, and I didn't offer. If I could manage it, I'd never thought about Bluewater again.

The pair of them visited me often, bringing me tools and supplies in exchange for my bracelets and baskets, which they sold in town. Soon I had the makings of a real home there on the beach. A place to stay forever and stare at the water. Neither on land nor at sea. Stuck in between, just like Hollis always feared.

What if?

"Have you ever been in love?" Miles asked one day. He had come alone, leaving Annaliese behind with her beau in town. He plucked the strings on his lute absently, adding a gentle melody to the rhythm of the waves.

I chewed my lip. "Once. You?"

"Not real love, I think. I've had my flings. The girls in town hear me sing and think themselves in love, but it's never true."

"What brought this up?" I asked, adjusting my position on my woven mat in the shade of the gorse bushes.

"Annaliese wants to marry her man. They plan to do it in the spring, when the cassia trees bloom again."

"It sounds lovely. Do you object to it or something? Don't like the man, maybe?"

He shook his head. "No, nothing like that. It's just that she's sacrificed so much to be with him, and I can't help but wonder if it was worth it."

"Maybe it was; maybe it wasn't."

"What would you do to have your lover back?"

"Gods, anything," I said. "I'd do anything."

"Would you even go so far as to wait by the sea forever? Hoping she'll come find you?"

I looked up in horror, but Miles only had a knowing smile.

"Word travels fast, Ayana. A crafter from Bluewater who fell for one of the merfolk? You didn't even change your name."

"Miles, please. You can't tell anybody. Have you told anyone?"

He put a calming hand on my arm, and I had to fight the urge to jerk away. Miles was my friend. But then again, Hollis had been my friend too.

"Don't worry. No one knows but me. Not even Annaliese has made the connection. And we haven't told a soul that you're here. We know better than to gossip about anyone living on the beach. You wouldn't be here if you wanted to be found. You have nothing to worry about."

I clenched the auger he had brought me a few weeks before. It had made my work go much faster. The one tool I couldn't make myself. I gripped it so tightly my fingers hurt against the steel. "Is that why you came here, then? To interrogate me?"

"Not interrogate. Just confirm my suspicions. I don't mean you any harm, Ayana. Honest."

"Well, they're confirmed." I tried to get up, but his hand on my arm held firm.

"Don't go. Stay here with me a bit. Tell me about her."

I hesitated. I could tell him about her hair, slippery as oil and dark as ink. About her blush gray skin, her iridescent tail with the flowing fins. I could tell him about her laugh, about the way she used to chase me with snails, giggling, until I tackled her. About how we used to lie on the rock below my house for hours, not saying anything at all.

"It doesn't matter anymore," I said instead. "She's gone. It's over. She's not coming back."

"Then why do you stay here?" Miles asked.

What if?

"Where the hell else am I supposed to go?"

"You could come into town with me."

I threw out both hands, gaping. "You say that. You make it sound so easy. Like I can just get up and go with you."

"What's stopping you?"

I opened my mouth, closed it again. Grunted in frustration. Conflicting desires clogged up my mind, like a drain swollen with debris after a hurricane. I wanted to be alone, to have company, to yell and scream, to beg him to take me along. I wanted to go, to stay, to wait, to start over, to go back.

He was right. Nothing was stopping me from moving on. Nothing at all. I had lost everyone and everything I had ever loved, and still I could not leave the beach. I couldn't let go of Miles any more than I could let go of my hope that Eden might come back.

What if?

Miles's warm hand squeezed my arm, and my face crumpled in unexpected emotion. It was the first time anyone had touched me in months.

"Tell me about her," he said again in a low voice.

So, I did. I told him everything, giving him the gift Hollis had always wanted: honesty. The words came pouring out of me in a torrent. At first, they came hastily, angrily. But as I fell into the story, my voice smoothed out, and the telling came easier. I talked about how Eden and I had met, how I had failed to save Kealan as a child, how Nikolas had grown up before my eyes, how Mama had done the one thing I never learned how to do: move on.

The ending was harder. I had to force the words out because I didn't want to relive the experience of betrayal and loss, of running away. But as I muddled my way through, the burden grew a little lighter.

We sat in silence for a long time afterward. The endless rushing of the waves soothed my raw soul. My voice was sore, and my heart felt empty.

"So, you're waiting for her, then?"

"No," I said, then chewed on my lip. The lie didn't feel as strong as it used to.

"What if she never comes?"

"She won't."

"How long will you wait?"

"I don't know!"

Miles had no response to that, just a helpless expression of hope. He wanted to help me; he just didn't know how.

"I'm tired, Miles. Come back another time."

We didn't talk about it again. I could tell he wanted to. It was in the way he sometimes opened his mouth, only to shut it again. It was in the way he took to staring at the water, just like I did.

But his compassion always won out, and he never brought it up. Not once.

Winter passed, and Annaliese married her man in the spring, just like she had planned. I sent a net of white Scotch bonnets to dress her hair with, but I didn't go myself.

Miles came a few times a week to sit with me and write his songs. "I just need to get away from it all," he said, sighing into the breeze. He helped me maintain my shelter, and I taught him how to dig for clams. We ate together, worked together. He became my only link to the rest of the world.

And one day in May, for no apparent reason, I thought it might be nice to go visit Miles in town. To try the bakery he always talked about and see if there were any fabrics for sale in the market that I liked. Maybe I could make a new shirt.

It was a surreal thought. Such a momentous change should have come with an epic battle or a valiant effort. It should have been difficult. Climactic. But it just happened. No fanfare. No one to even witness it.

Would it be so hard to start over? No. Probably not. People did it every day.

Miles noticed my changed mood that morning when he came ambling down the path. There was no hiding my shy smile of anticipation. "What's got you all worked up?" he asked.

I shrugged. "Nothing, really. Have you finished your new song?"

"It's not nothing." He pointed at how I clutched my fingers together.

"I want to hear your song!"

"Bullshit!" he said with a laugh. "What happened?"

"I just—" It was still hard to say out loud, but the time had come to be brave. "I was thinking I might go with you into town. If the offer is still good, that is."

Miles threw out both hands, grinning broadly. "Yes! The offer is good! Let's go!"

"No! No. Not now. Not today. But soon."

"Soon?" he asked with hope.

"I'm getting there."

He clapped his hands and rubbed them together. "I'll take 'soon.' This is good. You feel good?"

I took a deep breath and let it out in a huff. "I feel good. For the first time in a long time, I feel like me again."

Miles clapped a hand on my shoulder and nodded, pleased. "So, do you want to hear my song, then?" he asked.

"Yes, yes!"

And we settled down in our favorite shady spot under the gorse bushes.

He began to play. The notes poured out of his lute like it had a mind of its own. I leaned back against a palm trunk and closed my eyes, letting the music wash over me.

I had gotten so used to hearing him play over the past months that when his fingers stumbled on the strings, I almost didn't understand what had happened. The melody faltered for a few beats, then fell silent. I opened my eyes, confused.

Miles sat calmly next to me, staring out over the water. I followed his gaze. There was nothing remarkable about the shifting blue.

"What is it?" I asked.

He broke his stare and resumed plucking at the lute, but the melody had changed to a simpler tune I'd heard plenty of times before. "Can I ask you a hypothetical question?"

"Okay."

"This new excitement you have to go into town...It seems like a first step to starting over. Yes?"

"I suppose."

"Does this mean you finally believe Eden won't come back?"

I sighed. "She was never going to come back, Miles."

"That's not what I asked."

I chewed on my lip. "It's not that I believe it. I just want—It's just time to choose. The way I see it, I could live on this beach forever or turn my back on it and go inland, like Mama did."

Miles nodded without interrupting.

"I'm tired of being alone, of having to scrape and scramble. I love the sea. I love everything about it. But it's just not enough on its own. And I'm thinking, maybe it never was." I shrugged and half smiled. "Plus, I'd like a real bed. I've missed sleeping in a bed."

"So..." His fingers stilled on his lute. "So, if you left the beach, where would you go?"

I shrugged again. "I don't know. I'd figure it out."

"You could stay with Annaliese until you found your feet. Or you could...You could come with me. I'll be doing some traveling now that the weather is warm, singing all over Authe Ida. Maybe one day I'll even go north. Seek my fortune." He gave me a rueful grin. "You could come with me if you wanted."

The thought settled in my mind, sprouting idea after idea. All my life had been lived on the beach. I had never been anywhere. And now, here was my opportunity to go and see the world. Maybe we could even go far enough to visit Nikolas and Marta, see for myself that they were happy in their new home.

The idea drew a smile to my chapped lips. "Yeah. Maybe."

But Miles didn't return my grin. His worried expression doused the niggling excitement his offer had sparked.

"What is it, Miles?"

"I just—It's just that..." He trailed off, frowning at his lute. "I wanted you to think about it for a bit before..."

"Before what?"

"I wanted you to have a real choice. I wanted you to decide. I don't want you coming with me just because Eden never came back. And I don't want you staying here with her just because she did come. You should choose one or the other because it's what you want, Ayana. You need to choose. For yourself."

I shook my head. "I'm confused. What are you saying to me?"

"I'm saying...she came back." He gestured out to the water with the neck of his flute. "I saw her. Her face above the water, just like you described. Then she was gone before you looked. She's here. I think maybe she's waiting until I leave."

I stared at him for several seconds, my eyes wide, before rising mechanically to my feet. I stumbled toward the water, scanning the waves for any sign of Eden's face.

"But I don't want to go," Miles said from behind me. "Not unless you're coming with me. You're the best friend I ever had, and I want you to be happy. But I can't stand the idea of you wasting away here on this beach for the rest of your life. Not for her or anybody else."

I couldn't answer him. Was she really here? No. He must have imagined it. Saw a bit of seaweed and imagined the rest.

But then...

Yes! There, in the rolling water, was a face with eyes just above the surface. Too large, inky black, set in a pale gray face. Eyes I would have known anywhere.

I stood as if in a trance. My muscles moved, but I could only think about her. *She's here. Oh gods, it's her. She's here.*

My feet moved across the sand, and Eden rose a little higher out of the water. Her brow wrinkled in desperate hope, her smile broad and real.

My throat closed when I stepped into the water. "You're here," I croaked.

"I've been looking for you everywhere!" she said, reaching for me.

"I've been waiting for you." I collapsed into her arms, holding her as tightly as I could, determined never to let her go again.

"I found it, Ayana!" she said into my hair. Her voice was just like I remembered: musical, soothing, soft. "I found it, and I want you to come back with me. We'll be safe there. Come with me. Say you'll come! I've been looking for you to bring you back with me."

"Yes! Anywhere. I'll come with you. Where?"

Eden smiled at me again, true joy like I had never seen in her eyes.

"Eventide. Home."

I glanced back at the home I had built there on the beach. The shelter Miles had helped me create. My crafts half finished, lying about in tidy piles on their mats and in baskets.

And there was Miles himself, his lute laid to rest on top of its bag in the shade. He stood at the water's edge, a little line between his brows. Miles had heard every word.

"Wait one second," I said to Eden, squeezing her hand. Then I waded back to Miles and threw my arms around his neck. I soaked his clothes immediately, but he held me tight anyway.

"You've made your choice, then?" he asked into my hair.

I smiled up at him. "I think I made this choice when I was ten years old. I just wasn't ready for it yet."

He nodded and set me away from him. "Go, then. And live with abandon, mergirl."

"Write a song about me."

"What makes you think I haven't already?"

I laughed, but there was a sadness to it.

"Tell them about me," I said. "Then maybe everything that happened will mean something."

Miles nodded once, squeezing my hand. "I will."

I didn't know how to say goodbye. That was one thing I'd never learned. So, I simply turned away and waded back out to where Eden waited in the shallows.

"How will we get to Eventide?" I asked.

"We swim straight south. A person could never swim that far, but I can carry you. It'll take most of a day, but I can get you there fast."

An excitement I hadn't known in months welled up in my chest. "What if" had come true. Finally.

I kissed my hand and raised it to Miles, who gave me a knowing smile in return. He would miss me, just as I would miss him. But we both knew I'd been waiting for this. He would understand I couldn't stay.

I tucked the auger in my back pocket—the one tool I couldn't make—and turned my back on the shore.

With Eden's hand in mine, I set my eyes to the shimmering sea.

"Let's go and never look back."

Eden grinned. "Never look back."

~

What became of salt and hope?
Of girls who cannot stay?
Did love abide?
And brave the tide?
My friends, I cannot say.

But there upon the empty shore,
Where friendship used to be,
I sat alone
And smiled alone,
Staring at the sea.

EPILOGUE

As the hardwood floors, stiff chairs, and soppy drunks absorbed the final ringing notes, Miles almost wished it wasn't over. This was why he had written the song, after all. To help him stay close to Ayana. To tell her story. And every time the song ended, he was left on that beach all over again, watching her disappear into the water.

"Did you know her, then? Ayana of Bluewater?" asked a man in the crowd.

An expectant hush fell over the room. Miles chewed the inside of his cheek while he considered this. Ayana's story was common knowledge by then, and understandably so. The story of a girl accused of consorting with the merfolk had spread like wildfire through the country, picking up speed with each telling, with embellishments and outright lies added to the drama.

Unfortunately, kindness was not exciting, so by this point, Ayana had become little more than a victim at best and a villain at worst.

That was a big reason why Miles's version had become so infamous. To paint both Ayana and Eden as sympathetic? As the heroes of the story? It just wasn't done. And it certainly wasn't supposed to be so compelling.

"It's true I met a woman on the beach, and her name was Ayana," he said. "But the rest is simply the way I saw her. It is the truth I saw in her eyes."

The crowd held its collective breath, unsure of how to take his tale.

"Ayana was a criminal," someone said from the middle of the crowd.

Miles pursed his lips and cringed internally.

"It's just a story!" cried his wife next to him. "Merfolk aren't real."

Miles let out a heavy sigh and leaned back against the bar.

"Full well they are!" said someone else.

"Yeah, but they ain't like in the song! They're vicious. My mam told me."

"What does your mam know?"

"I saw a merfolk once...when I was a kid! She was just like Eden in the tale!"

"You saw a seal, you idiot!"

Miles tucked his lute close to his body and slid sideways along the bar to escape. This always happened after he sang the "Mergirl of Bluewater." The arguments started. The folktales and the anecdotes.

The voices overlapped each other like waves, sometimes swelling into yelling, other times laughter. But always, always, the story grew and passed from hand to hand, like gossip.

But sometimes, if he was lucky, someone really listened. Tonight, it had been a little boy about twelve years old. He sat at the back of the public house, his expression alight with hopeful wonder.

Miles escaped the growing argument at the bar and paused by the door to look the boy over. He wore a good linen shirt and held a fine straw hat in his hands. He'd probably been sent to fetch his father home for supper and had stayed to hear the song.

"Is it true, sir?" the boy asked in a quiet voice.

None of the arguing folk at the bar heard or paid them the slightest bit of attention.

Miles looped the strap of his lute bag across his body and squared his shoulders. He glanced back at the bar. None of the cheap bastards had given him a coin. Not one. But it looked like the night hadn't been a total waste.

Miles fingered the shark-eye bracelet and winked at the boy by the door. Then he walked out into the cool night air. On to the next town, the next crowd. Maybe someday, he would go north, find out what stories they had to tell. Maybe he would try to find the young man called Nikolas, who knew what it was to travel between the worlds.

But the boy in the pub...he would never leave. Miles knew it in his heart, like the girl in the story, that boy would never love anything like the sea. And someday, if he stared at the water long enough, maybe someone might stare back.

Starsong

ONE

The stars woke me.

Their voices sounded almost human. Or maybe like a bow drawn across the taut strings of a fiddle in a keening, pulsing song. A chorus of them, singing and shouting for joy, for beauty, coating everything in a silvery light. Joining the crickets, the toads, the wind, and the thrum of the earth itself, vibrating with life and magic.

They were so loud, I didn't understand how anyone could sleep through it. I sat bolt upright and peered at Sana's bed in the opposite corner. She lay in perfect tranquility, her face pressed into her flat pillow as if to a lover's chest.

Not that she'd ever had a lover. At least, not one she would admit to.

The stars never woke Sana. Not even when we were girls.

"Can't you hear them, Sana?" I would ask.

"Of course not, Lettie," she'd say, brushing a lock of my wavy brown hair away from my face. "Because there's nothing to hear. Sometimes people just wake up. There's no *why*. Go back to sleep."

She always said some version of the same thing. "No, Lettie." "There's nothing to hear, Lettie." "Go back to sleep, Lettie." So, after a while, I stopped asking her about it.

I didn't need her confirmation. I knew what I heard, and it was the stars.

The night was relatively warm for so early in the year, and I had left the window open to coax in the fresh air. That was one thing Sana and I had always agreed on ever since we were girls. There was nothing better for sleep than a pile of toasty warm quilts and the chill air biting at your nose.

Maybe that was why I'd woken up. With the window open for the first time that spring, it was easier for the stars to call to me.

I rose up on my knees and leaned against the window sill. Down below, the forest canopy shifted in the fidgety wind. The stars cast a wavering glow over the bustling trees, making everything look different. Everything *felt* different.

The rhythmic *shh* rustled through the dense trees on that side of the yard. I knew for a fact it was the stars making this music. The wind didn't sound like that during the day.

The Old Kind were out there in the woods. A tree spirit probably, or maybe a keeper of small animals. Or maybe it was many spirits, all chattering and dancing among the swaying branches in the starlight. Leaf sprites or fairies...or something like that.

I had never seen them, but they were there. That's why the stars sang—because the Old Kind should never be ignored. Even the stars knew that.

I eased the heavy quilts away slowly, careful not to disturb my sister. The night air bit right through my thin nightshirt, but I didn't dare try to fumble for my dressing gown. I could barely see in the pitch darkness, and I would be sure to knock over Sana's stool or trip over the trunk near the door before I managed to find it.

The stars might not wake up my sister, but my clumsiness certainly would.

So I slipped through the room, gritting my teeth against the cold, and did my best to make no noise. I glanced over at her when I reached the door, just to double-check that she hadn't stirred. Her dark hair tumbled like a thundercloud over the gray linen pillowcase, so beautiful and serene. This was the only time when the cares of the daytime didn't mar her face with worry lines and sharp expressions.

Imagine if Rafe could see her like this. If he could see that she wasn't all thorns, that she could be soft if she wanted to be. Maybe they wouldn't bicker so much.

Then again, I didn't really think Rafe minded the bickering. Why else would he come around so much?

I tiptoed down the stairs one at a time, leaning heavily on the banister to help me skip the third and fourth steps from the bottom, which squeaked horribly and threatened to give way underfoot. With light footsteps, I made my way to the narrow kitchen. There, on the workbench, our least-holey tea cloth was draped over the sourdough crock.

Oh, but I shouldn't. Not the sourdough starter. Not again. Maybe an egg?

No, Sana kept a careful count. She would notice if one of the eggs went missing from the basket on the sideboard.

But the sourdough? That would be easier. Surely, Sana wouldn't notice if I took just a little spoonful? I didn't need much. The Old Kind didn't count quantity, only remembrance. Only sacrifice.

That sourdough starter was the cornerstone of our kitchen. It always had been, even back when it had been Mama's. Sana counted her days around that starter, watching it carefully, feeding it flour and water when needed, taking from it when necessary to bake a fragrant loaf of bread or pancakes. It dictated how our limited funds were spent. Flour wasn't always easy to come by, and the starter could never be neglected.

"So long as we keep this starter alive, we'll survive another day," she liked to say.

But the Old Kind demanded sacrifice. If that sourdough was the center of our kitchen, that gave it more weight than a cabbage leaf or a stray bean could ever have. So much love and care had gone into it. And besides, Sana would never notice. She never had before. I just had to be careful.

I lifted the tea cloth away and breathed in the sweet, almost vinegar scent. It smelled like home, like safety. That's why I usually chose the starter as my offering. Because when I breathed it in, my chest filled up with warmth and love. That's what I was giving to the Old Kind. I was giving them my joy.

I dipped my finger into the crock and scraped up a dollop of the cool, sticky sourdough starter. A real dish was always best, so I took down a pinch bowl from the tidy stack at the back of the cupboard and wiped the starter onto it as neatly as I could. I dragged my finger against the cool ceramic, trying to get every last speck of it. What was left on my finger, I sucked off with determination and tried not to make a face.

"Blech," I said to the empty kitchen. I wiped my tongue against the roof of my mouth several times, trying to get past the acrid flavor.

But the starter couldn't be wasted. And the gods forbid if Sana noticed a stain on my shirt were I to wipe my finger off on my clothes. I could hear her admonitions in my mind.

What did you do, Lettie? Do you have any idea how hard it is to get a stain like this out of linen? I just washed this shirt too! I'll have to do it again. And she would add one more worry line to her forehead. Another weight on her shoulder.

No. It was better to just lick the finger.

With my little dish in hand, I eased the front door open and stepped out into the chilly night air.

The starsong struck me anew, and the wind kicked up in the

canopy of trees in the side yard, as if to welcome me outside. I breathed in deeply and forced myself not to shiver when my loose hair joined the dance around my shoulders.

With quick footsteps, I dashed across the thick spring grass toward the trees on the southeastern side of our yard. Our little acre sat on the very edge of town and butted right up against the forest, so there was no one to spot my white shirt glowing in the starlight as I disappeared between the heavy trunks.

These woods were mostly oaks, elms, and ash, but there was a solitary yew about a hundred feet beyond the tree line. Everyone knew a yew tree was a sacred thing, but ours was particularly ancient. It had a massive trunk with countless folds and narrow spaces in which a sprite might hide. It was old enough to begin hollowing out, with a small pocket around the back side of the trunk where I sometimes liked to sit.

Its majestic branches towered overhead and leaned noticeably to one side, as if it stood in a perpetual wind from the northeast.

If ever there was a place to leave an offering for the Old Kind, this was it. And so I had done for years, ever since the first time the starsong had woken me when I was six years old.

I tucked the pinch pot with its dollop of sourdough starter into a shadowy pocket in the trunk and pushed until it disappeared from view. All the while, I cast my eyes about, trying to see the spirits that must have been dancing overhead. But I saw only the swaying branches of the tree canopy in the starlight and heard only the wind, the stars, and the night birds calling.

But I gave the spirits a smile anyway. Just because I couldn't see them didn't mean they weren't watching me.

When I was little, I used to sleep out under the canopy of the great yew tree, but I had been caught sneaking back inside in the early light of dawn one too many times. So that hard-won lesson, along with the chilly breeze, chased me back toward the house after only a brief minute.

But when I reached for the latch on our front door, a male voice cut through the darkness. "Who's there?"

I started and jerked my hand away from the latch. The starlight wasn't bright enough to make out much besides the large shapes of our coop, the barn, and the lumbering oak tree that shaded the front porch.

Then, as my startled heart began to slow, recognition followed.

"Nik?" I whispered.

"Lettie?"

I let out a massive breath of relief and darted away from the front door, following a path away from our porch so familiar I didn't even need the starlight to guide me. Down the steps, under the oak, around the compost, along the short dirt track, and to the fence on the northern side of the yard.

Nik's tall form materialized out of the darkness, made even taller by his curling black hair. He and his mother, Marta, had moved into the tenant house next to ours nearly twelve years before, and he had been my best friend from the first moment we met. He came right through the gate to meet me.

"What are you doing out in your nightshirt, you idiot!" he said. "You'll freeze."

"Why are you awake at this hour, fully dressed?"

Nik let out a snort of mock superiority. "*I've* been down the laneway, helping Jedd Masters with a cow in labor all night. What's *your* explanation?"

I raised my eyebrows. "The same."

"The same?"

I crossed my arms over my chest, entrenching myself in this obvious lie with a confident nod.

Nik's voice was heavy with sarcasm. "You were at Jedd Masters's house too? In your nightshirt?"

"I'm surprised you didn't see me there. I saw you."

He looked me up and down with those wide, expressive eyes of his, and it struck me in that moment how brightly my white shirt must stand out in the starlight. And how short it was. My legs were bare from the mid-thigh and glowed nearly as brightly as my shirt.

"I feel like I would have remembered all this," he said with a vague gesture at my person, one eyebrow raised.

How did he do that? Just one eyebrow?

I uncrossed my arms and tugged at the hem of my shirt, wishing I could force it to be just a few inches longer. But I couldn't betray my self-consciousness. I shrugged once and shook my head as if to say, *I don't know what to tell you.*

"You don't even have shoes on."

"Listen, Nik," I said. "I'd love to stay and chat, but it's very late. I really need to be getting to bed. I was at Jedd's house all night, and I'm exhausted."

His white teeth glinted, just barely visible when he grinned. "Right."

"Okay. Good night."

I turned to go with a prim smile, but Nik's hand closed around my arm, stopping me. My heart jumped into my throat, just like always. Did he have any idea what it did to me when he touched me like that? So casually, like it was nothing.

I stared up at him for what felt like an endless moment, lost in the black pools of his eyes. The stars wheeled overhead, screaming their song for the Old Kind and for girls in love.

But the moment couldn't have lasted for more than a blink of the eye. If it had been any longer, he would have noticed too.

"What?" I asked with my usual nonchalance. But a little grin betrayed the corner of my mouth.

"You are infuriating." Nik pulled off his long coat and tugged it around my shoulders. It smelled like hay, smoke, and sunshine. It smelled like Nik. "Since you're up anyway, stay up a little longer. Mrs. Masters sent me home with some cinnamon cake. Let's go to the ridge. I'll never be able to sleep now."

Cinnamon cake! It was hard to hide my sudden excitement at the thought of cinnamon.

"But I'm so tired," I said—another obvious lie.

He only responded with a laugh and took me by the hand. But after a couple of steps toward the gate, I stepped on a stone and winced.

"Slow down, Nik. I don't have shoes, remember?"

"You're such a baby." Before I had a chance to object, he hoisted me up onto his back, like we were children again.

A little squeal of surprise escaped me, and Nik shushed me.

"Hush! You'll wake up your sister."

I wrapped my arms around his shoulders and tried to suppress a giggle.

Nik took off at a comfortable pace, not the least bit slowed by my extra weight on his back. He carried me through the gate onto his property, and I hissed for him to stop.

"The gate! The gate!" I reached back for the gate he had left open, and he retreated just enough for me to swing it closed behind us. "Okay, go, go, go!"

The ridge wasn't really a ridge. Rather, it was a large boulder the size of a house embedded into a steep hill at the back of Nik's property. One could walk right out onto it and sit in the open stars, with farmland and forest sweeping out below.

When Nik and his mother had come to Silmere when he was fourteen years old, I had taken him there on our very first day together. I had grown up in this town and delighted in showing off every path and interesting landmark within running distance of our houses.

We had been coming to the ridge together ever since, sharing secrets, jokes, and small concerns—and sometimes cakes and candies when Nik could get some. He and his mother did much better than Sana and me. Nik was the only reason I knew what honey cakes, caramel apples, and toffees tasted like.

The boulder was cold against my bare feet, worn smooth over the centuries and softened by sheet moss. Nik and I settled side by side on the very edge, with blackness below and a chorus of stars overhead.

He unwrapped the cinnamon cake and passed me a generous bite. I shoved it into my mouth with a groan of pleasure, and Nik just laughed at me. He ate his portion a little more slowly.

"It's a bit dry," he said, but he still took a second bite.

I'd been thinking exactly the same thing. "I don't even care. You could put cinnamon on a frog, and I'd eat it."

Nik nearly choked on his dry cake, and I grinned. That was exactly the reaction I'd been hoping for.

"What is cinnamon anyway? Is it a rock like salt is?"

Nik swallowed hard. "It's tree bark. They grow it in Authe Ida. It's too cold here in winter."

The mention of Authe Ida drew my eye to his profile, but I remembered myself and quickly looked away. "Oh."

The silence drew out between us. I didn't like it.

Nik used to live in a city called Bluewater, but I knew very little else. He didn't talk about it much, but sometimes, if I begged enough, he would tell me what the sea was like. And then, once he got started talking, his eyes would light up, and he'd go on and on about the tide pools, the shells, and the salty air.

But then, after a few minutes, the light in his eyes would die, and Nik would fall silent. That would be my cue to change the subject.

When my eyes fell on a specific stretch of farmland below us, just barely visible in the darkness by the shape of the trees surrounding it, I knew exactly what our new subject should be.

"Did I tell you Callan came to the house again today?"

Nik rolling his eyes was practically audible. "What does he want now?"

"He tried to buy the house again. And the forest on the south side as well, which we also technically own." I thought of the yew tree, with my little pinch pot full of sourdough starter. "He'd cut it all down, sell the lumber, and plant apple trees and pine there instead. Says he's always wanted to be an orchardist."

"Well, too bad for him," Nik said, not sounding sorry at all. "Poor fellow will just have to console himself with what he already has."

"Hm." My eyes fell to the vast swath of land below us, which already belonged to Callan. His property abutted ours on the east, where the hillside sloped more gently. If I walked straight from our back porch toward the rising sun, I'd be in his wheat fields in less than ten minutes.

Of course, his wheat fields were so vast it would take another half hour to reach his house.

Callan was a miller by trade, but his family had accumulated and passed down so much land over the generations that no one could rightly call him a tradesman anymore. He was one of the wealthiest landowners from the Sacred Wood to the capital, and his farms were all operated by managers and tenants.

"Where does he expect you to go after he buys your house out from under you?" Nik asked, agitated for my sake.

I snorted. "I don't suspect he cares."

"That man is such a snake. Did you know he mixes sawdust in with the flour he mills? Just to bring up the weight a bit so he can make a few extra pennies per sack. Pennies, Lettie. He does this for *pennies*."

"How could you possibly know that?" I asked. I thought back over all the flour we'd had from Callan's mill, but I couldn't recall it being especially woody.

"I just...I just do. People talk."

"What people?"

"Jebb said it tonight. Didn't you hear him? You were there, right?"

I shoved his shoulder with my own. "Shut up."

He nudged me back, hard enough that I nearly lost my balance. So, of course, I had to push him again, and more forcefully this time. And also throw a handful of old fallen leaves at him.

That set him yelling about his precious curls and "Watch out for the cake, you idiot!" and "You'd better run."

By the time we finally made it back to the gate between our houses, we were both filthy and out of breath, with smiles from ear to ear.

Two

"Lettie!"

I jerked awake and stared stupidly at the weak sunlight streaming in through the window over my bed. What time was it? Why was I being yelled at? What was going on?

Sana's voice intruded on my half-awake confusion. "What in the name of the sky above did you do last night? What is all this dirt from? Whose coat is that?"

My sister's pinched expression swam into view over me, and I collapsed back down onto the bed. "Sana, please!" I moaned. "It's so early."

"Whose coat is this?" She shook the garment in question, and her brown hair rippled with the movement.

"It's Nik's!" I said, annoyed. "Okay? It's Nik's coat!"

"Why do you have Nik's coat?"

I snatched it from her and rolled over in bed. "Why do you care?" I grumbled.

"Oh, no you don't," she said. Sana took fistfuls of my quilts and pulled so hard that I tumbled out of the bed entirely.

"Sana!"

"Just because you decide to stay up all night, rambling around in the dirt with Nik, doesn't mean you get to skip morning chores. Get up."

She threw my quilts in a heap on top of me and left without waiting for a response. I lay there on the floor, still clutching Nik's coat, and counted her footsteps down the stairs. As usual, she skipped the broken third and fourth and landed on the second with a heavy thump.

"When are we going to fix those stairs?" I shouted through the blankets.

"You're welcome to fix them any time, Lettie!"

"*Meh meh meh meh meh!*" I said to myself in a mocking tone. But then I got a whiff of Nik's scent from the coat I still held to my chest, and a happy memory of the night before chased a real smile onto my face.

I dressed quickly and hopped over the broken stairs on my way to the kitchen, just like Sana had done. There she was, inspecting the sourdough starter in its crock. I froze for half a second.

Had I left the cloth askew? Was there some other evidence that I had stolen some the night before?

"Does it need fed?" I asked innocently.

"Hmm," she said. "No, I fed it last night so I could make a loaf this morning. Pass me the flour, will you?"

I fetched a bowl and scooped flour into it from the bin in the corner. Sana didn't seem to notice anything amiss after all.

"Nik says Callan adds sawdust to the flour," I said.

"That's ridiculous."

I set the bowl onto the counter next to her and studied its contents. We never bought the fine white stuff the bakeries ordered. Ours was coarse and brown. Quickly milled and sold on the cheap.

"Do you think we'd be able to tell?"

"There's no sawdust in our flour, Lettie. Don't let your imagination run amok."

"It's not my imagination. It's Nik's."

"Well, don't let *Nik's* imagination run amok, then." Sana gathered her supplies to make a loaf of bread: her apron, a pitcher of water, the salt cellar. "We have enough going on without making up even more things to worry about. Did you know the wall panel in the back hall is loose again?"

"We just fixed that."

"Well, it's loose again. It was basically all the way off. Had to duck under it to get out the back door. So that's just one more thing in this shithole of a house that we need to fix. Again."

I hovered by the store cupboard, waiting for Sana to finish her diatribe so I could make my exit. It wasn't like I particularly relished mucking out the chicken coop or weeding the kitchen garden, but at least outside I could get sunshine and fresh air and get away from Sana's sour mood.

She scooped flour out onto the worktable and made a well in the center with practiced hands.

"We just have to buckle down even more," Sana continued, reaching for the crock of sourdough starter. "Tighten up. Aside from the damned wall panel, there's the hinges on the coop door, the leak in the sitting room roof—"

My eyes darted automatically to the bucket that had been in permanent residence by my favorite chair for the last six months. It was just easier to leave it there rather than put it out every time it rained.

"Maybe we just need some help," I said. "Do you think Rafe could spare a day to do some repairs for us?"

Sana nearly dropped the crock in her hands. The back of her neck went beet red. And when she responded, her voice was at least two notes too high. "Absolutely not."

An amused smile tugged at the corner of my mouth. "Why not?"

"I don't want that idiot anywhere near our house." She scooped out a healthy portion of sourdough starter and began working the starter into the flour with far more force than necessary.

I adopted a tone of utter innocence. "But you two are always together. And he's so good with his hands. He basically built that addition on their house by himself."

"I would rather eat glass than ask that man for help."

"I'll ask him," I offered, biting back a smile. "I like Rafe."

Sana swung around and brandished one flour-coated hand at me. "Don't you dare."

The look on her face was pure suppressed embarrassment bordering on fury. And because it was all for something as silly as her feelings for Rafe, I found it absolutely hilarious.

"Don't laugh at me!" Sana shouted, advancing, with flour everywhere.

I dodged her and fled for the door. "I'm not! I'm not!"

"He's an ass, Lettie!"

I laughed again and ducked under her outstretched hand, barely avoiding getting flour all over my shirt. "I know! Stop it, Sana!"

I ripped the front door open and hovered on the threshold.

"If that idiot comes here, I'll...I'll..."

"Kiss him stupid?"

"Get out!"

I slammed the door before Sana could get to me and turned to flee into the yard and my morning chores. But I was only able to make it three steps before I stopped short. The smile melted off my face when I spotted a familiar figure standing at the bottom stair of our porch.

"Callan," I said on an exhale.

"Hello, Lettie."

Callan was stout and strong, despite his advancing years. His salt and pepper hair was neatly trimmed, but not too prim. His farm clothes were rough, but not especially dirty. Callan only looked the part of a farmer—he had legions of employees who actually worked his fields and managed his animals.

But Callan had always been a miller by trade, and he never let anyone else run his mills. Most days, he could be found hauling bags of grain, refitting stones in the millhouse, and eyeing the flour pouring through the sieve. He checked every bag himself to make sure it was done right.

"Did you need something? I thought we settled our discussion yesterday."

Callan swept off his hat and shook his head, as if to excuse himself for insisting. "I know, I know. I just wasn't satisfied with how things turned out."

"Why? Because you didn't get what you wanted?"

Callan's laugh was humoring rather than amused. *What an adorable little girl,* his laugh said. "As a matter of fact—"

But just then, Sana opened the door behind me, obviously drawn outside by the sound of voices on the porch. "Callan." She wiped her floury hands on her apron.

"Sana," Callan said in greeting. "I was just telling your sister that I'd like to reopen our discussion about purchasing your acreage here."

"We haven't changed our minds, Callan. This is our home."

"Well now, what if I offered you double?" A conflicting smile crept onto his face. Pride, pleasure, arrogance, security, friendliness, and spite—all rolled into a single expression.

My own expression constricted at the sight of it.

How did a man get like this? So full of smug self-entitlement that he felt he could just go around, buying up people's homes like they were bags of grain? And then act like it was only our greed and bullheadedness that was keeping him from his goals?

Sana used the cleanest bit of her wrist to scratch at her forehead. She let out a weary sigh. "Callan, our land wasn't worth the ten thousand you offered yesterday. It's definitely not worth the twenty you're offering now. What in the name of all the gods are you doing here?"

He climbed our porch stairs with heavy footsteps, each *thunk!* its own death knell. Sana and I both backed up to make room for him in the narrow space, but it felt like retreating.

"Ladies, I just want to expand my farm. That's all. And help you both at the same time. With this money, you could easily find a small plot somewhere else, with a house that isn't falling apart around you." As if on cue, one of the wood planks groaned beneath his boot. Callan gripped the railing so tightly the wood creaked under his broad palm.

Gods, he could strangle a goat one-handed, couldn't he?

Sana braced her feet, as if refusing to back up anymore. The heel of her shoe nudged something that made a ceramic clinking sound against the decking. All three of us glanced down, and Sana bent to pick up the object.

It was the little pinch pot I had filled with sourdough starter and left in the cleft of the yew tree last night. It was sparkling clean, not a speck of the starter left.

Damn it all. In the chaos of the morning—and with our unexpected visitor—I had forgotten to collect it from the porch.

My dishes always found their way back home, freshly cleaned and sparkling. Sometimes it took a few days after I left my offering. Other times, only a few hours. But the Old Kind always returned my things.

"Why is one of our pinch pots outside on the porch?" Sana asked. She held the little pot up between two fingers. It was a sky blue color—one of my favorites in the house because it actually had a little brightness to it.

I schooled my expression to nonchalance and shrugged. "I have no idea."

"Well, someone must have put it here."

"Maybe it was a spirit." Callan gave a sly shrug of his shoulders.

A wide grin split his face, as if he had told an excellent joke that was sure to entertain two young ladies like us.

Sana and I turned to face him, neither of us the least bit amused. For Sana's part, she was probably just confused and annoyed because, *of course,* it hadn't been a spirit moving our dishes around.

But for me, it was disgust. Because people shouldn't make jokes of the Old Kind. They didn't care for it.

Sana found her voice first. "I'm sorry, Callan, but we're not selling our land. And if you'll excuse us, Lettie and I have work to get back to."

"Now, hold on," he said with a placating wave of his hat. "I'm not quite finished."

"I'm afraid you are." Sana took him by the elbow and led him back toward the steps.

"Aren't you girls tired of living in this shack? It's falling apart!"

"We manage."

"It's only going to keep getting worse and worse," he said, sounding very concerned.

But he was down the steps by that point, and Sana had already turned toward the house, effectively ending the conversation. She went inside, and the front door clattered against the jamb. The latch had worked itself loose weeks ago, and neither of us knew quite how to repair it.

"Lettie, my dear..." Callan continued in an ingratiating tone once we were alone. "Talk some sense into her. You and I both know that this house needs to be torn down. This is the only offer like this you'll get."

I pursed my lips and pivoted halfway back in his direction. "Tell me, Callan. Why are you so keen to give us such a large sum?"

"I told you. I have a dream of expanding my farm all the way to the river."

"And be the largest landowner in all of Silmere?"

"What's so wrong with that?"

"Because the landowners with the most resources often get a seat on the council in Valheid. That's why." I faced him fully.

His expression faltered for half a second.

"So, this isn't about having an orchard or a farming empire, or even about helping two sisters whose house is in desperate need of repair," I added.

He held my gaze and said nothing. His hands were relaxed by his side, but I couldn't get the mental image out of my head of him calmly strangling a goat. It was horrific and strange and random, and I couldn't shake it.

"It's a power grab." I forced myself to look away from his rough hands.

"Why can't it be both things? We could help each other."

"See, that's where you've gotten it all wrong, Callan. We don't need your help, and we don't *want* to help you." I shrugged. "So, I don't see why you're pushing the issue. Buy someone else's property."

Callan's mouth pressed into a thin line, and he took a deep breath, as if to respond, but I cut him off.

"Or is it"—I held up a finger—"specifically because our house is so wretched? That's it, isn't it? Twenty thousand is a steal for our acreage, compared to some others with a finer house, and we're desperate, right? We're the easiest mark?"

"You have a very low opinion of me," Callan said, ingratiating again. "I had hoped that with your sister and my son getting along so well—"

I laughed once. "I think you've got too high an opinion of Sana and Rafe's relationship."

Callan adopted that humoring smile. *Sweet little Lettie. Doesn't know passion when she sees it.* "I think there's more there than either of us expect, my dear."

"Right," I said, unimpressed. "Well, it was lovely talking with you, but Sana is right. I have work to be doing."

And without waiting for his response, I followed Sana into the house.

THREE

The stars screamed overhead.

I sat on my knees before the great yew tree, with a plate gripped tightly in my lap. On it was a generous slice of sourdough bread slathered with honey and butter. The deep gold and sunshine yellow were vivid and bright, even in the darkness. That was how I knew this was a dream.

Well, that and the voices.

I couldn't tell where they were coming from, but it wasn't the stars. The voices of the stars were familiar. That wasn't something you heard with your ears.

But these voices...they were real. Or was it one voice? Many voices together as one being?

"*Child*," they said in a deep, slow timbre. So low it would have been more at home in the throat of a bear than that of a man. It vibrated in my chest while I gazed upward at the yew tree. Its branches swayed permanently to the southwest, as always.

"Yes?" I asked. "I'm here. I hear you. What would you have me do?"

The wind picked up and buffeted my loose hair around my shoulders. I gripped the plate of food even tighter.

"*Beware,*" the voices said in the wind and in my chest. "*Beware the vandal in the night, and heed the word of the prophet.*"

The wind began to roar through the ordinary trees around me, but the yew stood perfectly still. I tried to stand, but my knees stayed stubbornly affixed to the ground.

"*Beware the greed of the rich,*" the voices said as one, clearly audible, even with the railing wind, the screaming stars, and the roar of the trees around me, creaking under the strain.

Then Sana's voice added to the din, barely audible on the back of my thoughts, calling me home. "Lettie! Lettie!"

I clutched the plate of honey bread even closer. It smashed against the front of my nightshirt and pressed right through the fabric to my skin.

"*Beware...*"

"Lettie! Come home!"

I kept smearing the honey bread into my shirt, trying to make it a part of me. That's what it was, after all. It was me, torn out to give to the Old Kind.

That thought triggered a mild panic. No...No, this bread was supposed to be a gift. I tried to make my hands scrape the ruined food off my clothes, but instead, I just ground it in even harder.

"*Beware the vandal in the night...*"

"Lettie! *Leeeettie!*"

"*Heed the prophet...*"

I finally found my own voice in the maelstrom. "What prophet? Who?"

The woods around me began to crack and break in the violent wind, but the yew tree remained constant.

"*Beware...*"

"Damn it! Stupid, useless thing. Lettie! Are you up yet?"

Sana's voice from downstairs jerked me awake with a gasp.

Weak early sunlight streamed in through the open window over my bed.

I lay back down on my pillow with a sigh and laid a weary hand over my eyes. What a strange dream it had been—so real, so vivid. The voices of the Old Kind still echoed in my memory.

Beware the vandal. Heed the word of the prophet.

It never occurred to me that it was *only* a dream. It had, without a shadow of a doubt, been the Old Kind themselves reaching out to me, giving me a warning. That meant that not only was there a vandal in my life, but there was also a prophet.

Excitement and foreboding warred in my gut, tempered only by Sana's voice, which still echoed up the stairs.

"Lettie! Please tell me you're up."

"I'm up!" I shouted back.

But then an unexpected voice joined Sana's downstairs. I couldn't hear the words, but the rumble of a familiar male voice said something that set my sister to seething.

"Lettie!" she yelled.

I wrapped myself up in my robe and finger-combed my hair as I plodded down the stairs. "I'm coming, I'm coming." I skipped the third and fourth steps. "Hello, Rafe."

"G'morning, Letts," Rafe replied cheerfully, which made Sana roll her eyes at the washbasin.

Rafe was the spit and image of his father—or at least how his father must have looked in his youth and if he'd had a better personality. Thick brown hair, twinkling eyes, and a rakish set to his mouth.

"Isn't it just like you to be here at the crack of dawn," I said in a deadpan tone.

"He won't leave," Sana hissed, for his benefit more than mine.

"That's right. I won't." Rafe crossed his arms over his chest and leaned back against the workbench.

Sana brushed past him toward the fire, where some eggs were

roasting. He watched her progress through the room with an appraising eye.

"Your father was here again yesterday," I said to him while I poured myself a glass of water from the pitcher.

"Oh, yes. I know. He sent me here this morning to talk some sense into you two."

"Which is why I told you to leave!" Sana said.

"I wasn't going to do it!" He gave a defensive shrug of his shoulders. "Have I said even one word in favor of his insane plan to buy up half the town? No!"

He ruined the fire of this statement by plucking a piping hot egg from the plate in Sana's hands. She swatted at him but did very little else to deter the theft.

Rafe tossed the hot egg between his hands to cool it a bit before he began to peel it. "It was just an excuse to...Ouch!" He waved his burnt fingers in the air, tossed the egg back and forth a couple more times, then proceeded to peel it again. "Just an excuse to come annoy you."

"As if you need an excuse." Sana pulled three plates down off the shelf, but there was no fire in her tone. In fact, because I knew to look for it, I spotted a little smile tugging at the corner of her mouth.

I shook my head in a silent laugh. She thought she was so aloof.

Rafe bit the egg in half and blew out a mouthful of steam. He sat in his usual chair.

We had slices of yesterday's sourdough, new cheese, and roasted eggs for breakfast. And Sana even poured a little milk for each of us.

"Very fancy," Rafe said appreciatively when Sana set a mug in front of him.

"Don't get used to it," she replied, which was stupid because he had eaten breakfast with us countless times.

"I'd like to see you try and stop me." Rafe laughed, and his eye twinkled.

"What are you, twelve? Are you going to pull my pigtails next?"

The glimmer in Rafe's eye darkened slightly, and his smile widened. "If you ask nicely."

Sana's face flushed purple with embarrassment, rage, and something else I didn't want to think about—at least not with my sister involved. But I had to admit, Rafe was very good at pushing Sana's sore spots, and by all the gods, she needed to be goaded once in a while.

But that didn't mean I wanted to sit around and be subjected to it.

"Okay," I said around a mouth full of food. "I think I'll eat in the other room."

"Don't be ridiculous!" Sana's face was still glowing.

"No, no." I laughed, picked up my plate, and shoved my chair back. "You two clearly have some stuff to *argue* about, and it has nothing to do with me."

"Just—" Sana started but clearly didn't know how to finish that statement. Her hands fluttered around the table, fussing with everything in her reach, as if she could put the whole world to rights if the milk pitcher was turned *just so.*

"It's fine!" I said again, heading toward the sitting room.

But then Rafe stood so abruptly that his chair threatened to topple. "No, Lettie! Don't!"

I turned with a start, and even Sana's hands stilled, hovering over the plate of cheese.

Rafe had never so much as raised his voice at us in jest, much less with the fear and command his tone now carried. What had gotten into him? Why in hell shouldn't I go into the sitting room?

He seemed to quickly realize his error. Rafe adjusted his posture and expression. He leaned back on his heels and gave a casual shrug. "Stay here and eat with us. I promise I'll be good."

But neither Sana nor I were that easily shaken off.

"What's wrong, Rafe?" Sana asked, her voice sharp again.

I, on the other hand, went straight to defensiveness. "I'm just going to go eat in there. What's the big deal?"

Rafe tried to answer us both at the same time. "Nothing's wrong. Just sit with us, Lettie. There's nothing wrong. Just sit."

"No!" I said, annoyed. What right did he have to tell me what to do? "You two are being gross."

"Rafe..." Sana's voice was even sharper somehow.

I turned back toward the sitting room, which caused Rafe to abandon his casual posture and jump in alarm. He lunged for me when I edged toward the door. "Lettie, stop!"

"Rafe! What is going on?"

"Lettie!"

"Get off me!"

"Oh my god!"

Rafe reached for my arm, and I jerked away from his grip. Milk sloshed over the side of my mug, and my anger ratcheted up another notch.

"Look what you made me do!"

"Don't go in there!" Rafe commanded.

"Rafe!" Sana shouted again, sounding like a big sister and a wife at the same time. Protective of me and a warning to her lover.

For half a second, Rafe seemed to falter at her tone.

"Lettie, just don't," he said in a pleading tone.

"Why not?" I asked.

"Just trust me."

"Pfft." I rolled my eyes. Clearly, he was just pulling another prank.

Rafe was always trying to make us laugh or surprise us. Maybe he had some kind of surprise in the sitting room. Perhaps a gift for Sana laid out on the faded cushions of her favorite armchair. Something pretty to soften the drab furnishings and faded wallpaper.

Oh! Maybe he was finally going to promise himself to her, and he wanted to make a big show of it!

That thought made me giddy. I had the impish desire to both ruin the surprise and bring it about even faster. To include myself in it and make it fun. Of course, I would excuse myself once the intimate bits started, the confessions of love and the inevitable kissing. But the beginning could be boisterous! I was Sana's sister. I had a right!

"What are you hiding in there?" I asked with a sly grin. I moved with even greater haste.

"Lettie! Don't!" Rafe lunged toward me, his arm outstretched to pull me back.

Confusion and fear overtook me. What was going on? Why was he so afraid? I lurched away from his grasp, and this time, I backed into the archway between the kitchen and the sitting room with a breath-stealing thud.

"Ow!" I hissed.

My first thought was to make sure I hadn't spilled my food again. But then a strange sound echoed through the house. A creaking, groaning, cracking noise. It sounded like the third and fourth steps in the staircase but much bigger. Room-sized. Disastrous.

Rafe's hand closed around my arm, and he yanked me back toward the kitchen. The milk sloshed out of my cup and arched through the air in a graceful curve, suspended in an endless instant. Like smoke wafting through the air.

At the exact same moment, everything went to chaos.

Crumbling, crashing, incomprehensible *cacophony*. So loud I couldn't make sense of it. Someone screamed. I think it might have been me, but I couldn't be sure in the moment.

I saw it happen at the same time—a downward tumbling, ruining, disintegrating. The sitting room compressed to nothing in a great tumble of plaster, broken wooden beams, roof tiles, dust, and shattered bits of house.

But it was several seconds later before my brain started to make sense of everything.

The roof of the sitting room had caved in. Not the entirety of it, but enough. All it had taken was me knocking into the archway to trigger the avalanche of debris.

One minute, our sitting room had been there—quiet, peaceful, ragged but home.

And then it wasn't.

I stood gasping, still clutching my plate and my now empty mug, as the dust settled. Another couple of roof tiles clattered into the mess at my feet. Rafe stood next to me, mutely horrified.

"My gods! Lettie! Are you okay?" Sana's hands were all over me, searching for injury. She guided me toward the kitchen table, and I let her do it without even noticing what was happening.

The sitting room had collapsed. I could have been sitting right there. I could have been buried under all that debris.

I could have died.

Someone took the plate and mug from my hands. I was vaguely annoyed that my food was now covered in plaster dust and my milk was splashed across the floor. My knees bent, and my backside hit the seat of my chair at the kitchen table.

Breathe, Lettie. Just *breathe.*

"Is she hurt? I can't see any blood. Lettie?"

"She's okay, Sana."

"Are you hurt? *God* Rafe! What just happened?"

"The roof collapsed!"

"I *know* the roof collapsed! Look at it! Lettie, can you hear me?"

"She's in shock. Just give her a minute."

Their words washed over me like the wind. My chest heaved with the effort of driving air in and out of my lungs. It tasted of dust and mold.

"It was that damn leak," Sana said. "It had to have been. We've been meaning to repair it for ages. It must have weakened the beams."

"Ye—Yeah," Rafe said with a heavy swallow. "Must have been it."

Finally, I found my voice. It came out in a tight squeak, but it was mine.

"How did you know?"

They both swiveled their heads toward me, but Rafe's eyebrows were a bit more pinched.

"What?" he asked.

"How did you know it would fall?" I asked.

"I—" He cast about the room, refusing to look at either of us. "I don't know. Just a guess."

My brain had begun to operate again, though my hands still shook. "That wasn't a guess, Rafe. You were terrified. How did you know?"

"I—I saw it, okay? When I came in. The ceiling looked a bit... saggy...in there." He shrugged.

That was an absolute lie, but Sana didn't seem to notice. She began wiping up the kitchen table with angry swipes of her rag. The falling dust had settled all over the bread and what was left of the cheese, ruining it all. Even the pitcher of milk had a thick layer settled on the top. We couldn't afford to lose so much food for nothing.

I, however, stared at Rafe. He had known the ceiling would collapse. Rafe had *known* I was in danger. He had *known*.

Heed the word of the prophet.

He met my eyes only briefly, then cast away again. All his spark was gone, and the only thing left was a poorly hidden fear.

Was Rafe a mindwalker? One of the sibylline, able to see into the future and suss out the truth of a person's thoughts? Had he been hiding it from us all this time? Had he just outed himself, trying to save my life?

Did Sana know? Did his father?

My lips pressed closed on this new idea. If Rafe were sibylline, then I wouldn't be the one to spread his secret.

The damage to our sitting room was substantial, but the house itself was still sound. We had several of our neighbors out to help us assess the damage. It was decided that the water leak must have been much worse than we realized, with the rain soaking into the beams and rotting them from the inside.

The kindness of our friends was a blessing. Tins of food were passed to us one after the other. We would be eating better over the next couple of weeks than we had in years.

Mothers sent their teens inside to help clear away the debris, and Jedd Masters climbed onto our roof, along with Nik and Rafe, to board up the gaping hole and seal it against more water damage.

Even Callan made an appearance in the early afternoon, bearing gifts to boot.

"This is for you." He passed me a sack of the most expensive flour I had ever seen. It was so finely ground it would probably float away on the wind before we even got a chance to use it.

The sack was deceptively heavy, and I sagged under it a bit. But Callan had passed it to me like it was nothing but milkweed fluff. Gods, he was stronger than he looked.

"Thank you. Very kind," I said, and I meant it.

"I was very sorry to hear what happened to your house this morning."

"It wasn't your fault." I immediately regretted the bite in my tone. "But thank you. Honest."

"Do let me know if there's anything I can do to help. I see my son is already hard at work on your roof. Rafe is a good man."

"Yes." I thought of how hard Rafe had tried to save me that morning. "He's a credit to you."

Callan gave me his best humble smile. "Aw. He'd say he's his mother's son more than mine. But don't let me keep you, my dear."

He patted me once on the shoulder, and I had to force myself not to cringe away from it. Fortunately, he didn't linger and, instead, moved away to chat with a group of lookers-on by our front gate. In a small town like Silmere, the partially collapsed roof of a neighbor was a high point for the local gossips, and they were happy to sit and watch the excitement all day long.

I hugged the bag of flour to my chest and gazed at the house I had lived in my entire life. It appeared so broken, so sad. A shell of its former self. There had been a time, when I was little, when the shutters were painted a bright poppy red, the lines of the eaves were crisp and straight, and the roof tiles were uniform and free of moss. But we had been girls then, with a father who knew how to repair and build and improve. He had begun to teach us, but he died when we were so young. We had been on our own, with Sana becoming the parent at thirteen.

And that had been us ever since. Two girls, just eking along while the house crumbled around us, so slowly that we hadn't noticed until the entire roof came crashing down.

My fingers dug into the bag of fine flour as frustration and shame crept in around me. No more. Something had to be done. We couldn't keep on like this.

So, I stashed the bag of flour on the sideboard, ignoring Sana's questions. She scrubbed out the kitchen, but I scurried upstairs to change into a pair of stout work pants. Then I went outside and climbed the ladder to the roof, ignoring the instinctual fear of being up so high.

"What's up, Letts?" Rafe asked, swiping the back of his hand across his forehead to get the hair out of his eyes.

Nik darted forward to help me onto the roof. "Not there. Watch your step," he said in a gentle voice. His hand was hot in mine, guiding me away from the weakest places, where I should avoid putting my feet.

"I'm here to help," I said, determined. "Tell me what to do."

So, I spent the rest of the day with Nik, Rafe, and Jedd, learning the best methods for tying the repair into the existing roof so as to avoid any new leaks and practicing my accuracy with a hammer.

It felt good to work and use my muscles. To laugh and joke and learn something useful, something important. And judging by the look Sana gave me when she called us down for a supper break, the joy of it must have shown on my face.

She had been working herself to the bone all her life, just to keep us alive—and so had I, if I was being honest. But she had always borne the brunt of it. Too much for one person. But now, together, maybe we could start making a little headway.

Sana said nothing but passed me a plate full to bursting with leafy greens, fresh red tomatoes drenched in a tart dressing, a slab of beef, and rice swimming in a rich broth of onions and mushrooms.

I caught her eye over the delightful meal provided by our neighbors, and she gave me a little smile and a nod of approval. We all ate together on the lawn, shooing away curious chickens and laughing over a hard day's work.

And yet, despite all the warmth, the camaraderie, and the hope of rebuilding after a disaster, my dream from the night before kept finding its way back to my mind. We finished up the repairs on the roof just as the sun began to set, and my eyes strayed more often toward the darkening forest on the south side of the house.

If I looked carefully, I could just make out the slanted upper branches of the yew tree, always reaching toward the southwest, among the canopy of ordinary trees.

Heed the word of the prophet.
Beware the vandal in the night.

FOUR

fter a day's work like that, I expected to sleep like the dead. But the starsong was too loud through my open window. So loud—how did Sana always sleep through it?

I dragged myself up, sore and aching, wanting so desperately to go back to sleep, but the Old Kind should never be ignored. The stars were calling me. I had to go.

So, I left the temptation of my comfortable pillow and slipped out of bed. My bare feet kissed the cold wooden floor, silent as always to avoid waking Sana. I slipped a robe off the headpost and draped it over my shoulders.

The house was quiet when I eased myself down the stairs, skipping softly over the third and fourth steps by habit, and made my way to the kitchen. I reached for a tin of peach cobbler left by one of the neighbors—a perfect gift for the Old Kind—but just as my fingers brushed the ceramic dish, I froze.

Movement out of the corner of my eye. A shifting in the shadows.

I whirled around, peering into the dark corners of the kitchen.

At first glance, everything appeared to be exactly as it should have been. The waxing moon outside cast shadows through the large window over the washbasin, throwing the narrow shape of the table into sharp relief. Behind that, the cupboards, piled boxes, stacks of pots and pans on their shelf, a basket piled high with dirty laundry stashed near the door—it all seemed correct.

But then, the shadow of the table changed. Its boxy shape moved before my eyes, creeping across the floor, stretching away from the window and toward the archway of the ruined sitting room.

And it didn't just move. It morphed into an entirely different figure. Straight lines curved, corners smoothed, and the entire thing grew more dense, more solid, climbing up the wall in the unmistakable form of—

A wolf.

I stood near the wall, unable to move, my heart pounding, breath caught in my throat.

The wolf swelled until it was no longer just a shadow, but a real, three-dimensional beast. Four paws moved silently across the rough floor, eyes like yellow embers peering toward the sitting room.

A dream. It was just another dream. That was all.

Wake up, Lettie. Just wake up, and you'll be in your bed. Everything as it should be. No moving shadows, no wolf creatures made of light and dark.

But when I backed away, the sharp corner of the worktop jabbed into my lower back, and the pain was very, very real.

The shadow wolf pivoted, its glowing eyes clear and warm. It gazed at me for several endless seconds. The starsong swelled outside, screaming to me. Screaming for the Old Kind.

Then the shadow wolf turned away, breaking the spell, and faced the sitting room once more. It bared its teeth, and a low growl vibrated through its belly. I couldn't hear it, not with my ears, but I could feel it—the same deep undertones as the voice that had prophesied in my dream.

Beware the vandal in the night.

There was someone in the house. And the shadow wolf was telling me that they were in the sitting room. There was danger there.

The shadow wolf growled again. Its glowing eyes narrowed.

Beware.

I eased myself away and slipped around the sharp corner of the worktop.

I should wake Sana. I should run. I should scream.

What about a weapon? There was a knife block just across the kitchen, but that was the wrong way. I couldn't bear to move toward it, closer to the danger. My heart pounded in my chest and froze my feet to the floor.

The shadow wolf strafed, stepping sideways toward me, edging me away while maintaining a narrow focus on the empty maw of the sitting room archway, putting itself between me and the danger.

I backed away obediently and slipped closer to the hall and the stairs, trying not to think of how relieved I was to have the decision taken away from me. The shadow wolf wanted me to retreat. That's what I wanted as well, in my heart of hearts.

A hot hand closed over my mouth, and I sucked in a sharp breath of shock through my nose. But then the hand adjusted itself, covering my mouth and pinching my nose in one fierce grip before I could make any sound at all. An arm snaked around my waist and pulled me back against a lithe, firm body.

A young man's body.

My first thought was of betrayal. I had trusted the wolf. It was supposed to protect me. I thought it would keep me safe! But the wolf had driven me right into the arms of the intruder. A murderer or a thief...or someone worse.

Fight, Lettie! Fight him! But I was frozen in fear. Even without the hand over my mouth and nose, I wouldn't have been able to breathe. Things like this didn't happen to us. Men didn't hurt us. Wouldn't dare. They'd be lynched in the street for such a crime.

And yet here was some man sneaking around in my house where he shouldn't be, touching me, hauling me against his body. I tried to look to the wolf for help, advice, anything. But the hand on my face held me tight.

You're a fighter, Lettie! Fight! Do something! But it turned out, when it came down to it, I wasn't a fighter. I was a helpless little creature too terrified to move. I even quivered like a kitten when a set of lips and hot breath pressed against my ear.

"Don't move. Don't make a sound."

My knees nearly gave out with the wash of intense relief.

Nik. It was Nik who gripped my mouth, who held me close to his body. His arm around my waist immediately became an anchor instead of a binding, and I relaxed against him.

I glanced back toward the kitchen, but the shadow wolf was gone. The table's rectangular shadow lay still and quiet against the floor, like it had never moved at all. But that made perfect sense. The wolf had done what it came to do. It had kept me from danger and had pushed me toward Nik, who would keep me safe.

Nik's next words—so quiet against my ear I could barely make them out—brought all the terror right back again.

"There's someone in the house."

Beware the vandal in the night.

His hand loosened from my mouth and nose, and I forced myself to breathe slowly, quietly. I gripped his arm tightly, begging him silently not to let me go.

A sound echoed from the sitting room, so hushed it would have gone unnoticed if we weren't listening for it. A step, then another. So soft. Whoever it was clearly didn't want to wake anyone who was supposed to be sleeping upstairs.

"He's not here for you." Nik's mouth was still close to my ear. His hot breath sent shivers down my spine. It was too much, too many things to feel and keep track of. "Upstairs. Quick. Go."

At first, I couldn't move. I stood clutching at Nik's arm, trying to melt backward into his body heat. He would keep me safe. We just had to stay still. Don't move. Be quiet. He would keep me safe.

"Now. Go, Lettie. It has to be now." He pushed me toward the stairs, and this time, my feet obeyed.

We crept back up the stairs I had only come down a few moments before, both of us careful to make not a single sound on our way up. In my room, I turned to question Nik.

Who was it? Why is he here? What is he doing?

But the look on his face, only just visible in the light of the stars, stopped the words in my throat.

His eyebrows, usually quirked in a teasing expression, were drawn together in determination. And his eyes were blown wide with terror. He didn't give me even half a second to speak, but ushered me directly to the bed. Nik yanked my dressing gown off and dropped it on the floor so that my bare legs flashed, momentarily visible, in the dark.

"In," he hissed, pulling off his own shoes. He climbed right into the bed after me, tucking us both up to the chin.

I scooted closer to the wall to make a bit more room for him, but it was a very small bed. We lay on our sides, facing each other on the pillow. Nik even threw an arm around my waist to pull me closer. Our breaths mingled, and our knees knocked together under the blankets.

"What—" I began, but Nik cut me off.

"Close your eyes. Whatever you do, don't open them. No matter what you hear. He's not here for you or Sana."

"Nik!"

"Be asleep!" he hissed. He gripped my hand tightly and held it close to his chest so that I could feel his heart pounding erratically against his ribs. Nik shut his eyes and went still—the perfect picture of a young man sleeping casually in his lover's bed.

It didn't matter that we were only friends. No one would think twice seeing two young people sharing a bed. And anyone who knew us? Well, they would hardly be surprised, would they? I'd been teased more than once by the local gossips about how close Nik and I were.

The barely there scuffs of careful boots on the stairs edged into my consciousness, and my heart picked up its pace again.

What was happening? Who was in the house? And why was Nik so afraid?

I should get up. Should find out what's happening. Confront the man. There was an old dagger in the top drawer of my dresser. I could be brave. I could do the right thing. I could—I could do it.

"Don't!" Nik hissed, his eyes still shut. "You won't get it in time. Just be asleep, and he'll leave us alone."

Muffled footsteps sounded on the landing just outside the door.

Nik gripped my face, his fingers wrapping gently around the back of my neck. He opened his eyes, begging me to listen. Desperate.

Trust me, he mouthed.

Heed the word of the prophet.

The latch on the bedroom door scraped against the doorframe.

Trust me.

I did. I trusted him. I trusted Nik so much that I would have done anything he said. Absolutely anything. So, I scooted closer and ducked my head under his chin, cuddling close in a way I had only ever dreamed about before. I closed my eyes.

Nik had never let me get this close before—close enough to kiss his throat and breathe in his scent. I had just enough time to acknowledge the way he held me tightly against him, like he'd done it a thousand times before. Like it was easy. And the stars kept up their song, bathing us in their light through the window, like we really were lovers.

But then the door opened, and time stopped.

Breathe.

In. Out.

Nik's thumb stroked across my spine.

Relax.

I couldn't see the man, but I sensed him. He took up all the air in the room. The man had to have been twelve feet tall or a wall of solid muscle. And judging by his light-as-a-feather tread, he was also skilled, careful, and meticulous.

My imagination supplied a wide range of terrifying images. Glowing red eyes, blood-stained hands, knives and hammers and clubs and...

Nik sighed into my hair, a sleepy sort of contented sound, and he snuggled me closer under his chin. His thumb began a regular soothing path across my spine in time with his breaths.

Relax.

I can't. I can't. I can't do it.

He was going to know. The man would be able to tell Nik and I were awake, only pretending. The footsteps moved toward the other side of the room, where Sana slept, oblivious. They paused, as if the man were hovering over her bed.

He had better not touch her. I'd kill him. I'd claw his eyes out. I didn't need the dagger in the top drawer. I had teeth and nails. I would...

Nik's hand closed around my upper arm. A warning.

Don't.

I forced myself to breathe. Nik had said the man wasn't there for me or for Sana. I had to trust him. So I choked my rage into the back of my throat, compelled my breath to be slow. I focused on the way Nik's thumb moved over my back, the way his leg lay casually over mine.

How was he this relaxed? How was he this good at appearing calm?

I felt him smirk against the top of my head, and I made a mental note to ask him later what the hell was so funny.

The man spent a long time at Sana's bed. Doing what, I could only guess. When he finally moved toward us, he paused for only a moment, as if to check that Nik and I really were asleep.

Breathe. Just breathe.

Then, seeing nothing to alarm him, the man stepped away. He exited the room just as quietly as he had entered and eased the door closed behind him.

I immediately dropped all pretense of sleep and only just barely managed to keep my questions to a whisper. "What in the name of the gods above is happening?" I pulled away just enough to be able to look Nik in the eye.

"*Shh.* He's still in the house."

"Answer me!"

"I don't know, okay? I don't know!" Nik's hand fisted into the fabric of my nightshirt at my back, as if he were desperate to keep himself under control.

"Then tell me what you *do* know."

"I—"

"Who is it?"

"I don't know."

"How did you know he was here? Why were you in my house? How did you know we'd be safe if he thought we were asleep?"

"Lettie, quiet!"

My voice dropped to the barest breath. He could only hear me because we still lay so close on the pillow. "Answer me! Now!"

Nik clamped his eyes shut, as if afraid I might see too much in his expression. "I saw him!"

"Where? When?"

"I—"

"Nik!"

"A vision, okay? I had a premonition. There." He shrugged, daring me to comment. "I saw it all. I saw it…You were going to run into him in the kitchen, and he was going to hit you over the head and run. You were so hurt, Lettie. *So* hurt. You'd be broken.

Forever. Your life would be essentially over. I couldn't let it—I couldn't—"

He gripped my face again and pulled our foreheads together. Nik wasn't so calm and collected anymore. He scrunched his eyes closed, breathing hard. He hooked his leg around mine, holding on.

The pain in his posture, in his expression, snapped the taut line of righteous fury that had kept me whispering questions at him rapid-fire. Nik was hurting. He was afraid, upset. I had to comfort him, make him feel good again. Nik didn't deserve this pain. He was supposed to smile and tease and laugh.

Nik was supposed to feel safe.

"*Shh.*" I returned the pressure he was putting on my leg, anchoring him to my body. Then I pulled his head down, kissed his forehead, and tucked him under my chin. It was my turn to comfort him.

He accepted the embrace with something close to desperation. Nik clung to me, buried his face in my collarbone, and battled with his breath. It came in heavy sobs, panicked and wild.

I carded my fingers through his curls. "*Shh*, it's okay. I've got you."

"I'm so sorry," he whispered against my skin. "I should have told you. But I didn't know how."

My eyebrows furrowed. Told me what? The thought passed through my mind only half a second before another. *Mindwalker.*

Heed the word of the prophet.

In all the confusion and terror, it had never occurred to me that Nik had been keeping a secret from me. He had responded to my thoughts, answered my unasked questions, had seen visions of the future...

"You're sibylline," I said against his forehead.

He nodded against my mouth.

"That's why you and your mother left Authe Ida."

Nik nodded again.

"Because in Authe Ida, they used to burn the mindwalkers."

Nik shuddered in my arms and let out a tortured gasp of horror. This wasn't the response of someone who had *heard* the horror stories, like Sana and I had. Like everyone did in the north. This was the remembered fear of someone who had *seen* it done in person.

How many of Nik's people had he watched burn? How many nights had he lain awake, wondering when it would be his turn? And he just a child at the time?

"*Shh*," I said again, hugging him tighter.

Downstairs, something squeaked, like a nail being wrenched out of a plank of wood. Something metal clattered to the floor, so quiet I probably wouldn't have noticed it if I didn't know what was going on downstairs.

That was two sibyls I had discovered in a single day. Both of the young men in our lives? Both of them mindwalkers?

And yet the Old Kind had told me of only one. The prophet. Singular.

If Nik was the prophet, what did that make Rafe?

FIVE

Nik and I lay in bed for what seemed like ages, saying nothing at all. Just being together. I listened to the starsong coming in through the window, punctuated here and there by the sound of another nail being removed somewhere downstairs.

I counted them—the ones I could hear, at least. The stars were *very* loud.

Nineteen nails were pulled from their holes. Wrenched out and taken away. The man made very slow progress, easing each nail out one by one, trying to cause as little noise as possible. The vandal downstairs was sabotaging something. But what? And why?

"Can you hear his thoughts?" I whispered.

Nik sniffed once and kept his eyes firmly on my chin. "No."

"But you could hear mine before?"

"I hear yours always."

That set a sting to the back of my eyes, like I might cry if I blinked enough.

"Why?" The word came out as mere breath.

Sana slept across the room, entirely unaware that anything had happened—or was still happening, more like.

"I'm not very strong," he said with a sigh. "I only hear people I'm close to. Or if someone is very emotional. Or if they touch me. Mama, you, Ayana..."

People I'm close to. People I'm close to. I latched onto those words and held them tightly to my heart. If they were all I ever got from him, no matter what happened next, at least I knew this was real. It wasn't just me.

"Who is Ayana?"

He shifted his weight, then settled back against the pillow. "A friend from back home. I haven't seen her in ten years. Not since I left Bluewater."

"What was she like?"

And so, Nik told me all about the woman he had known as a child, who was as good as family. He told me about how she was never afraid of him nor of the sea. Of how she was fearless and would have done anything to save someone who needed saving. Of how she had fallen in love with one of the merfolk and was, therefore, stuck between the land and the water.

"What happened to her?" I asked.

Nik shrugged. "I don't know. I don't guess I'll ever know." His eyes found me in the dim light of the stars. "You're not afraid."

"Why would I be afraid?"

"Because I—Because of what I am? I'm in your head—"

He broke off, and his eyes darted away again.

I pressed a hand to his cheek. "No. Don't look away. Don't hide."

But he couldn't meet my eyes anymore. He clenched his own tightly shut, battling some kind of ongoing war within himself that I would probably never understand.

Downstairs, the vandal finished his work. We both heard the unmistakable sound of the front door easing gently open, then closing again. He was gone.

"You're safe now. I should go," Nik said, and to my horror, he began to scoot out from under the blanket.

I gripped him tightly with my hands and knees. "Don't you dare leave me here alone. Don't you dare."

He opened his mouth to reply, but his expressive eyebrows gave it all away. Nik didn't want to go, not really. But he thought he should. But he didn't want to. But he should. But—

"Stay with me," I said. "I can't bear to be alone tonight."

"Lettie, I—"

I gripped his hand tighter, pulled it close to my chest.

Stay.

"You shouldn't want me here."

"But I do."

He opened his mouth to argue again, but finally, Nik gave in and settled back against the pillow.

I clutched his hand between both of mine, possessive.

"You hear my thoughts always?"

He nodded.

"So you know I'm in love with you?" My stomach knotted up, trying to snatch the words back. But it was too late. It had been said. I had put it all out there.

A fearful downturn to his lips broke my heart a little.

"Yes, I know."

"How long have you known?"

He tucked his chin down. "Since before you did."

I reached up a finger and traced along the angle of his jaw, scruffy with the day's growth in the best way. "That's not fair."

Nik shook his head and tried to draw away from my touch. "I know, Lettie. That's what I keep trying to tell you. You *shouldn't* love me. You can't love a sibyl. You can't."

"But I do. And it's not fair that you know my feelings but I don't know yours. You owe me that much."

"I can't keep out of your head, Lettie. I've tried."

"I didn't ask you to."

His eyes shot to mine finally—*finally.*

That was when I knew. That's when I finally understood.

Why I had been flirting with him for years and he hovered just out of reach. Why he'd carried me in the dark to Ridge Rock so I wouldn't hurt my bare feet. Why he'd shared his cakes with me, helped fix our roof, always been there for me when I needed him. But he had never closed the gap. Never kissed, never touched, never admitted anything.

Nik loved me. He did. But he didn't think he should because of his mindwalker abilities. Because he'd been trained all his life to hide it, that he was something to be feared and scourged. So, Nik couldn't get close, but he couldn't bear to stay away.

I saw it all in his eyes, or maybe it was a hint of his powers passing the knowledge directly to my mind. But I knew.

I pressed my hand against his neck, fingers scraping just under his ear. "Do you love me, Nik?" I whispered.

He swallowed hard, his eyebrows drawn together. "Yes."

Say it.

"I love you."

I wasn't sure who moved first. Maybe it was both of us. But the kiss that followed was achingly sweet. The first brush of lips sent a surge of unbridled joy through my chest, puffing me up until I could hardly bear it. If the stars had their song, then mine would be a burst of sunlight, bright and loud and joyous.

It wasn't even that scandalous, our kiss. Just a soft parting of lips. But it was everything.

Then Nik shuddered a breath into my mouth. A desperate exhale of relief. He gripped me tightly and held me close with shaking hands. The kiss changed into something a little less harmonious, just a pressing together of mouths while he clung to me and breathed. Like he was scared to move, like I would disappear if he shifted an inch.

But I didn't want him to move. Not one single bit. Never before had I felt so beautifully held, like he more-than-loved me. Like I was something precious and fragile. And maybe I was. At that moment, I could believe it.

As we lay there, sharing each other's air, still as statues with our open mouths barely brushing, another profound truth hit me. Where this was a moment of joy for me, it was something else for Nik. For him, this was a release. He was free. Nik no longer had to hide. He could have what he wanted.

He could have me.

"Is this real?" he asked against my mouth.

My lips curved into a smile. "This is real."

Six

Six

"Lettie, get up."

Sana's voice was less annoyed than usual, considering it was so early. She sounded grim, resigned.

I opened one eye against the dawn shining in through my window but didn't move in Nik's arms. I wasn't ready to leave the little nest we had made the night before.

"What is it?" I asked in a voice still gravelly with sleep.

Sana's face was pinched in a strange way. What was that expression? Pain? Was she hurt?

I sat up with alarm, and Nik sucked in a gasp, suddenly awake as well.

Sana grimaced and shifted her weight in a way that looked suspiciously like a limp. "I need your help. I fell through the floor in the hall this morning. Got my leg pretty good. Surprised you didn't hear me."

"Oh my god," Nik said, his voice thick with sleep.

I scrambled out from under the tangled blankets and over Nik's warm weight sagging the mattress down, ignoring his protests in my haste to free myself.

"Sana, shit," I said breathlessly.

Blood ran down her calf in thick rivulets from a nasty gash stretching ankle to knee, surrounded by angry red scratches and swelling flesh. The blood had already begun to pool around her foot, where she rested it gently against the floor.

"Oh my god," Nik said again, fully awake now.

"Sit down. Sit!"

Nik and I ducked under Sana's shoulders and helped her toward the stool near her bed. She let us manhandle her without complaint, wincing at the pain of her injury. I ran to the cupboard to fetch the basket of fabric scraps—saved pieces of linen, cotton, and wool we used in patches, quilting, and on occasion, bandaging.

"I'll go get Mama," Nik said once Sana was settled. "She's stitched me up more than once. Get this bleeding stopped."

I fashioned a hasty padding from cotton scraps and pressed it against Sana's wound to staunch the blood.

"What happened? Did the floorboard break? Why didn't you call for me?"

Sana sucked in a breath through her teeth when I pushed too hard on her wound.

"I can't believe you would climb the stairs like this!" I said.

"Don't lecture me right now, Lettie!"

I let out a growl of frustration.

Nik returned with his mother, Marta, in record time. Marta had always been good to Sana and me. She was short and plump, with a warm expression that contrasted sometimes with sharp eyes. Marta always had an extra slice of pie for me when I wandered over to her house. She was a leatherworker by trade, and she always smelled like it. Like the lye baths, the stain, and the brown scent of hide.

Today was no different. She bustled in behind her son, a basket of tools at the ready, and immediately got to work.

"Put your leg here, sweetheart." Marta guided Sana's foot to rest on her thigh. She was probably the only person alive who could get away with calling Sana "sweetheart."

Sana's leg was a rash of torn skin, but only one of the cuts needed stitching. Marta cleaned and mended the leg quickly and efficiently, sending me downstairs again and again for fresh water, spirits, and once, a new knife.

The first time I went, my stomach rose into my throat. Sana had left a trail of blood across our room and down the steps. A gory account of how she had hauled herself up the stairs for help with only one good leg.

She had always been so prideful. Probably thought she could handle it herself. Just like always. Never let me in. Not until she was so badly injured she could have fucking died from it.

I brought up the supplies and held Sana's hand through the stitching, then helped Marta wrap fresh bandaging around the whole thing. A few spots of blood showed through, but no more. We were all satisfied that the bleeding had well and truly stopped.

Nik spent that time cleaning up the mess Sana had trailed up the stairs. And when I found him downstairs a little later, he was in the hall, examining the place where the floorboards had given way.

I crouched down next to him and took in the sight. One of the floorboards had come loose, and it had clearly fallen into the crawl-space below when Sana had stepped on it. There were no broken boards, only the jagged edge of the floor supports in the crawl-space, where Sana had cut herself.

"What do you think?" I asked, though I knew exactly what he would say.

His expression didn't change. "I think there are some nails missing."

"Hmm," I said.

"We should tell Sana," he added with a grim expression.

I chewed on my lip. "That would mean telling her about you being a sibyl. Are you okay with that?"

It was Nik's turn to hesitate. Old fears passed over his expressive face. "Do you think she would..."

"I don't know. I don't think so." I shook my head and picked up the loose floorboard. "And even if she did, we don't lynch the sibylline here. Not like in Bluewater. Not in this day and age."

Something creaked overhead, followed by a hiss of pain and a muffled swear.

Nik and I both craned our heads back and peered at the landing at the top of the stairs. There was no one there.

"Sana?" I asked.

An annoyed sigh floated down to us. "What?"

A strange combination of irritation and guilt flooded my chest. "Were you eavesdropping?"

Sana's head appeared over the railing. "So what if I was?"

Nik's tawny skin flushed darker with a deep bush. Shame? Fear? Whatever it was, I didn't like it.

"That's incredibly rude!"

Sana's expression contorted. "Rude? You want rude? Try keeping secrets!"

"We were going to tell you," Nik said, but I spoke over him.

"We're not keeping secrets!"

Nik sat back on his heels with a deep sigh. He had seen enough of our sister-fights to know better than to insert himself.

"Like hell you're not!" Sana started easing herself toward the stairs one-legged, leaning heavily on the banister.

Marta appeared on the landing just as Sana began trying to go down the stairs. The older woman raised one eyebrow and cast a knowing glance at her son.

"Should we..." she began.

"No. Wouldn't do any good," Nik said.

"How much did you hear?" I asked Sana, ignoring both Nik and his mother.

"Enough to know you're keeping something from me! Ow! Damn it!"

That was enough to break Marta's resolve. "Sana, sweetheart..."

But I had no such sweetness to spare for my sister. "Stop it! Stay there! You're going to hurt yourself!"

Sana hopped down another step with a grimace. "Oh, like you'd care."

Somewhere in the back of my mind, I knew she didn't think of me that way. She was in a tremendous amount of pain, she was hurt by our whispering, and she was stressed and broken and feeling excluded. Alone.

I knew all of this, rationally speaking.

But I was anything but rational in that moment. Furthest thing from it. I was angry, seething. I was hurt too. Someone had snuck into my house and had caused my sister pain. And she had the gall, the spite, to say I didn't care?

"I don't care?" I hissed.

Nik reached for me with soothing words I couldn't focus on. I jerked my hand away, determined to be angry. He let out a resigned sigh.

"I don't care?" I said again, my voice rising.

Sana clambered down another step, cursing again when she jostled her injured leg too much. "Lettie..." She sounded even more annoyed now.

"I spent all day yesterday fixing the roof," I shouted, really getting going, now. I ticked the items off on my fingers, bending them so far back it almost hurt. "All night last night fighting to stay silent to keep us safe while some *asshole* ransacked our house. All morning holding your hand while Marta stitched up your leg. And *I don't care?*"

"Someone was in our house?"

I turned on my heel and stalked toward the back door, which we didn't often use because it stuck horribly. But it was the closest exit. I put my weight against it with a growl of rage until it finally opened enough for me to squeeze through. Then I ran out into the unseasonably hot morning sunshine.

My feet churned over the grass, which the chickens and our two goats kept cropped short, carrying me further from Sana's muffled shouts. Said chickens came running up to me, expecting to be fed, but they scattered with a flutter of flapping wings and indignant cackling when I powered right through their little flock. Somewhere deep in my gut, I cursed myself for being careless with my chickens, who were always such good company.

But the fear and stress of the last twenty-four hours came crashing down on me, crowned by three awful, terrible, little words: *Like you'd care.*

And so, my feet kept moving to the south side of our property, past the chicken coop, toward the trees protecting our property on that side. I went without thinking, following the same path I had traveled countless times before, usually in the dark when the stars woke me up. The yew tree was a quiet place—a solemn, divine sanctuary. I could think there. Be alone. Get myself together. Away from Sana. Away from that damned house.

At the last moment, I remembered myself. I couldn't go to the yew tree without a gift. Not even now. So, I veered back a bit and stormed into the chicken coop. The rooster flapped angrily at me for the disruption. I reached under a hen in the nest box, ignoring her growls of protest, and drew out a fresh egg from the modest pile.

So stupid. She would probably start laying in the woods now that I'd annoyed her on the nest.

But what difference did it make, really? It wasn't like *I cared* at all. Fuck!

I charged back out again, grumbling to myself, dodging chickens, and clutching my egg so tightly it might break.

I stomped into the forest, distantly grateful for the cooling shade, and followed an invisible path. Around the crooked oak tree, a large step over the wet weather spring, under the briar stretching out into the open air from the bramble lurking among the denser trees...I could have done it blind and often had in the dark of night, with only the starsong to light the way.

The yew tree looked different in the daylight. Darker somehow without the shine of the stars overhead. Its branches thrust aggressively away, completely still in their desperate reaching for the southwest, always straining for something far away. Maybe another yew tree somewhere far, far from Silmere. A sister tree. A sister spirit.

I hesitated at the edge of the clearing and gazed up at the tree. Never before had I realized how black the bark was, almost like rot. It usually seemed so bright and alive at night.

Sure enough, when I stepped cautiously closer and placed my hand on the tree, it was very much alive. Its wood was twisted but firm, with thin strips of papery bark fluttering against my skin. Ants crawled up its surface, and a lark sang cheerfully in one of its upper branches before taking off with a flurry.

The anger I had been clutching so tightly finally began to ebb away, and I sank to my knees at the base of the tree. My lungs expanded for the first time in what seemed like days, drawing in cool, verdant air down to the very core of my body. The buzzing in my head eased, and I let my head fall to rest on my hand, where it lay against the tree.

I didn't know how long I sat there like that, just breathing with the yew tree. But it was long enough that, when halting footsteps crunched through the old leaf litter, I couldn't bring myself back to anger if I tried.

The footsteps drew nearer. The lopsided gait made it perfectly clear who had followed me.

"Why did—" I said, but there was no bite to my words. "You're such an—"

"I'm fine," Sana said through gritted teeth.

"You have fifteen stitches in your leg, Sana." I finally looked up at my sister, incredulous. "Why did you walk all the way out here?"

Sana eased herself down on the ground next to me, stretching her injured leg out to the side. She laid an old cane across her lap with a sigh.

"Where did you get that?" I asked with a shake of my head.

"It was in the back of the closet. Grandad's, I think."

"You're being ridiculous. You should have stayed at the house."

"I'm *fine.*"

I let out a huff of indignation. It felt like expelling the last of the poison I had left in my body.

"How did you even know I was here?" I asked.

"Oh, please. As if I didn't know where you sneak off to most nights? We share a room, Lettie. You think I never caught you creeping around?"

I scrunched up my mouth, unsure of what to do with this reve-lation. Silence stretched between us, but it was the comforting quiet of two women who knew each other very, very well.

"I'm sorry I eavesdropped."

"We weren't keeping secrets from you," I said.

"I know. Nik told me."

"I'm sorry you got hurt."

"I'm sorry you were scared."

I opened my mouth to say something else, to address the one thing that had hurt me more than anything else, but it was too big. I couldn't get it past my lips.

Like you'd care!

Sana's hand closed over my own, where it rested comfortingly in my lap. At first, I thought she wanted to hold my hand, and I didn't quite know what to do about it. But then her fingers pried into my fist to pull away the stolen egg.

She held it up, turning it gently in the dappled sunlight, as if the simple brown shell were a work of art to be admired. "I know you've been stealing food from the kitchen," she said in a soft, thoughtful tone.

"I—"

"I've known it for years." Sana cut off my protests before I could get started. "I used to follow you when you were smaller... Make sure you didn't get hurt in the dark."

A warm...*something*...bloomed in my chest. Like a gust of wind through the trees, maybe. Or the weight of a friendly chicken sitting on my knee. Or Nik's smile against my skin.

But this was different somehow. This feeling—it was bigger.

"At first, I didn't know what to do about it," Sana continued. "Didn't know if I should stop you or talk to you about it. It's not like we could always spare what you were taking. But you have such faith, Lettie. I didn't want to take that from you. So, I figured I'd wait. Wait until the time was right. Wait until—I don't know. Until you opened up on your own. When you were ready."

The *something* in my chest stuttered slightly. A small flame, barely caught, gusseted by the wind.

"But you never did." Her voice was even lower now, almost sad. She lifted the egg and nestled it into a large dip in the bark of the yew tree, just big enough to contain it. Like that spot had been made specifically for this egg.

I breathed in carefully, terrified to break the little soap bubble that was this moment with my sister. "I thought you didn't believe." I swallowed hard, tried again. "You said...all the time...You couldn't hear them. Eventually, I stopped asking."

"Hear what?"

"The st—the stars."

Her eyebrows knitted together. "What stars? *The* stars?" She cast a finger upward in a question.

I couldn't look away from her curious stare, terrified of the inevitable laughter. Or worse, the pity.

But she only shook her head. "I can't hear any stars. What do they sound like?"

I frowned, not quite ready to believe we were having this conversation. "Like singing. Many, thousands, millions of voices. Far away but so close. All different notes, just sustained and... worshipful."

I let out a heavy sigh. I'd never tried to put this into words before. Who would have listened?

"I don't hear them with my ears. Not quite."

"What do you mean?" she asked with a gentle, encouraging tone.

"Like...I *feel* them more than I actually *hear* them. I hear the sun too. But it's different. Just one voice...and so overwhelming. It sings all day long, cradles us all in the song."

"You hear the sun?"

I nodded. "Sometimes, I can't believe no one else hears it." I pointed up at the sunlight on the leaves overhead. It transformed the leaves it struck, making them glow like fire. "Look. It helps when you look with your eyes too. Brings it into focus."

"Look at what?"

A small grin played at the corners of my lips. Were we really talking about this? Me and Sana, sitting in the dappled sunlight at the base of the yew tree, just chatting. Doing nothing useful. No chores, no broken house, no one else around to intrude. Just us.

"At the sunlight," I said.

But then I remembered something Nik had said the night before.

I only hear people I'm close to. Or if someone is very emotional. Or if they touch me.

That was certainly an idea, wasn't it?

I stretched out my hand and took Sana's, where it rested gently in her lap. Squeezed hard. "Look at the sunlight. *Feel* it. Listen."

We sat there together for several long seconds, her eyes on the sun-brightened treetops overhead.

I knew when she heard it, recognized the change coming over her face. Her eyebrows rose a fraction of an inch, and her mouth cracked open in a silent gasp. A half sob, half laugh punched its way out of my chest. She heard it. *She heard it.* It wasn't just me. It was real. Sana could hear it too.

I turned my face up to the sunlight and really focused on it, willing myself to hear the gentle hum, the warm vibration, the nurturing energy of the sun. It sounded like a mother singing to her child, like a father laughing, like sisters holding hands in a sacred place. Filled us up, caressed, lifted, settled.

Sana gasped again as the sunsong swelled around us. And for a while, nothing existed at all except for a pair of sisters and the sunshine on the leaves.

I didn't know how long we sat there, listening. Minutes, hours...It didn't matter. But eventually, Sana shifted positions, wincing at the pain in her leg. We gathered ourselves up and made our slow, steady path back to the house.

Nik was still there, just spooning some oatmeal out into bowls, but Marta had gone home ages ago. Nik sat down next to me and held my hand while we ate.

Afterward, the three of us sat in stewing silence for a long time until Sana broke it by saying, "Well? What the hell are we supposed to do now?"

Nik squeezed my hand and cast me a sympathetic look. Gods above, his great big cow eyes could write sonnets on their own. And right now they were saying, *Be brave. I'm here.*

Because clearly, he had heard my thoughts and knew exactly how hard it was going to be to say what I had to.

"Sana." I took a deep breath and adjusted my position in my seat. "I have an idea who is behind this."

Sana sat up a little straighter. "Well? Spit it out."

I swallowed hard and gripped Nik's hand tighter. "The other night, the Old Kind gave me a warning. *Beware the vandal in the night. Heed the word of the prophet. Beware the greed of the rich.*"

When I paused again, Sana grew impatient. "And?"

"Nik is the prophet," I said. "And I think we can all agree that Callan is the rich man. We're already wary of him."

"And you think you know who the vandal is?" Her eyes darted between me and Nik.

"Sana..." I said.

"Why are you looking at me like that? Just say it!"

I didn't even try to school the sympathetic expression off my face. "How did Rafe know the ceiling was going to collapse yesterday?"

Sana stared at me, her eyebrows drawn together and her lips in a tight line. Any second now, she would start yelling. Any second, and she'd tell me how wrong I was, how fanciful, how the Old Kind must have been wrong, or I had interpreted their warning incorrectly. Any second now...

But Sana said nothing. Her eyes darted over the table, not focusing on anything in particular. Then, just as her eyes started to go red, she got up abruptly to stare at the sitting room instead.

I dropped Nik's hand and followed her, wrapping my arms around her middle and resting my temple on her shoulder from behind. She drew in and let out a big, shaky breath. That was it.

But I knew better.

One breath? No.

She and Rafe had been circling each other for years, coming together, dashing apart, rushing back in. I had caught them more than once in a dark corner or walking down the road with their pinkies linked like children. And more than once, Sana had smiled over the sourdough with a secret delight, which she would tuck away into the dough where no one would ever find it.

And now, all she had to say for her broken heart was one breath, in and out. Because she was herself and always would be. Too strong for her own good.

"I want to hear it from them," she said. "I want them to admit it to my fucking face."

SEVEN

Originally, Sana wanted us to send for Rafe and Callan immediately, bring them to the house, and confront them. She was a mass of simmering rage bound to a chair by the leg that couldn't bear her weight. So when I refused to send the message, she could do nothing but yell about it.

"Why not, Lettie? Why the hell not?"

"What do you think would happen if we brought them here?" I spat back. "They'd deny it. We have no proof. I didn't even see Rafe last night. All we have to go on is a prophecy I got in a dream and Rafe's warning about the ceiling yesterday. And he's already explained that away by saying he saw the ceiling sagging."

"Lettie's right." Nik leaned back against the table with his arms crossed over his chest. "We need to catch them in the act."

And that was how we ended up huddled in the newly repaired sitting room that night, in the back corner where the shadows were the deepest. Just waiting. We dragged Sana's chair over so she could sit comfortably with her leg propped up on a cushion. Nik and I lay cozy in a little nest of blankets and pillows on the floor by her.

"Don't be gross down there," Sana said with a grumble as we settled in.

"Hypocrite," I said, but there was no bite to my tone.

At first, I thought I'd be far too keyed up to sleep, listening intently for every creak of the house and puff of wind hitting against the unlocked door. The stars sang their very best, calling me outside, but for once, I ignored them.

"Can you hear them?" I whispered into Nik's shoulder.

"Only because you do," was his reply.

But that was good enough for me. I hugged his arm close and nuzzled into his shoulder, reveling in the bright glow of validation.

I must have fallen asleep eventually, though, as wrapped up in Nik as I was. One moment, I was lazily tracing the collar of Nik's shirt with my finger, listening to the whoosh of his breath through his lungs, and the next...

Beware.

My eyes snapped open.

The voice was deep as thunder, but it was like the starsong: not quite a part of the real world. It was the voice of the Old Kind threading through my dreams, just like it had done a few nights before.

I listened hard, trying to hear them again, trying to feel them. But the voice was already gone, even before I'd woken up.

There was another sound, though, and this one was real.

A creak of the porch steps, a sharp intake of breath outside, halted so quickly it might not have even been there.

It was time. Rafe had come again.

I patted Nik's chest sharply to wake him, then reached up and tugged on Sana's wrist, where it hung over the side of the armrest of her chair. She gasped softly and sat up to peer down at me.

"*What?*" Nik breathed, but I put a finger to his lips.

That got his attention. I placed a finger to my ear and pointed at the front door.

The porch creaked a second time, and we all heard it. Nik and I eased out from under our blanket and huddled close with our eyes trained on the front door. Any second, the intruder would come in. We had all agreed to let him break in, let him get on with his vandalism. That way, we could catch him red-handed. There would be no doubt.

But the minutes ticked by with nothing more than the occasional creak of the porch decking or the scratching sound of fingers raking over fabric. The restless movements of someone with nothing better to do but wait in the dark.

Nik, Sana, and I glanced at each other. Their baffled expressions made it clear they didn't understand what was happening any better than I did.

After another few minutes, Nik had had enough. He crept forward on bare feet toward the front door. I followed close behind, but Nik guided me to the left, where I would be out of sight.

He put a finger to his mouth and his other hand to the latch. I glanced back at Sana, and my heart clenched at the look on her face: hope, fear, shaking anticipation. Maybe it wasn't Rafe outside, preparing to sneak into the house. Maybe her heart didn't have to be broken after all. Maybe it wasn't anyone at all, but a stray dog or something equally harmless.

Nik opened the door just wide enough to slip outside, and all Sana and I could do was listen.

"What are you doing here?" Nik asked.

The other person let out a hiss of surprise and then came the growl of a familiar voice. "You can't be here, man. Go home."

Rafe.

I squeezed my eyes shut at his words, and Sana let out a huff of air, almost like a silent sob. With a single word, all our fears were confirmed. Rafe—*Sana's* Rafe—had been sabotaging our house for weeks. Months, maybe. And all the while, he'd been coming over for breakfast, romancing her, inserting himself into our lives.

The bastard.

Outside, the conversation between Nik and Rafe continued,

both oblivious to the turmoil inside. Well, I supposed Nik was perfectly aware, considering he was sibylline.

"And why can't I be here?" Nik asked.

Rafe spoke over him, his voice ragged with some unknowable emotion. "Are the girls awake? Please tell me they're upstairs, asleep. Nik, please tell me."

"What difference does it make?" Nik asked.

But Rafe ignored him again. The door suddenly opened right in front of me.

I stumbled backward to avoid being hit and found myself staring into Rafe's wild eyes. Fury swirled in my gut, knotting up my tongue and clenching my teeth shut so that only a sharp hiss escaped.

"Shit fuck." Rafe breathed in shock when he locked eyes on me. "No, no, no, no..."

"Come to pull out some more nails, Rafe?" I asked. "Maybe poke another hole in our ceiling?"

"Lettie, you have to get upstairs now." Rafe reached for my arm, but I jerked away. He put out his hands and began to crowd into my space, almost like he was trying to herd me toward the stairs.

I sidestepped him. Nik drew me closer with a firm hand on my elbow.

"Are your daddy's ambitions really that important to you, Rafe?" I asked. "Did you really think you could get us to sell the house this way?"

"Lettie, you don't understand!" Rafe reached toward me again.

Nik jerked me back a step. "Don't put your hands on her."

"She has to get upstairs. He's going to be here any minute!"

"Who?" I asked with an angry frown.

He snarled his response. "My daddy and his *fucking* ambitions, Lettie. That's who."

An icy cold washed down my gut at Rafe's words, and Nik's hand tightened on my arm.

"What does that mean?" Sana asked, speaking for the first time.

Rafe whirled around to face her, clearly unaware she was in the dark corner until that very second. "Sana..."

Her voice was abominably steady. "What does that mean, Rafe?"

"It wasn't me, Sana. I swear. It was my father."

"Bullshit," I said.

"It's not."

I took a hesitant step forward, Nik's hand still firm on my arm. "You knew the ceiling was going to collapse the other day. How could you have known that if you weren't the one to sabotage it?"

"I caught Father coming home the night before. I called him out on it. I made him tell me everything." Rafe turned to Sana again. There was a pleading note in his tone. "That's why I came to breakfast that morning. I was going to tell you, but I didn't know how. I was going to fix it, Sana. I swear."

I was going to fix it.

An image came with that thought: one of Nik and Rafe on our roof that very afternoon, both working tirelessly through the entire day and evening to repair the damage.

Rafe barreled on. "But then Lettie was going to walk in there, and I could already see it bowing down. The ceiling...It was...I couldn't..."

He cast about, as if he might find the proof he needed to clear his name hanging in midair. Then he took an entirely different train of thought and ran with it.

"He's done this before! The Harrods...The Kemp brothers last year? You think it was an accident their house caught fire just before Father bought their property? And the Halloways about five years back? It wasn't a burglar that broke in that night."

The chilled wash in my chest nearly froze solid. It was hard at first to picture Callan sneaking around our house, silent and soft, breaking things with precision. But now that the image was in my head, I couldn't shake it. He was so careful, so calculating—two things Rafe had never been. It didn't take much at all for my mental image of Callan to pivot from sleazy businessman to outright criminal.

Sana hauled herself out of the chair, balancing on one leg.

"Sana, my gods," Rafe said. "What happened to your leg?"

"She fell through the floor this morning." I still had a good bite to my words. "Nearly took her damn leg off."

I couldn't make out Rafe's expression, but his shoulders tensed, and his breath caught in his throat. He took half a step toward Sana, hands outstretched, but she shrank away from him.

"Tell me it wasn't you," she said with a shaky breath.

His response was a low, desperate plea. "It wasn't me."

She sniffed once. Or was it a sob? It was so hard to tell in the dark.

"Make me believe it, Rafe."

We all waited for Rafe's response. He was a talker. Rafe had spent the last several years regaling us with stories, both true and imagined, at that very kitchen table. He'd spoken with such gusto that I would sit rapt in my chair, my full attention on what he'd say next.

But now, all that came from his mouth were two words. "I can't."

Only Nik could have seen what came next, and even he was too late to do much about it. The only warning he had time to give was a hiss through his teeth and a tight hold on my hand.

And then Rafe grunted in shock and pain.

But I couldn't see why. Not at first. It was still so dark in our sitting room. Not even the starsong penetrated the shadowed house. We had all been so rapt on Rafe's tales, on our anger and our confusion, none of us had noticed another man creeping in through the door behind Rafe.

But we saw him now.

Callan had a fistful of Rafe's hair and the collar of his shirt all bunched up in one punishing grip. He drew his son back, entirely unfazed by Rafe's struggling, prying fingers.

And judging by the grim lack of surprise on Rafe's face, this wasn't the first time Callan had handled his son this way.

"Well, well," Callan said, as calm and charming as ever. "It seems the con is up, doesn't it? And my own son betraying me? That's rich."

"Let me go!" Rafe gritted out.

"Stop being so difficult, my boy," Callan said, as if he were trying to get a toddler to eat his greens at dinner. "We've talked about this. I thought I made myself clear. Our security—*your* security—it doesn't always come easily. Sometimes, we have to bend a few rules."

Nik, Sana, and I stood frozen, staring at Callan and Rafe struggling near the open front door. I couldn't imagine what they were thinking, but my brain had entirely whited out. Only now were a few of Rafe's earlier explanations becoming crystal clear in my mind.

...their house caught fire...

It wasn't a burglar...

You think it was an accident?

By all the stars above, Callan was going to kill us. He was going to set fire to our house, kill us, call it a freak accident, and purchase our property from the city for pennies.

He was going to push his property line out a couple more acres. That much closer to becoming the largest landowner in Silmere. That much closer to his seat on the council.

And of course, Nik heard every thought passing through my mind. His hand squeezed mine once more, and he whispered in my ear. "Get Sana and run."

That kicked my brain into gear. I dashed toward Sana and tugged her in the direction of the stairs, but she was so slow.

"And where do you think you two are going?" Callan asked.

I turned frightened eyes toward Callan while Sana and I limped as far away from him as we could.

"Run!" Rafe yelled, still trying to pry his father's fingers out of his hair. "Run, Sana!"

Callen's patience finally snapped. "You ungrateful little shit," he said to Rafe, who continued to struggle against him. "I have given you *everything*. You'd be nothing without me! And you have the audacity to get in my way? Uh uh." He shook his head, trembling with rage. "It breaks my heart, boy. But if I can't trust you, I can't trust you."

Callen let out a frustrated yell and threw Rafe with all his might. The younger man stumbled, completely off balance, and cracked his head against the end table near my chair.

"Rafe!" Sana screamed, stumbling against me.

Nik planted himself between us and Callan.

Rafe groaned on the floor, trying to rise, his eyes like coal fire on his father.

But Callan, determined as ever, knew how to stop his son in his tracks. All it took was one violent stomp, aimed with precision at his son's knee.

The horrendous crack of splintering bone was chased out of our ears by Rafe's scream of pain.

"Rafe!" Sana shrieked. "You fucker! I'll kill you myself!"

My sister fought against me, trying to lunge toward Callan on one good leg, with enough rage to resurrect a bull.

I did my best to haul her back toward the stairs. "Stop it, Sana! Let's go!"

But Sana had never been one to be stopped once she set her mind to something. She couldn't get far on one leg, but she managed to lean enough to one side, hauling me with her, to snatch the crock of sourdough starter off the workbench. And then, with the rage of a mother bear, she threw the ceramic pot at Callan with everything she had.

"Aargh!" he yelped when the heavy pot collided with his collarbone and his chin, nearly knocking him off balance. The sharp, vinegar scent of the sourdough bloomed through the room, and the sticky starter splattered across his front in a messy stripe.

His gaze went dangerous and dark as he took in the mess Sana had made, and he shook off the pain of the blow. Some of the starter had smeared across his left cheek like war paint.

Nik helped me push Sana back before resuming his position between us and Callan. "Run, Lettie! Get her out of here! I'll slow him down!"

Callan laughed at that and advanced casually toward Nik. Rafe groaned on the floor behind him.

"Let's go, Sana!" I said again. "We can't help him if we're dead!"

At first, I thought to drag her toward the back door, but it would be too difficult to get open. Callan would catch us easily. We needed distance. We needed time.

The only other option was the stairs.

Sana screamed in frustration and finally let me haul her away.

Callan lunged toward Nik just as we turned away. We climbed the stairs one at a time. Sana leaned heavily on me and the banister, pulling herself along with determination.

By the gods above and below, I couldn't just leave Nik, could I? He was sacrificing everything, knowing he could only slow Callan down. Had he seen another premonition? Did he know how this would end?

Or would Nik end up on the floor, screaming in pain next to Rafe?

That thought had me glancing back, and with a thrill of pride, I saw Nik giving back as good as he got. Nik and Callan were of the same height, but Nik was younger and had more to lose. They grappled at the bottom of the stairs, both of their expressions twisted with fury.

I could only catch glimpses of the fight. Sana was grunting in pain with every labored step she climbed. But I caught enough to understand what was happening.

Nik got in a good, solid punch. Callan's hands closed around Nik's throat, and Nik pressed his thumb into Callan's eye.

But then I must have missed something. The next time I glanced back, Nik was on the floor, gasping for breath.

"Nik!" I yelled, but I didn't go back. I had to get Sana to safety.

Callan didn't even glance up at us. He just grabbed Nik by the ankle and dragged him toward the cast iron stove, where we cooked our meals and kept away the winter frost. It was supposed to be the heart of our house, and Callan had the nerve to turn it into something ugly.

He yanked Nik's arms around and bound his wrists to the cold stove with what looked like corded rope.

"No," I whimpered.

I glanced between the incapacitated Rafe in the sitting room and Nik tied to the stove. So neat, so tidy. And if Callan could manage to truss up Sana and me just the same, all it would take is one house fire to eliminate every witness to his crimes.

But he would have to catch us first.

"Go, go." I urged Sana up the next step even faster.

We were almost to the top. If we could just get to our room, we could barricade the door.

But then what?

No, one step at a time. Just get up the stairs. Sana clawed her way up another step.

A crunching sound cut into my brain, followed by Callan's yell of anger.

"Ahh! Fuck!"

I glanced back, and a grin of satisfaction pulled at my lips. The old bastard had fallen through the third step on the stairs—the one we always skipped. Served him right.

He struggled and dragged himself out of the broken stair, only to crash right through the fourth step next.

"Fuck!" he yelled again.

"Go, go. One more!" I said when Sana and I finally reached the landing outside our door.

"Stop!" Callan yelled after us. "I'm coming for you! Don't think you're safe! I'm coming!"

I shoved Sana into our room and slammed the door shut. She helped me push her dresser in front of it with a groan of effort. We both backed away, staring at the door as if it would slam open at any second, even with the heavy dresser blocking it.

"Now what?" Sana asked, her breath ragged in her chest.

"Um…" I glanced around, unsure.

"Because he could just as easily fire the house with us here as anywhere else."

That sent my mind hurtling toward Plan C. Because what would be our escape in case of fire?

"The window!"

"What?"

"We go out the window! Now! Go, go!"

"Lettie, no!"

"It's the only way out of here," I said.

And then, as if to prove my point, three thundering bangs sounded against our bedroom door. "You can't hide in there forever!" Callan shouted.

The door rattled in its frame, and it even opened half an inch. The dresser shook.

"Okay, okay, the window!" Sana agreed, and she dove for my bed.

The window was still open from last night, when Nik and I had shared confessions and kisses under the starsong. I knelt on the bed and peered out into the darkness. The starsong clattered down at me, and in the deep shadow under the tree line, two yellow eyes glared back. Two yellow eyes set in the deep dark fur of a wolf made of shadow.

But when I blinked, the shadow wolf was gone, disappearing among the trees. That was all the confirmation I needed. This was the right path.

"You first," I said, my mouth in a grim line. "I'll lower you down."

"Oh gods," Sana muttered.

She eased her legs out over the windowsill, inched herself out, feet first, and grabbed my hands tightly. Sana was so heavy, but I held on with everything I had until I was halfway out the window as well. The sill dug into my hips.

Callan shoved against the door again, and the dresser scraped across the floor another few inches. He'd be in the room any second.

Sana dangled below me, still way too high up. This was so stupid. She was going to tear open her leg.

But we were too far gone now to come back. There was no way I could get her back up to the window.

"Ready?"

"No!" Sana squeaked. Her eyes held mine, fear and trust warring in her expression.

"One, two, three!" I counted way too fast, and she only barely kept in a yelp of shock when I let her drop.

She hit the ground with a thud and rolled.

"There's no point in running!" Callan shouted through the inches of open space, where the door pressed against the dresser. The stench of sourdough starter leached into the room, making me dizzy.

I spared him only half a glance before turning around and easing out the window properly, feet first. I lowered myself as far as I could, my fingers going numb against the hard wood of the windowsill, and let myself drop.

"Oof!" I gasped when I hit the ground. Pain radiated up through my ankles.

If I broke my ankles, it was all over. Sana couldn't run without me. This was it.

But then Sana was scrabbling at my shoulders, hauling me up. And I found that I could stand. The pain in my ankles subsided to a dull ache after a few stumbling steps, and we both disappeared into the shadowy tree line as fast as two injured and terrified sisters could go.

I glanced back when we reached the trees.

Callan's face appeared in the window we had just exited, still smeared with sourdough. His calculating expression seemed to glow in the light of the starsong he would never be able to hear. The stars screamed their anger down on us, their song furious and vengeful.

They didn't like what was happening. They shouldn't have to see this, but they couldn't look away.

Callan, entirely unaware of how much he had angered the stars above, hissed at us through the open window and disappeared.

But he wouldn't be giving up that easily. He was probably just too old and too smart to go jumping out of windows when there were two perfectly good doors downstairs.

Well, one perfectly good door and one very, very stuck back door.

Sana and I stumbled through the trees, our feet following the invisible path I had traveled so many times before. I didn't know why we went to the yew tree, but where the hell else were we supposed to go? To Nik's house? Where his mother, Marta, slept peacefully in her bed? Callan wouldn't hesitate to kill her too.

And the next nearest house was Callan's.

So, our only option was the woods. To hope we could hide well enough that he would miss us. And then maybe, when the sun rose, we could go for help.

And besides, there was the shadow wolf. I caught occasional

glimpses of his tail between the trees and the flash of his glowing golden eyes. Far ahead, leading the way.

The second I saw the shadow wolf, my resolve settled. My reasons for fleeing into the woods were moot. The Old Kind wanted us to go this way. And that was all that mattered.

I couldn't think about leaving Rafe and Nik behind. I didn't even know how badly Nik might have been hurt. But there was nothing we could do for them, not with Callan still on the warpath. I had Sana to look after, and I couldn't risk her life just to help them. They wouldn't want me to.

And so we followed the shadow wolf, and we ran.

The yew tree loomed out of the darkness, its bark even blacker tonight than ever before. Its branches swayed in the gentle wind, but they always returned to their preferred slant toward the south-west. The starsong overhead grew even louder, bathing us both in its silvery light. They screamed and screamed, filling my head with such noise I couldn't think.

"Over here." Sana dragged me behind the yew tree.

Toward the back, it had begun to hollow out with age. Not enough for us to hide inside, but we could tuck ourselves away. It was better than nothing, but I hated the fact that I couldn't see anything more than a narrow slice of the woods.

We wouldn't be able to see Callan coming.

Sana and I clung to each other. The rough bark dug into my skin through my thin shirt, but I ignored the discomfort and leaned even harder back into it.

Our breaths came in ragged, desperate gasps, loud in the tight space. It sounded even more amplified out of the fear of being heard. If Callan came anywhere close to the yew tree, he would hear us immediately.

"What if he comes this way?" Sana whispered.

Then we'll fight him. We'll run. We'll—

I clutched her closer. "The Old Kind will look after us."

Sana let out half a whimper, as if this was the last thing that could ever reassure her. But she had placed an egg in the tree that very morning, and she didn't argue with me now.

We heard him from a long way off. He moved through the woods like a thrashing, heedless bull plowing through everything in sight. His footsteps sounded like he was wading through the forest rather than walking along any kind of path. The old leaf litter crashed about like it was breaking against his shins.

Sana and I sucked in our breath and did our best to make no sound at all. Maybe Callan would just walk by. Perhaps he wouldn't see us at all.

Gods, maybe he would give up, go back, and set our house on fire with Rafe and Nik still inside.

I nearly bit clean through my lip, trying to keep still.

But of course, the shadow wolf had led us to the most noticeable place in the entire forest. Even Callan couldn't help but stop and admire the majestic yew, with its leaning branches and broad trunk. His crashing footsteps stopped just on the other side of the tree, and we listened, hearts in our mouths, while he gaped up at it.

"Fucking shit," he mumbled under his breath.

Just keep walking. Move on. We're not here.

Sana's hand found mine in the darkness and gripped tightly.

Then Callan's footsteps started up again, and my heart sank into my gut. He was coming toward the tree, then around it. Oh gods, he was going to come right to the back, circle the whole thing.

We smelled him first. The sharp vinegar of the sourdough. Sana stiffened against me and threw a hand over her mouth and nose, as if to force her breath to stop.

But that wouldn't help. Because Callan had come right around the back of the tree and into our narrow view. His eyes were fixed upward, staring at the branches reaching toward the southwest.

Maybe he wouldn't look down. Maybe he would miss us in the dark.

But then he *did* look down. His gaze landed on mine, and his mouth opened in a startled *oh*. As if shocked and delighted that he had managed to find us where he least expected.

And there was something in his eyes that sent fire through my veins. That arrogance, confidence, superiority—that calm.

He would never stop. Not ever. Not until he had everything he wanted, and then his hunger would grow even further. If Rafe was to be believed, Callan had done this to several other families in Silmere before us. And what would stop him from doing the same to someone else?

Maybe Nik and Marta would be next after all. Adding their acres to ours would make for a tidy property line along the road, wouldn't it?

My body acted before I had a chance to fully decide. My thighs bunched, my hands gripped the tree to haul myself up, and my lip curled. Sana screamed my name, but I barely heard her over the starsong above and the thrum of blood in my veins.

I didn't feel the moss, stones, and sticks under my bare feet. I didn't hear the snarl that worked its way out of my throat. All I knew was that I had to stop this man. Had to stop him here and now and forever.

I launched out of the crevice in the yew tree and tackled Callan around the middle, catching him by surprise. The air was forced from his lungs with a startled grunt. We both toppled to the ground, gasping.

I didn't have the strength to hurt him on my own. I had no delusions about that. My shoulder might knock the wind out of him, but he would just swat away my flailing fists like mosquitos.

So, the first thing I did after knocking him off his feet was scramble up and scan the ground for a weapon. I dove for the first solid-looking branch I could find and hefted it up like a club. It was a little unwieldy, but I might do some serious damage with it if I tried.

The fury in my gut had turned my blood to fire. I stalked

toward Callan with the branch raised, the bark digging into the soft flesh of my hands.

But he was faster than I expected. He was an older man, but he was hardy and strong after a lifetime of working his mills. Callan rolled away and scrambled to his feet before I could reach him with my weapon, and my advantage was lost.

He bent his knees, all smugness gone. Now he was just angry. Callan wiped a hand across his face, trying to smear away the smelly sourdough.

"You were always such a pain in my ass, Lettie," he said.

"I never did a damn thing to you, Callan. You're the one who kept insisting on bothering us at home."

"I will have this property, no matter what it takes." He gave me a patronizing nod. His graying hair had gone a bit wild when I tackled him, and the sight of it flopping only added to his generally unhinged attitude. "Especially now I see there's a yew tree to be had."

"This tree doesn't belong to me, you idiot. And it will certainly never belong to you. Don't you know anything about the world?"

"Oh, I know," he said with a smug smile. "I know that magic is strong at a yew tree. I know that if I can harness it, if I can catch myself one of the Old Kind, I could do great things. Greater than getting onto a council. I could be one of the sibylline."

I laughed out loud at that. Ambitions indeed. "That's not how any of that works."

Callan circled a little, pacing like a panther in the darkness. "And what would you know of it?"

"What difference does it make? Quit stalling and come at me, you old bastard. I'm gonna cave your head in with this tree branch." I raised the limb a bit higher to illustrate my point.

Callan laughed at me. He *laughed*. And I remembered how small and soft I was, how I had frozen in the kitchen when Callan had been sneaking around in my sitting room in the dark, the unknown intruder. I remembered how strong he was after a lifetime of hauling grain sacks and millstones. This man whom I had always dismissed, he'd been a monster all along.

The branch was so damn heavy, and my hands were smarting against the rough bark. If I hit something with any amount of force, I'd probably gash my hands to ribbons.

Callan must have seen the doubt in my expression because he straightened up and closed his mouth in a smug grin.

Fuck. Fucking shitting fuck. I couldn't do this. I *had* to do this. He wouldn't stop with me and Sana. He would kill Rafe and Nik to keep his secret. And probably Marta too. And anyone else who got in the way of his precious ambition.

But I could stop this here and now. I *had* to stop this.

So I raised the tree branch once more, and my expression hardened with determination. I took two deliberate steps toward him, ready to swing with everything I had. I was going to do it.

Callan's expression faltered, and he stumbled backward as I approached. His fear emboldened me even more. Maybe I did have it in me to be fierce after all. This was working.

But then Callan let out a strangled yelp, his eyes wide and terrified. They rose above my head to stare at something behind me.

A terrible, deep, bone-rattling growl erupted just over my head, and I stopped in my tracks. I didn't need to look up; I knew what I would see: the underside of a great shadow wolf, tall as a house, black as night, with glowing yellow eyes. The tree branch in my hands lowered and dropped to the ground when two massive paws planted themselves on either side of me. I could have reached out and brushed the coarse, night-black fur if I wanted.

The shadow wolf stood over me, teeth as bright as starlight and bared at Callan. And the stars themselves, oh they *sang*. They belted out their glorious song as the shadow wolf faced Callan down. This man who would burn everything if it meant he could earn a few more pennies.

This man who was covered in sourdough—my favorite gift for the Old Kind.

A hard choking gasp burst from Callan, and he stared up at the shadow wolf looming protectively over me, growling like thunder.

Then Callan ran.

Or at least, Callan *tried* to run. He made it about one and a half steps before the shadow wolf lunged.

I didn't cower, even when the air stirred my hair up with the motion. But I did flinch when Callan's strangled cry of fear was cut off with a wet crunch. Those jaws snapped shut around Callan, and I was grateful that I could see very little around the bulk of the wolf's powerful body.

And just like that, Callan was gone. No trace of him left behind. Not even a lost shoe or a drop of blood on the mossy ground.

One moment, he'd been standing there, and then he wasn't. An entire life snuffed out right before my eyes. I couldn't breathe. I couldn't think. Couldn't...I was going to—I would have done it. It might have been me who did that. Oh gods, I would have been a murderer. I had been so ready to do it...

When the shadow wolf turned, he seemed smaller somehow. He stepped forward, his nose level with my forehead. My spiraling panic stopped in its tracks. I stood as tall as I could, gazing into his deep yellow eyes with reverence.

He closed the distance between us and hovered his snout near my face, his hot breath huffing against my skin. I raised my hands, shaking with adrenaline, and paused an inch away from him. Gave him plenty of time to back away, to say no.

But he didn't. He watched me passively, almost curiously. I buried my fingers into the thick fur of his jaw.

Incredulity burst from my throat in a gasp. "Huh..." My eyes began to water.

I worked my fingers through the shadow wolf's glorious fur. He was hot against my hands, blazing as the sun itself.

He gazed down at me, imperious, kind, and...so many things I could never hope to name. So beautiful. And then, to my great surprise, the wet press of a wolfish tongue grazed across my nose. There and gone before I could react.

Peace, the gesture said. *Peace, child.*

The shadow wolf turned toward the yew tree next, and thoughts of Sana surged back in full force. Had she been there the whole time? Hiding? Safe? Hurting? Scared? Was she okay?

Sana sat awkwardly in the crevice of the yew tree where I had left her, her bandaged leg stretched out in front. Her face was a mask of fear and wonder, and she gazed up at the shadow wolf as it approached her.

Sana had one hand pressed to the bark so hard it looked like she was trying to hold up the entire tree with her palm. But then I noticed a splash of deep red in the starlight. It ran down her wrist in a gentle drip, spattering to the grass one drop at a time.

"Sana," I breathed.

The shadow wolf lowered his head to her hand, where she was pressing her blood into the yew tree—the ultimate offering. He had become even smaller and was on her level now. The wolf nosed at her hand until she drew it away from the tree and held it out for him to investigate.

He sniffed at the bloody mess in her palm, then licked her as well. The shadow wolf's bright pink tongue worked until every trace of blood on her hand was gone, swept into his mouth. It was so matter-of-fact—of course, this blood was his to take. She had offered it to him, after all.

And when I stepped up to look closer, the gash on her palm, dug there with the sharp rock still clutched in her other hand, had disappeared as well. Healed without a mark or scar to remember it by.

I knelt by my sister and looked up at the shadow wolf. His eyes were calm once again.

"Thank you," I whispered.

The shadow wolf only blinked his glowing eyes and was gone. Smoke on the wind.

EIGHT

S ana and I made our way back to the house under the singing stars. I tucked an arm around her waist, and she clung to me, limping but determined.

The front door was open when we got back. We heard Rafe's moans and grunts of pain long before we made it to the porch. There was another voice as well, murmuring indistinctly in what sounded like a soothing tone.

"Rafe?" Sana lurched away from me, hopping the rest of the distance as fast as she could.

I trailed after her with feet that felt like stones. The uproar in the house only increased when Sana stumbled in. And if Nik hadn't appeared in the doorway, I might have run forward as well.

But when Nik's eyes caught mine, I couldn't hold myself up anymore. He strode toward me on steady feet. I ran my hands over his arms, his chest, looking for any sign of injury. But aside from a few bruises from his fight and the redness around his wrists from the rope Callan had used to tie him to the stove, there was nothing.

"I'm okay, I'm okay," he murmured, pressing kisses over my face and mouth. "We're okay. It's over."

"How did you get free?"

"Mama," he said simply. "Sometimes, if I really need her, she can hear me too."

Nik held me close and squeezed tight, as if to prove to himself that I was real.

I just stood there and let him do it, going slack against him. "Did you see?"

He nodded against my hair. "I saw it all. You did so well."

Thank the gods. I didn't think I'd ever be able to tell the story of what happened at the yew tree.

"Come inside. Mama and Mrs. Masters are taking care of Rafe, and the kettle's on. And I sent Jedd for the guard."

I nodded once but didn't get a chance to say anything in reply. Nik went stiff in my arms, then snaked his hands up to clamp them over my ears. I stared up at him, alarmed, unable to hear anything over the thrum of blood in my veins and the white noise of his hands shifting over my ears.

"What is it? What's happening?" My voice sounded wrong in my blocked ears.

Nik dropped his hands away, breathing hard, and let them rest against my neck in a comforting hold. I could hear Rafe inside the house, gasping on every breath. Sana's voice kept up a running ramble of soothing words that I couldn't pick out, and Marta's tone added measured, calm instructions to the general noise.

"They just set his leg," Nik explained. "Didn't want you to hear that."

That did it. After the stress of running for our lives, Callan's death, Rafe's injury, general fear and worry, it was Nik's instinct to protect me from something as simple as a distressing noise that finally sent me over the edge. I collapsed against his chest, and the tears finally hit me. My shaking legs gave out, and I sagged against him, completely spent.

Nik's arms went around me, and he half dragged, half carried me toward the porch steps. We sat there for a long time, me sobbing in his lap. He curled his body over me, rubbing soothing circles along my back and stroking my hair. Nik held me close. Let me cry.

By the time the neighbors started showing up, I was nearly empty. I sat with heavy eyes, staring out over the grassy yard, ignoring everyone who filed into the house. I let Nik answer questions, give explanations. He never left my side.

At some point, there was an argument about what to do with Rafe. Someone wanted to carry him into town on a stretcher, but Sana clung to him, screeching at anyone who came close.

"I'll take care of him! He's staying here!"

"You can't walk either, Sana!" someone said.

"He's staying *here!*"

Fortunately, our neighbors knew Sana well enough not to push the issue any further. There was a big to-do while a pallet was made on the floor for him, then another when he was moved onto it. But Rafe was to stay, and I could almost picture Sana hovering over him like a mother cat, hissing at anyone who looked at him wrong.

"Mama will stay and help," Nik said to me.

Good, I thought. Sana had always liked Marta. She would allow that.

Eventually, Nik had to nudge me awake. I must have fallen asleep against his shoulder.

"Inside," he said gently. "To bed."

Most everyone had left by then, with only Marta left behind, sleeping in Sana's chair just in case she was needed in the night. Sana herself lay curled up against Rafe on the floor, both tucked under a set of cozy quilts, dozing fitfully.

Nik led me through the kitchen toward the stairs, and I took in the house for the first time. The neighbors had done their best to clear up the mess and the damage, but it felt wrong somehow. It was spotlessly clean, with everything in its place.

But there, by the door...That was where Callan had broken Rafe's leg. And look...The third and fourth steps were missing entirely. Someone had cleared away the debris, leaving a gaping hole where the steps should have been.

And on the counter, the empty sourdough crock...Scrubbed clean. Not a drop of starter left. That crock hadn't been empty in decades. When I saw that, I found I had a few tears left after all.

Nik led me upstairs and helped me undress. He eased me down onto the bed and crawled in after. Nik tucked me under his chin and relaxed against me.

Outside, the stars sang the softest lullaby. I closed my eyes and focused on it, imagining how the trees below the house would be coated in silver light. How the yew tree would sway in the breeze. How the yellow eyes of the wolf had gazed down on me. How his fur felt under my hands.

That night had etched itself into me forever. Yesterday, I'd had something of innocence. I thought a man would never dare to hurt us, wouldn't *dream* of it. I knew better now.

But I also knew that Nik was real and solid and *good*. His heart beat sure and steady under my hand. His warmth wrapped me up, held me safe.

And I could still hear the stars and feel their joy. Tonight, they sang for me, I thought. They sang for the Old Kind and for girls in love. They sang for sisters, for neighbors, and for faith.

"Do you hear them?" I breathed against Nik's chest.

A beat of silence, then simply, "I hear them."

I couldn't quite smile, but I wanted to. And somewhere deep down, I knew I would remember how to smile again properly. Someday soon.

Because the stars still sang, even after everything.

They sang for us.

RAVEN'S END

ONE

What a stupid fucking way to die.

I expected something a bit more dramatic: mauled by a bear or fallen in battle for a great cause. After all, I had done so much over the decades, made so many friends, helped people who were struggling, and brought joy and adventure where there was none. There should have been a parade in my honor—or at least a few toasts to my bravery in the local pub.

"To Fletcher!" They would call my name like invoking a hero. "The bravest of us! He lived his life to the fullest to the very end! That bear must have been *huge*!"

Fuck's sake, I deserved *something*.

But instead, I slipped in some mud and fell onto a broken tree branch, alone in the woods, for no reason except for a bit of slick after an unremarkable drizzle of rain. There wouldn't be a funeral. No one would even know. I would bleed out in the mud, and that would be that.

Fucking stupid.

The gentle rain continued to patter on my face. It slicked my red hair flat against my skull and weighed down my short beard. I gritted my teeth and forced air to continue in and out of my lungs at a steady pace.

A few inches of gory wood protruded from my upper belly. I had fallen backward onto the damn thing after sliding along the slope a few feet, and it had gone straight through me.

It was survivable. For me, at least, it was all survivable. If I got stitched up fast enough, if the blood loss could be stopped quick enough, my body would mend itself like this disastrous day had never happened. Just like always.

But I had to get up first. I had to get this branch out of my gut. And then bind it up tight until the wound closed. And then something this deep would have me laid up for at least a few days. I would need care.

I needed help, but there was no one around to help me.

"Don't travel alone, she says," I muttered through gritted teeth, chastising myself while somehow still managing to blame my sister back home. I stretched my arm out toward another branch of the same tree I'd fallen on. "What if you get hurt, she says? I should come with you, she says!"

My damn sister, always fucking right. And every time she got on my case, I just kept telling her, "No, Isla. I'll be fine, Isla. Don't worry so much, Isla."

Maybe I shouldn't have been so dismissive of her worrying, if this was the sort of mess I got myself into. Bit late to do anything about it now, though.

I pulled on the branch above me, lifting myself with a scream of effort. Fucking...shitting fuck. The pain was like nothing I'd ever felt before. The adrenaline coursing through my blood dulled most of it, but my body still rebelled against every movement.

I screamed, then kept pulling. Wanted to pass out, wanted to relax and just let it take me. Maybe death wasn't such a terrible fate. At least it wouldn't hurt anymore. And besides, I'd lived more than long enough by now. I'd already had two lifetimes, going on three. Maybe it was just time.

But no one in all of Lujor or Amau would say Fletcher of Mitsmooren was a quitting kind of man. So, I didn't let up. I pulled until the branch sank into my gut, until I could reach the higher limb with my other arm as well. I kept pulling until the damn thing slid out of my back with a sickening slurp. And finally, with a choking gasp of relief, I let myself fall to the ground.

The world spun around my head, and I let myself focus on breathing for a little bit. With grim satisfaction, I glared at the bloody branch that had been inside my body a moment before.

"Fuck you," I said on a sigh. "You're not going to be what kills me, you fucking tree."

I allowed my head to rest against the trunk of the offending tree. Overhead, perched on a branch of a sprawling oak, two ravens sat side by side. They watched me, beady eyes curious as their heads quirked at an angle for a better view.

Ravens were ominously large when viewed up close. Too large. Birds of prey.

This mountain was known for its ravens—and for the Old Kind spirit who lived there. The Raven King, they called him. A great black bird taller than a man, lurking between the trees.

In the east, we just called him Death.

That was the entire point of coming here in the first place. I had wanted to see the area for myself, hear the legends. Maybe sit in the forest at Raven's End if I could find it. The story went that if you lingered there long enough, if you were quiet enough, the Raven King would come to you and tell you when you were going to die. He might even hasten your death along, if you asked him to.

Of course, the idea had caught my interest. After all my decades, could there be an end to it someday? If anyone would know, the Raven King would. Death himself

The irony of my current situation wasn't lost on me, though. Imagine traveling to meet the Raven King to ask about my long life, only to die a few miles short of reaching his forest. Impaled on a tree, with his ravens watching me.

While the pair of ravens and I stared at each other, a third flew in and landed on the fallen tree I was leaning against.

"What the..." I said.

For some reason, I was offended. What right did these ravens have to come watch me die? If they were useful, they'd go get some help or something. But no. They were just going to stare at me while I lounged in a pool of my own blood.

Two more ravens flew overhead and disappeared into the treetops. They talked to each other from somewhere outside my field of vision with their gurgling, croaking calls, passing messages, telling secrets.

"Get help," I growled at the one closest to me.

It shifted its feet on the fallen tree and tilted its head toward me.

"Get help," it mimicked in an almost perfect echo of my voice. Its glossy black feathers shone in the soft sunlight filtering through the clouds.

The pain in my gut grew in waves as the adrenaline subsided. My hands were cold in the misty, drizzling morning. Too much blood loss. I was so fucked. Such a stupid way to die. Death by tree. Give me a fucking break.

"Get help."

"Yes, go get some fucking help." My eyes were heavy. It would be so easy to just close them, to rest for a bit.

"Get help," said the raven closest to me again.

"Get help," echoed another in the oak tree overhead.

"Get help."

"Get help."

"Get help."

I peeled my eyes open while raven after raven began repeating the message. It sounded from deep in the leaf canopy overhead as more unseen ravens took up the chant.

"Get help. Get help."

How many of the damn birds were there? My numb hand fell

heavily on the hilt of my knife. The ominous chant spread around me.

"Get help."

Was I dead already? Surely I was hallucinating this massive cloud of ravens hidden just out of sight. That must be it. I came to the mountain looking for tales of the Raven King, and this was the hallucination my dying brain provided.

The bird closest to me fluttered its wings, agitated. *"Get help."*

What was left of the blood in my body rushed through my ears, muting the eerie echo of the ravens. Whiteness clouded in the corners of my vision. The quiet, dripping forest wavered around me, the mossy greens growing a little grayer with every struggling heartbeat.

"Get help."

"Daddy! Help!"

That...That wasn't a raven.

"There's someone down here!"

I pried my eyes open when the unmistakable sound of footsteps punched into my consciousness. There was movement on the incline above me, where the road sloped down into a ditch. I'd been walking up there just five minutes ago, perfectly fine. No gut wound. No fucking tree. No ravens. Why were there so many ravens? That couldn't be normal.

Must be hallucinating.

Another raven flew in on a graceful glide and perched on a branch above me. Two more winged by overhead.

But nearer to, something definitely real was moving. A person. Had to be. Someone was sliding down the incline from the road. I forced my eyes to focus. It was a little girl with fair skin and dark hair curling about her delicate shoulders. Behind her stood a great shadowy figure. Death probably. The Raven King himself. Come to take me away after all these decades. It made sense he would collect me in person.

"Finally," I said to Death on the road, though much too softly to be heard by either of them. "The hell you been, then?"

"He's hurt, Daddy!" the little girl wailed when she reached me. She hovered a few feet away, uneasy with the sticky blood the rain hadn't managed to wash away.

"S'not your daddy," I mumbled. "Tha's Death. I came here looking for him, and there he is."

"No, that's my dad." The little girl had to be less than ten years old, but her eyes were steady on me. They were unremarkable eyes, deep brown with a hint of gold when the light hit them just right. But they were so confident, so piercing, I couldn't look away. Those bright brown eyes became the only thing in the world to look at.

"*Get help,*" a raven said overhead.

"Back up, Zoya," a male voice said. "Let me see what's the matter."

And then the piercing brown eyes that had taken up my entire field of vision were replaced with vivid black ones set in a pale face. Dark eyebrows narrowed with concern over them.

Strange. All the stories described Death as a giant black raven taller than a man. But this was just...a man. Or at least, he looked like one.

"You're in a bad way, friend," Death said.

"You come to take me away?" I asked, my voice little more than breath.

"If you want me to."

I should be afraid of him. I tried to make myself afraid, to remind myself of what happened when I was too weak to fight people off. But I couldn't spare the energy. Besides, this was Death. He was one of the good ones. He had to be.

"Where you gonna take me?"

"My house is a little ways further up the road. But I think we need to address your injuries before we can move you anywhere."

"Weird thing for Death to do—patch me up before taking me away."

He didn't seem to hear me.

The man began pulling at my shirt and hauling me around. The world came into much sharper focus. He was trying to get an idea of how bad my injury was. Which, considering an entire tree branch had gone through me, it was pretty damn bad.

I groaned, helpless.

"You've lost a lot of blood," Death said in an undertone.

The girl hovered near my feet, peering around her father's shoulder to get a better look. "He's going to be okay, right Daddy?"

"I hope so, darling." Then he continued in a lower voice only I could hear. "I'm going to have to stop this bleeding before we can move you. I'll do my best, but it may already be too late."

"No such thing as too late." I gave him my most wolfish grin, one that had a reasonably high success rate in charming the pants off basically anyone I threw it at.

The dark eyes hovering over me lifted with a smile. "A charmer, eh?"

"Only for the handsome ones," I said and winked.

Well, I tried to wink. It might not have worked, because both of my eyes were closed now.

"A flatterer too," Death said, amused. "Come here, Zoya. Help me wrap this. Tight as you can. That's right."

I grunted when something was drawn tightly around my middle. Some kind of bandaging, though fuck if I knew where the man had gotten it from. The world slipped in and out of reality around me.

All I could feel was the pain in my gut. All I could see were those deep black eyes. All I could hear were the murmuring voices of my saviors and the ravens croaking to each other in the canopy above.

Two

My eyes felt like sandpaper when I blinked slowly awake. Everything hurt. Not just the deadly wound in my gut, but my head, my arms, everything. My dry throat clicked, and I swallowed against the awful taste in my mouth.

"Fuck..." I said to the empty room.

I was lying on a firm bed, tucked neatly in with a soft, multi-colored quilt and wrinkled, linen-gray sheets. I rolled my head to the right and took in my surroundings.

The room was simple but tidy: a rough-hewn wooden floor, paneled walls, and a high ceiling with drying herbs hanging in bunches. There was a table with four chairs, an economical kitchen complete with a squat black stove, and a smaller bed in the far corner. The quilt on that bed was every color of green imaginable, pieced together in spirals. At least ten stuffed animals were lined neatly along the foot of the bed, and a stuffed rabbit sat pride of place against the pillow.

Right. There had been a little girl. That must be her bed.

And there had been a man. I couldn't picture his face, but I remembered his piercing black eyes and the amused quirk of his eyebrow. And I could recall the feel of his hands on my chest while he moved me about, if I thought hard about it.

I took stock of my body next. Weaker than I had been the day before–severe blood loss would do that to a person. But I felt more lucid, less addled by adrenaline and panic. And though I could feel the pain of my injury, I felt whole. I was no longer dying.

My body was knitting itself back together, just like always.

"You're awake," said a familiar male voice.

My scratchy eyes peeled back open. Standing next to the open door of the one-room house was the man I had mistaken for Death on the road. Now that I was able to get a good view of him, I could understand how my dying brain had made such a mistake.

The man was very tall, with fair, clean-shaven skin. Jet-black hair curled around his ears where it had come untucked from a hasty tie at the back of his head. He wore a dark cloak, which he proceeded to take off when he entered the house. Underneath was more dark clothing, though now there was some color: a deep purple tunic, aged leather pants, a thick homespun scarf.

The man approached the bed, and my insides clenched with remembered fear. I didn't like being so weak and under the power of others. You never knew which ones were nice and which weren't.

But the man simply came close and studied my face. "We were beginning to worry you'd never wake up. Are you thirsty?"

One of the nice ones, then. Hopefully. I dry-swallowed again and nodded.

The man fetched a wooden cup from the kitchen sideboard and filled it from an ewer of clear water. He sat down on the edge of my bed and held the cup to my mouth. His cool hand on the back of my neck helped raise me enough to drink.

I swallowed gratefully and wished for more. But I said, "Thank you," instead and lay back down.

"You should take it slow." The man's voice was gentle. "It's been two days. Too much too fast could turn your stomach."

Two days. I had never been out so long in my life. The injury must have been far worse than I realized. That was the closest to death I'd ever gotten. And hopefully, it was the closest I'd ever get.

"My name is Pace."

I swallowed hard. "Fletcher."

"Good to know you, Fletcher. Good to see you alive."

"Take more than a—more than a tree—" I couldn't finish the sentence, but Pace seemed to get the idea.

"I'd rather noticed," he said with a smile. "How are you feeling? How's the pain?"

"Feel like shit, man. Not gonna—Not gonna lie."

"Does it feel infected? You don't look feverish, but you'd feel it long before I'd see it from the outside."

I almost laughed. Infected? Me? If I'd made it this long, there was nothing to worry about anymore. But Pace couldn't know that, so I answered the question as simply as I could. "No. I'm good."

Pace picked up my hand from where it rested at my side. He pressed my fingers between his hands, as if to feel for a fever. How many times had he checked me like this in the last two days, while I slept on his bed?

I looked down at where my hand disappeared between his. His skin was fair, but not as fair as mine. There were white patches on the back of his right hand and up his wrist, tinged a little pink across the knuckles.

When he casually released me, satisfied I still had no fever, I grabbed his hand instead. I ran my thumb over the patch of white skin on the back of it, mesmerized by the change of color.

"I've had it most of my life," Pace said. "The white bits spread over the years, but it doesn't hurt or anything."

"Pretty." Which was true, but it was a stupid thing for me to say. Didn't make sense to get attached to people or throw out unnecessary compliments. I let my hand fall to the bed but didn't take back my words. That would just be stupider.

"Well, I don't know about that," Pace said with a rueful smile. "But thanks all the same. How about another drink of water?"

I must have fallen asleep in the time it took Pace to refill the cup, because he had to nudge me awake to drink it.

~

The next time I opened my eyes, Pace was gone. The light had changed in the room, with bright streaks of it spilling in at a steep slant through the large open windows. It was either late evening or early morning. And judging by the pain levels and how badly I needed a piss, I had to guess late evening of the same day.

But with the first movement of my arm to draw back the blankets, something flopped over that had been propped up against me. It was a stuffed rabbit. The same one that had sat proudly on the other bed across the room. There were also a handful of wilted wildflowers, a teacup made of brass on a matching saucer, and a spreading wet stain of water that had spilled from the cup when I moved.

"The hell?" I breathed in confusion at the impromptu tea party soaking into my side.

But before I could investigate further, running footsteps approached from outside, and the little girl from the woods came bounding in. She held more flowers in her hands, along with a little ceramic jar. The girl stopped abruptly when she noticed me looking at her.

For about ten seconds, we just stared at each other, her startled, me alarmed. Instinct told me to be afraid of everyone when I was so weak, but she was just a little girl. I didn't know how to feel.

"You're awake!" she said, delighted. Her expression brightened, and she approached the bed. The girl immediately began straightening up the mess I'd made of the tea party. "Daddy said you were thirsty earlier, so I brought you something nice to drink. But you knocked it over! Don't worry. There's more. And it's only water, so it won't stain."

The girl hopped over to the kitchen and struggled with the same ewer Pace had used earlier that day. She was only just barely strong enough to pour it without splashing too much on the sideboard.

What I needed to know was how to get out if I had to. I gingerly tested sitting up and found I could move a little if I went gently. Not a good sign. The pain of my gut wound radiated up my stomach and into my chest, making my arms and legs feel weak. And the dizziness—that had to have been the blood loss. I'd never lost that much in one go before.

The boisterous little girl approached the bed with her copper teacup, and I fought the urge to recoil. I took the teacup carefully, trying not to wince with the movement.

"Thanks. Where's your dad?"

"He's outside. He has a visitor."

"Oh, okay."

"He should be done soon. They've been talking a long time."

"Okay, sure."

"My name is Zoya. I'm nine. What about you?"

"Fletcher. I'm a hundred and forty years old. Give or take." I snapped my mouth shut the moment the words were out of my mouth. Why the hell did I say that?

But Zoya only laughed. "That's funny! You're funny. Why's your hair that color? I've never seen hair that color before. Looks like carrots right after you dig them up. Do you want more tea? Don't worry. It's just water. But Daddy can help me make real tea in a minute if you want that too. He usually makes tea for his visitors, but they won't come inside today. So I can ask him to make tea for you if he's not too tired."

I relaxed a fraction when Zoya paid no attention to the absurd age I'd just admitted to and downed the water she had given me in one go. "More water would be good. Thank you, Zoya."

She reclaimed the cup and bounded back toward the sideboard. Zoya kept prattling away while she struggled with the ewer. "You were sleeping a long time, Fletcher. Can I call you Fletch? Do you make arrows? Is that why you were named that? My daddy says sometimes names come from jobs, but now they're just names. So maybe you don't make arrows."

I relaxed against the pillow and watched Zoya with astonished wonder while she rambled on, no fear. "I've made a few arrows in my time."

"But that's not why you're named that. Did your mama give you that name? My mama gave me *my* name. And because of that, someday, when I have a daughter, I'm gonna name her Edith. Because that was my mama's name too."

Was. Past tense. So I had every reason to expect that Pace and Zoya lived alone. There were only two beds, and there had been no sign of any third person.

Zoya continued her rambling chatter. She didn't require much input from me, so it was easy enough to just lie there and listen, with the occasional one-word answer to keep her going.

After a few minutes, heavy footsteps sounded on what I assumed was a deck outside the front door, and Pace entered the house. A dark raven perched on his shoulder, its wings spread to keep its balance as the tall man moved.

"Zoya darling, didn't I say not to bother our guest?"

"He's awake, Daddy! Can you help me make him some tea?"

The raven glided off Pace's shoulder and perched on the ewer of water. I eyed it, wary.

"Some tea, huh?" Pace asked, ruffling his daughter's hair. "We can do tea. But first, why don't you run outside for a bit and let me check on Fletcher? Give him some privacy? Why don't you go collect eggs for us?"

Zoya readily agreed, but she made sure to press her stuffed bunny into my hands before disappearing outside with a little basket over her arm.

I turned the rabbit around and studied the faded stitching that made up its eyes and pink nose. "She's cute."

Pace laughed. "Yes, she is. She likes to help."

"I noticed." I gestured at the remains of the tea party still littered across my blanket.

"I want to check your wound. Make sure it's healing well. I stitched it as best I could after I brought you back, but it's going to leave a nasty scar. I want to make sure it's holding together."

Well, fuck. That's what happens when you pass out, Fletch. Someone goes and puts stitches in your gaping wounds.

If I had been awake, I could have stopped him. Now they'd have to be taken out, and that always hurt like a wretch.

I sat up gingerly and waved away his hands when he reached for the blanket. "No, don't. It's fine. I can feel it. It's holding well."

"I don't trust your feelings on this, Fletcher," Pace said, determined. "These things can turn nasty fast. We probably need to do an onion poultice at least. You're not out of the woods yet."

I closed my eyes, torn on what to do. On one hand, I could just get up and leave. I could duck out into the woods for a few days until the wound healed. But it would be a shitty, shitty few days. And with a wound this bad, I wasn't sure how many days it would take. Weeks, even.

But if I stayed? If Pace recognized what I was, maybe he wouldn't be so nice anymore. And hell, I wanted him to be as nice as he seemed.

"What I really need is a piss," I said, ignoring the twinge of anxiety in my gut.

"Right. Can you stand at all?"

It was a difficult business. Any movement pulled at the wound in my stomach, so Pace had to do all the heavy lifting. He bent over, breath warm on my neck, and had me wrap my arms around his shoulders. Pace hefted me to sit up. My sore legs dangled off the side of the bed.

"Where are my pants?" I asked with a cheeky grin. I clutched the blanket around my middle.

"There's that charmer," Pace said with a smile. "They're clean and folded up on that shelf back there. But how about a robe for now? Keep things simple."

He produced a long scarlet robe with sleeves that swept the floor dramatically. It had faded a bit from being dried in the sun after too many washings, but it was as soft and cool as rose petals against my tender skin. Pace helped me thread my arms through the sleeves and cinched it closed around my front.

Getting to my feet was another tricky business. Pace put my arms around his neck once more, braced his knees wide, and helped me to a standing position. I grimaced with the movement, but standing upright felt so good after laying for so long. I held onto Pace's neck a little longer, my forehead resting on his shoulder, and I reveled in the delicious stretch of the muscles in my thighs and lower back.

He braced his hands on my waist, careful of the wound in my gut. "Steady?"

"Yeah," I said into his shoulder.

Pace was warm. He smelled good too. Strong, wide shoulders kept me safe. Soft black hair tickled my ear. Firm hands gripped my waist, grounding me. I found myself letting out a bit of a sigh at the easy intimacy of it, then startled back when I realized what I was doing.

Get it together, Fletch, you horny old goblin. You don't know this man, and you're half dead, besides.

The corner of Pace's mouth curled up with amusement, which was a relief. At least he wasn't horrified at my behavior. Maybe we could just chalk it up to me being out of my mind with blood loss and pain.

"Outhouse is out this way," he said.

Fortunately, I could walk without hurting myself too much.

But I was weak, and my feet felt like clubs, so Pace kept a supportive grip on me as we exited the house.

The cabin sat in a forested glen, with a stony creek running down the center. The rain had finally stopped, and sunlight reached the mossy ground in dappled patches. The house itself was picturesque, with a steep thatched roof, bright blue shutters, and two comfortable rocking chairs on the front porch. Close to the tree line stood a tidy row of beehives. Several outbuildings dotted the yard, including a chicken coop, where Zoya was chatting to the hens. Her basket of eggs lay spilled and forgotten on the grass behind her.

The scene was absolutely idyllic—or it would have been, if it weren't for all the ravens.

The midnight black birds perched on every conceivable flat surface. A dozen preened along the fence that kept a trio of goats contained. Two more sat directly on a goat's back. It grazed, unconcerned, despite its feathered passengers.

They crowded on the roof of the house, foraged along the creek bed, and took treats from Zoya's hand as if they were just another chicken. They croaked at each other in the tree canopy and flew by in odd groups of three or four, disappearing as fast as they appeared. One landed directly on Pace's shoulder, and I jerked my hand away just in time to avoid the talons.

"Don't be afraid. They won't hurt you," Pace said.

"Not afraid." I stared around. "Concerned, maybe. Curious, I'll admit."

Pace grinned at the ground and continued leading me toward the outhouse on the back side of the property. The raven on his shoulder spread its wings to keep balance while Pace moved.

I gripped his shoulder a little tighter, careful not to nudge the raven. "So, you're not going to explain, then?"

"Nothing to explain," Pace said. "This is just where they live. It is Raven's End, after all."

"*This* is Raven's End? These woods? Raven's End?" I looked

about me, oddly expecting to see the Raven King moving between the trees in the distance.

"That's right. Well, technically, it borders our property to the north. Over there."

"I didn't know people lived here."

"People don't. Zoya and I do."

"You're people." My foot slipped on the loose gravel, and I sucked a hiss of pain through my teeth.

Pace neatly avoided the subject. "Here's the outhouse. Can you manage on your own?"

I wanted to keep pressing the issue, but my bladder was incredibly insistent. "Yeah, I can handle it. Don't go far."

"I'll be here," Pace said.

The outhouse was...Well, it was an outhouse. But it was clean and orderly, and I felt much better when I emerged a moment later.

Pace stood a few feet away with his back to me, watching Zoya with the chickens. The raven still balanced on his left shoulder, and the pair made a dramatic image in the dewy sunlight.

I couldn't stay here. It was too dangerous. I could feel the pull of the idyllic homestead, the dramatic clusters of ravens, the adorable little family living in the shadow of the Old Kind in Death's own forest. It was sweet, dramatic, domestic, and adventurous. A potent mix of everything I had ever wanted and never bothered to chase.

And of course, there was Pace, with his broad shoulders, steady smile, and soft hair. If I had run into him at any tavern, I'd have spent the entire night wooing him—and hopefully getting him to ruin me in a back alley.

No, not an alley. He was too put together for that. In an inn, with a bed and soft candlelight. Sweetness with the ruin, with a warm cloth to clean us up afterward and his nose pressed to the nape of my neck as we slept. That's what Pace would do.

Sweet hell, I really was a horny goblin.

No, it was all too dangerous. I couldn't stay here, even though Raven's End had been my goal the entire time. No adventure—no sighting of the Raven King—was worth getting trapped by my own desire for a cuddle. Because the Old Kind knew, if I ever let a man like Pace hold me, I'd never leave his arms. That would be it. No more adventures for me.

I cleared my throat to signal to Pace that I was done, and he turned, as if startled. The raven on his shoulder took flight and landed on the branch of a nearby oak tree. I opened my mouth to ask again about the ravens, but no.

Don't dig too deep. It would only make it harder to disentangle myself and leave once my wound had healed enough.

"Back to bed?" Pace asked. He tucked his supportive shoulder under my arm once again.

"Bed!" mimicked the nearest raven.

I tried not to let my wariness show on my face. "Yeah. Think so."

"And then we'll check your wound and get you something to eat. Are you hungry?"

"You don't need to check my wound."

Pace slowed to a stop only halfway back to the house. I turned to look at him, confused.

"Fletcher…" Pace had a Very Determined expression on his face. This wasn't the sort of man to be swayed on any topic.

It was endearing. It made me want to argue with him, just to see what he'd do.

"I can't begin to understand why you don't want me to examine your injury, and I won't pry about your reasons. But you have to understand…I have a small daughter to think about."

My eyes fell on Zoya at the mention of her. She continued with the chickens across the yard. She had one cradled in her arms and appeared to be scolding the rest of them for what must have been very poor chicken behavior.

"What—" I began, but Pace spoke over me.

"I am happy to care for you as long as you need it. And if you don't survive, then that's just how it is. But I cannot have you wasting away on purpose in front of my daughter in her own house. I won't allow it. So, if you're going to stay here, you will let me care for you and do my best to make you better."

Something tightened in my lower belly, and my eyes widened. Pace turned his Very Determined expression on me at full volume, and my mouth answered without permission from my brain.

"Okay."

"Don't worry about me, I've seen it all," Pace continued, still in that there-is-no-argument-here tone. "So, whatever is going on under that bandage, you won't scare me off."

I cleared my throat and forced my fingers to unclench where they gripped the fabric of his shirt at his shoulder. There was no way he'd seen what I had going on—that was for *damn* sure. But I needed help, at least for a few more days. And if I wanted that help from Pace, this appeared to be the price.

He was one of the good ones. Wasn't he?

"Fine. You can look at it."

Pace nodded, his dark hair falling into his eye. We continued walking toward the house.

"Good. We'll do it now."

THREE

As soon as I was back in bed, with the blankets pulled up over my tired, aching legs, Pace set about unwrapping the bandaging around my midsection.

I let him do it, my eyes focused on a cobweb in the upper corner of the far wall. It seemed out of place in the tidy little house.

"Does it hurt?" Pace asked while he worked.

"A bit."

Pace smiled, rueful. "You don't have to play it up for me, you know."

"I'm not playing it up." I caught his eye, my expression serious and my breath already coming too fast. I did not like this. I was too vulnerable.

His smile fell away at the look on my face, but he didn't reply.

My lips compressed into a thin line beneath my beard, and I returned to studying the cobweb. I lifted my arms when Pace directed me to and leaned forward so he could reach the bits on my back. Even though he was pressing quite close to me and smelled warm and welcoming, I wasn't thinking of candle-lit inns, soft sheets, or strong arms anymore.

I didn't tell people about me very often. It rarely came up, and when it did, it was easy enough to sidestep. "I'm just a fast healer," I would say. Or else I'd claim to have used Athorum on the wound, and that's why it healed so quickly. Athorum was rare and expensive, but not unheard of. And what else were people supposed to believe? That I was *actually* immortal?

The handful of times my immortality had been proven to people...Well, let me just say it hadn't gone well. Pace seemed like a good man, but good men had been soured by less. I'd seen it plenty of times.

I clenched my hands into fists at my sides when the last of the bandaging fell away. Pace leaned in to examine the wound, his eyebrows drawn in tight together. He gently poked at the skin around the wound and then sat back.

"Huh," he said, sounding both pleased and very, very confused.

I made no reply.

"It looks..." he began again but finished that thought with another, "Huh."

"Can the stitches come out yet?" I was aiming for a conversational tone, but the words came out too high and too fast. "I've never been injured this bad. It can be hard to tell how long it will take to close up."

"I don't understand," Pace said. "This wound looks weeks old, but it's only been two days."

I shrugged a little too hard. Get it together, Fletcher. You are not being subtle!

"I'm a fast healer," I said. And this time, my voice sounded almost normal.

Pace studied my face, his expression unreadable. He was piecing it together—I could see it. He knew I hadn't given myself Athorum because I'd been unconscious the entire time and my travel bag was on the other side of the room. If he'd gone through the bag, he'd know there was no Athorum anyway. And Pace hadn't given me any. My wound should be weeping, angry, red, and a single sneeze away from bleeding freely again.

But instead, it was cool to the touch and bright pink around the edges of the sore, raised scar. The stitches were still there, but they didn't seem to be holding anything together. They just sat in my skin. Hell, those were going to sting coming out.

Pace was extrapolating the timeline in his head. Give it another few days, and the scar would be gone. Not even Athorum could do that.

His gentle, discolored hands urged me to lean forward with a press on my arm, and he looked at the entry wound on my back. "How does it feel internally?" he asked.

I swallowed hard. "Listen, I don't have to stay here. Thank you for taking care of me, for saving my life. But I'm going to be okay now. I'll just get out of your hair." I began pulling the faded red robe back up, pushing the loose bandaging out of the way as I went. I scooted toward the edge of the bed with a grimace, but I did it anyway.

I would survive. I always did.

"Whoa, whoa. Take it easy." Pace extended his hands as if to herd me back to a relaxed sitting position.

"I'm okay. I'll be fine. I can move on. Just give me a minute to get my clothes on."

"And where do you expect to go?"

I paused, dread flooding my chest in a hot wave. His no-nonsense tone wasn't so endearing now. Not in this situation.

"You can't keep me here," I said, my voice shaking.

That was a lie. He could absolutely force me to stay. I wasn't dying anymore, but I wasn't myself yet. My whole body shook with the effort of keeping myself upright. If Pace decided to restrain me, I could not fight him off.

I blinked, and visions of the past blurred behind my eyelids. A dark room, too small with no windows. The foul bedding, the damp floor, the door that never opened except to let *him* in.

Pace shifted his weight from one foot to the other. "I don't—"

"I'm leaving. You can't stop me." Despite my best efforts, the fear was plain in my tone. I didn't even care anymore. All I could think was to get out. Get up. Don't even need the clothes or my bag. Just start walking. Get away. Maybe a knife? I could stop him if he tried to grab me.

There was a knife on the kitchen sideboard, but Pace was between me and the weapon.

"I'm not going to stop you!" Pace put his hands on my arms—to steady me probably—but my body remembered the fear instinctually, and I flinched away from him, hard.

Pace jerked his hands back. His wounded expression only made things worse.

This wasn't his fault. Somewhere in the far corner of my brain, I knew he wasn't going to hurt me. But my body shook anyway. My vision blurred. The panic...

Hell, the panic. I couldn't think straight through it, and that didn't help my chances. I needed to calm down.

But I couldn't calm down. I couldn't breathe. Couldn't think. Couldn't get my hands to unclench on the robe. Couldn't stop myself from scrambling toward the wall, as far away as I could get.

Pace wasn't going to hurt me. And as if to prove it, he picked up a stool, carried it several feet away, and sat down near Zoya's bed. He had deliberately left a clear path between me and the front door.

The shaking subsided immediately. I slumped against the wall, clutched the robe around my body, and closed my watering eyes. Mercifully, the old memories didn't make a second appearance. I breathed slowly in through the nose and out through the mouth.

Pace waited calmly on the other side of the room. He braced his elbows on his knees, his fingers loosely interlaced in the gap between them. They were such pretty hands, with long, slim fingers and a sharply angled thumb. He wore no rings, but the bright patches of white on his right hand and wrist stood out in the shadowed corner where he sat. More beautiful than any jewel.

I came back to myself slowly. And as my heart slowed, the pain increased. In my panic, I had pulled something inside that wasn't quite healed. That would set me back a day, at least. I grimaced and eased myself into a less rigid position.

Pace continued to wait. He didn't seem to be in any hurry.

At one point, Zoya bounded inside with her basket of eggs. She ran right up to Pace to tell him all about her adventures with the animals and then called a cheerful "Hi, Fletch!" to me on her way back out the door a minute later. Zoya hadn't seemed to notice my pale face, my pinched expression, or the sheen of sweat all over my body.

Pace settled his elbows back on his knees after Zoya left. He continued waiting.

"I'm sorry," I said, when I couldn't stand the silence any longer.

"No need to apologize."

"I had a, uh...a bad experience...the la—the last time." I swallowed hard, my hand still gripping the robe for dear life. "Sometimes it sneaks up on me."

"I'm sorry that happened to you. Do you want to talk about it?"

Fucking hell. "No."

"Okay," he said simply. "What can I do to make you more comfortable? What do you need?"

I closed my eyes, not wanting to see the rejection on his face. "Can you just—Can you just tell me what you're thinking? Please?"

"Thinking about what?"

I let out a huff of unamused laughter. "About me. About what I am."

"What are you?"

My eyes popped open in surprise. I couldn't *not* look at him.

Pace sat calm as ever on his stool, his fingers still laced together between his knees. His expression was neutral but open. He didn't look afraid or worried, or even all that curious.

"Immor—" The word broke off in my mouth. Holy hell, I didn't think I'd ever said it out loud to anyone outside of the family. "Immortal."

Pace raised his interlaced fingers to rest against his mouth. "Fascinating."

My heartbeat picked back up. Interest was never a good sign. It led to questions, which led to conclusions, which led to decisions made without my input. And I was not in any shape to push back and stand up for myself. Not by a long shot.

"Perfect healing, then?" Pace asked.

I gave a small nod.

"And you would have survived if we hadn't found you in time?"

"I don't know. Haven't tried very hard to find out what the limit is. Don't *want* to find out."

"Of course." He sat back on the stool, still studying me. "How did it happen? The immortality? Or have you always been this way?"

"I, uh..." How much should I tell him? I'd never really talked about it to anyone before. There hadn't been a need to. "It's a long story. No, we weren't always like this."

"We?"

"My siblings and me. And there was one other man there that day."

"So, you're not the only one?"

"Hm."

He allowed me to shut down the conversation and didn't pry further. Instead, he changed the subject. "Can I come closer?"

"Why?" I bit out immediately.

Pace's expression softened. "You're shaking and pale. You need to lie down. Can I help you?"

One breath, then another. "Okay."

He approached the bed slowly. I tracked him with my eyes.

"Can I touch you?" he asked.

I nodded.

Pace put his hands on my shoulder and helped guide my body around so I was straight on the bed again. Then he braced me while I lay back on the pillows. I grimaced against the pain in my gut as I moved, but his support helped.

His touch was firm, grounding, steady. And he let me go immediately when it was done. Pace cleared away the bandaging still littering the bed and drew the quilt over me. I sighed in relief when the warmth spread through me, and my body relaxed into the mattress.

Pace sat down on the foot of the bed, far enough away so I didn't feel crowded but close enough that I wasn't alone. He cleared his throat, appearing indecisive for a moment, then finally spoke.

"My family has lived in Raven's End for generations. We are caretakers for the forest, and someday, when I'm gone, Zoya will take over for me. There isn't much to do. Mostly we make sure people don't linger too long and disturb the spirits here. I'm sure you've heard the rumors about this place, about the Raven King."

He paused for a moment, and I nodded.

"He's real, you know?" Pace continued. "I've seen him myself several times. Spoken to him once. He is—He's indescribable. People come here to visit him and ask for their deaths. And if they want it bad enough, the Raven King grants their wish. And I thought maybe that's why you came. That's why you didn't want me to help you get better. But I don't think that's true anymore."

"No. I don't want to die. That's not why I came here."

"I'm glad to hear it." Pace gave me a soft smile. "I'm not going to ask you about your reasons for coming here or about what happened to you in the past. But if you want to talk about anything, I'm here. I've heard it all. You won't surprise me. And if you need space or anything else to feel safe and comfortable, please tell me. Can you do that?"

I watched him with wide eyes, and once again, my mouth answered for me. "Yes."

"Good." He stood and slipped his hands into his pockets. "And I won't make you stay here, not ever. But I think you *should* stay, at least for a few more days until you can get around on your own without pain."

I shifted in bed and studied his dark eyes. He really meant it, didn't he? In all my long life, it had been proven to me again and again that people were not to be trusted—especially not with your most vulnerable bits. But Pace had taken those vulnerable bits when I was too weak to protect them, and he'd been so gentle.

"Are you real?" I asked.

Pace laughed. "Only just barely."

He had a warm laugh. It loosened something in my chest that I'd been holding on to way too tightly.

"I'll stay. Just for a few more days. Then I'm gone."

Pace nodded, pleased. "Good. I'm glad to hear it. Now, how about something to eat?"

Four

Supper that night was cabbage, beans, and sausage. Pace only filled my plate halfway, suggesting we take it slow on my empty stomach. I glowered at him when he passed me the scant meal, annoyed and starving half to death, but by the time I'd eaten half my portion, my stomach began to cramp. So maybe he'd been a little bit right.

Pace and Zoya pulled their dining table right up to the bed so we could all sit together while we ate. Zoya regaled us with stories about witches and their familiars, about "potions" she had brewed near the creek, and a dozen other things. Any time she slowed a little, Pace offered a new scenario for her imaginary witches, and Zoya would perk up and trot down yet another tangent with delight.

It was peaceful, domestic, and full of laughter, and minute by minute, the tension in my body eased away.

Four ravens had decided to roost in the rafters for the night, and Pace had to gently relocate them outside one by one after supper.

"They'll just be up there, shitting all night long, if I leave them there. We learned that lesson years ago, didn't we, Bug?"

"Yeah!" Zoya said with an exaggerated grimace of disgust. "They'll just poo and poo and poo all night long. They're worse than the chickens!" She stuck out her tongue and pretended to gag.

Pace encouraged the last raven to perch on his hand. The great bird stepped easily from the rafter, as if they'd done this every night for years.

"Poo!" it croaked.

"I dunno..." I said. "I don't think there's anything worse on this earth than chicken shit. That's a smell that sticks with you."

Pace grinned and walked toward the door with the raven. It was the first thing I'd said all night since my panic, and it looked like he'd been patiently waiting for me to join the conversation. To prove that I was still with them.

Well...I was. I was still here, and honestly, maybe that wasn't such a bad thing.

Pace tucked in with Zoya in her bed that night. He'd probably been sleeping there with her since I arrived, seeing as how I had taken over his bed. I lay there in the dark for a long time, trying to ignore the discomfort in my gut and the general achiness of blood loss and of lying down for too long.

Zoya talked in her sleep. Mumbling impossible-to-interpret nonsense. But it was soothing, hearing her little voice. She was so safe here. Zoya had clearly been encouraged to talk and create and imagine all her life, and I was struck with the fierce desire to make sure she experienced that kind of safety forever.

The rush and wave of her mumblings eventually soothed me to sleep. I dreamed of happy little witches darting about the woods with ravens on their shoulders. I dreamed of dappled sunshine and warm hands on my shoulders. I dreamed of peace.

Over the next few days, we fell into an easy routine. Pace and Zoya woke early to feed the animals and make breakfast. They left the dining table next to my bed, and we ate every meal there together.

After early chores, Pace spent the morning teaching Zoya reading, math, and history. The afternoons were spent outside with the animals. Pace would repair a fence or a feed hopper, while Zoya flitted about, scolding the goats and hand-feeding the chickens. I sat outside with them, bundled up in a comfortable chair on the porch, where the sunshine slanted over me.

In the evenings, we went inside. We traded stories from their small stash of novels, or I told them of my adventures. Sometimes, we made up our own tales from nothing. Those were the silliest and had us all doubled over laughing by the end.

It only took a couple of days for me to be able to get up on my own, and only a few more to start helping Pace with his work about the homestead. Pace took my stitches out only five days after he put them in. I clenched my fists and yelled at him all through it.

"Don't be such a baby." Pace pulled out yet another stitch, with his lower lip between his teeth.

"Why don't we try sewing through *your* gut, huh? Maybe then you'll see how it feels!" But I gritted my teeth and let him get on with it. And soon enough, it was done. The pinprick wounds were healed up and barely visible by dinner.

I was well. I could pack up my bags and move on. But there always seemed to be something to do. The beehives needed inspected or a frame repaired. A doe required processing so the meat could get drying in the sun. Zoya just *had* to show me her favorite swimming hole about half a mile downstream.

I thought, "I'll just go tomorrow," every day for two weeks, and somehow, "tomorrow" never came.

Pace said nothing about it for a long time. But one morning over breakfast, about three weeks after I had arrived, he did have a suggestion.

"Why don't we build you your own bed today, Fletcher?

There's room on that far wall under the window if we move the dresser a bit. And we have a guest mattress in the loft. It's due for a good airing and maybe some fresh straw, but it's still perfectly good. What do you think?"

I chewed my oatmeal slowly, considering. My own bed? A place that was...mine?

I had a bed, of course. Back home in Mitsmooren Keep, in the room next door to my sister, Isla. I slept in it maybe one month out of twelve, but it was mine, and I could always go back there for any reason, at any time.

But now Pace was offering to give me a second bed, here in his house.

I shouldn't. I needed to pack up and move on. After all, I was strong and well and could travel as much as I liked. The same as always.

"Okay," I said. "Yeah, let's build me a bed."

"Good." Pace smiled. "I'll bet you'll be glad to have your bed back to yourself, won't you, Bug?"

Zoya announced herself to be very excited. She needed that space for her various stuffed animals.

And so, we built me a bed. It took a couple of days, and the little house was a bit more cramped than we expected once the furniture was all rearranged. We had to push my new bed end to end with Pace's, or else none of it would fit.

My bed was quite a bit lower to the ground, but it was sturdy and comfortable. Pace pulled out another quilt from storage, this one constructed with a dozen scavenged fabrics of many different patterns. The light and dark pieces contrasted to make a pinwheel in the middle.

"Did you make all these?" I asked, holding up the quilt to study the pattern.

"Edie did," Pace said. "My wife. Before she passed. She loved to do all the patterns. These light pieces here were from Zoya's baby clothes."

Zoya was outside, off on some adventure or another, or else I wouldn't have pushed the topic. "What happened to her? If you don't mind me asking."

"She got sick. That's all." Pace turned away to straighten the quilt on his own bed—the one I'd been using for the last month. "It happened very quickly. Zoya doesn't remember her."

I chewed my lip. "I'm so sorry."

He pasted on a gentle smile. "It's been a long time. We're okay."

"I'm still sorry."

Pace helped me spread the quilt out over my new bed. "I'm glad we have these quilts, though. It's like we still have a piece of her. And I tell Zoya stories about her. Edie was a good woman. A firecracker. A talker too. That's where Zoya gets it from."

I laughed, and the smile on Pace's face became a little more real.

That night, the three of us lay in our own beds for the first time. I clutched the pinwheel quilt to my chest and stared up at the dark ceiling, listening to Zoya mumble in her sleep.

Pace wasn't asleep. I could tell. He was too quiet. With our beds situated end to end, our heads were only a couple of feet apart, with him a little above me. That close, I could basically hear him thinking. But about what, I couldn't possibly imagine.

I'd be lying if I said I had stopped being a horny little goblin about this sweet, beautiful man. But at the same time, that didn't matter so much anymore. What mattered was his smile, Zoya's endless imagination, and this bed we had made together, just for me.

A week later, while walking alone in the woods to the north, the noise of people came from the road leading up to the house. Two sets of footsteps, plus the grating of cart wheels on the gravel.

At first, I didn't realize what I was hearing. I was so lost in my own thoughts that I didn't notice the general birdsong and rushing wind were being slowly overtaken.

Suddenly alert, I jogged toward the road and broke out of the woods ahead of the strangers. We were very close to the house. So close the roof of the goat barn was clearly visible through the trees.

Two people appeared along the road, walking steadily up the hill. The first person was average height, with a slim build and dark hair cut close at the sides but curling jauntily in a mop on top of her head. She wore bright, loose clothing and thick boots. The woman hummed to herself while she went, eyes on her feet. She pulled a cart behind her loaded down with parcels, burlap bags, quarter casks, and small crates.

The second person trailed behind, shoulders hunched. A middle-aged, fair-haired woman with her shawl pulled tightly around her shoulders despite the mild weather. Her clothes were high quality and had some intricate stitching along the bodice, but it all looked to be at least two sizes too big.

These were the first new people I had seen at Raven's End in all the weeks I'd spent there, and I didn't like not knowing what was going on. Not when it came to Pace and Zoya's safety. Strangers were dangerous.

"Stop there, ladies." My voice cut over the noise of the cart-wheels. "Who are you?"

They both stopped. The cart puller's foot dragged through the gravel on the surface of the narrow road. The rattling of the cart stopped, and the ambient tones of the forest and birdsong resumed.

"Hey," the cart puller said, looking alarmed. "I'm Quinn. Not a lady. I'm a friend of Pace."

The woman behind them stared at me with wide eyes and echoed, "They're a friend of Pace."

"Take it easy, buddy." Quinn spread their hands to show they were empty.

I deliberately unclenched my fists and adopted a slightly less menacing stance, though I didn't clear the road.

"And who's that?"

"That's Mistress Harper. She's come to visit with Pace. That's all."

"I just want to speak with him for a moment," said Mistress Harper, placating.

"What do you have there?" I asked.

"In the cart? Supplies. I'm doing the usual supply run. Where's Pace?"

"Quinn!" Zoya's familiar voice cut through the roaring alarm in my head. The little girl came sprinting down the road from the direction of the house.

I had half a mind to throw an arm out to block her path and keep her as far away from the strangers as possible, but she darted right past me and launched herself at Quinn.

The stranger caught Zoya mid leap, and they shared a big hug. I wanted to snatch Zoya back but stopped myself at the last minute. I barely knew Pace and Zoya. I'd only been there a month. If Zoya recognized Quinn, then that probably meant they were a friend.

"I was waiting and waiting for you! We have some new baby chicks, and Miss Pickles has started brooding *too*. You have to come see. Did Remy not come with you?"

"No, Bug," Quinn said. Their use of Zoya's nickname was reassuring. "Remy stayed home. Hey, who's your friend over there?"

Zoya squirmed out of Quinn's arms and ran up to me. She grabbed my hand between both of hers. I squeezed her fingers tightly, possessive.

"This is Fletcher. He got hurt and is staying with us."

"Oh, hey! I thought you looked familiar. I met you in the bar down at Wainstown more than a month ago. You did say you were coming up to Raven's End, didn't you?"

I thought hard, tried to place Quinn's face, and yes...a bar did sound right. The night before I set out for Raven's End, I had spent the evening at a local pub at the nearest village and had met lots of people. We'd swapped some stories about the Raven King and had a few pints. The next morning, I had left for Raven's End and nearly died in the mud.

And yeah, now that I thought about it, Quinn had made an appearance that night. They had even mentioned having friends up this way and told me the best path to take.

"Right," I said, relaxing a little more. "Yes, I remember you."

"So you made it!" A broad smile took over Quinn's face. "Good. I'm glad to hear it. Not hurt too bad, eh?"

"No," I said, wary. "Not too bad."

"He had a whole tree through him!" Zoya said with eyes wide as saucers at this juicy gossip. "But he's doing okay now."

My face flushed hot. "It wasn't that bad, Zoya."

Yes, it had been that bad. And if Zoya had any more attention to spare for literally anything, she probably would have argued the point. But instead, she was already grilling Quinn about someone named Remy, who was apparently her very best friend in the world, though she had never mentioned him to me before. That last bit stung, but I tried not to analyze that strange reaction too closely.

"I can't believe Remy didn't come with you!" Zoya said, scolding. "He said he would!"

"Well, what if you come home with me tonight?" Quinn offered. "You two can play as much as you like. Why don't you run up and ask your daddy, huh?"

Zoya brought two clenched fists up to her little face in a show of pure, unbridled excitement. "Yes! Yes! Daddy!" She called for Pace even before she belted off in the direction of the house.

Once Zoya's bright energy was gone, I was left with Quinn and Mistress Harper on the road. The awkward silence stretched between us, with Mistress Harper shifting from one foot to the other. She had a pinched look to her face, as though she were just barely done with a nasty illness.

"Right," Quinn said after a moment. "So, we're just going to..."

They gestured in the direction of the house and resumed pulling the laden cart up the road. Mistress Harper trailed after them, and they both passed me with a watchful eye.

Right, indeed. I cut through the yard and beat them to the house. Inside, I found Zoya already packing a bag while still explaining the proposed plan to Pace.

"And I can stay with Quinn and Remy, and I can help them at the store during the day, and me and Remy can practice riding in the back pasture some. I'll be lots of help and won't get in the way, and Fletcher can come get me any time if you need me to come home! So can I go, Daddy? Can I go?"

"Yes! Yes, of course you can go," Pace said with a chuckle. "But I'm not volunteering Fletcher to go anywhere, Bug. That's rude."

"He doesn't mind! You don't mind, do you, Fletch?"

"Nah," I said, even though I honestly didn't want to go anywhere at all. But I could never tell Zoya no. I'd walk to the end of the earth for her if she asked me to. It wasn't like I hadn't done it before anyway, just for the fun of it.

"Hello!" called a voice at the door, and my entire body tensed.

"Quinn!" Pace called and embraced the stranger with a friendly pat on the back.

My body stiffened even further. Every single muscle clenched at the sight of Pace casually hugging this random person who I'd never even heard of before.

"Good to see you! I was wondering when you'd make it up. We expected you days ago. Fletch, this is Quinn."

"We've met." I did my best to relax, but Pace noticed.

He softened his expression. "They bring us supply runs about once a month. And they sell our furs and honey at their general store in Wainstown. Their son, Remy, is Zoya's best friend, as I'm sure you've heard. He usually comes with them. Remy stayed home today?"

He directed this last question to Quinn, probably on purpose, to shift focus away from me.

They talked for a moment about small matters, and I barely heard any of it. Mistress Harper hovered just outside on the grass below the front deck. She shifted her weight back and forth and wrung her shawl between her hands. Mistress Harper watched Pace and Quinn talk and seemed like she wanted to interrupt but didn't know how. She glanced between the house and the road they had arrived on, like she was considering running back down to Wainstown without ever talking to Pace at all.

"I'll go speak to her. Just give me a moment. Why don't you stay here and get to know Fletcher a bit?"

My name in Pace's mouth caught my attention. He patted Quinn on the arm and then descended the porch steps. Pace held out a hand to Mistress Harper but didn't actually touch her. He led her away from the house and closer to the stream, where they could talk without being overheard.

"Hey," Quinn said, and I nearly jumped out of my skin.

I was so focused on watching Pace and Mistress Harper, wondering what they could be talking about, that I had forgotten Quinn was even there.

"Oh, hey," I said.

"I'm surprised you're still here." Quinn gave me an open grin. They seemed like the kind of person who was always ready to smile. Joyful. "Back at the pub last month, it seemed like you were the kind of guy to never settle down anywhere for long."

"I haven't settled down." What a fucking lie. I purposefully did *not* glance over at my bed with the pinwheel quilt.

Quinn nodded, their smile still perfectly easy. "Gotcha. You, uh...Where do you plan to go next? Any big adventures planned?"

I ignored this question entirely. "How do you know Pace?"

"Oh!" They seemed delighted to have something to talk about. "Edie and I grew up together. Best friends. Pace's wife, you know."

"Yeah."

"Zoya's just like her," Quinn said with a fond smile.

Zoya was at the goat pen, probably reassuring the animals that she was going on a trip but would be back very soon, so don't worry.

"I love having her stay with us. Remy does too, of course. But I love having her around. Reminds me of when Edie and I were little."

"She's a good kid."

Quinn's grin broadened. "Yeah. A little firecracker, just like her mom. But she's got Pace's sweetness too."

Outside, Pace squeezed Mistress Harper's shoulder in a show of comfort. Her expression was one of great resignation and relief.

"She lost her husband last year," Quinn said, their voice solemn. "They'd been together fifty years. She's had a very hard time ever since."

I said nothing, only watching while Mistress Harper turned away and began walking back down the way they had come. One of the ravens seemed to catch an interest in her and hopped from branch to branch, following her along the path.

"She's not gonna wait for you?"

"Nah, probably not." Quinn scratched the back of their head. "I'm sure she's ready to get home. I usually stick around for lunch after a supply run. I brought cinnamon buns!"

Pace climbed up the porch steps, hands in his pockets. He sniffed hard, his eyes looking a little tight, but he shrugged his shoulders and pasted on a smile. "All right! Shall we unload the cart?"

Quinn had brought wheat, oats, beans, and salt. The quarter casks were all empty, apparently to refill with honey the next time Pace harvested from the hives. There was also a small box packed tightly with straw to protect ten perfect blue chicken eggs. Zoya exclaimed over these and ran off to put them under Miss Pickles, the chicken who had just started sitting that week.

"You need more chickens?" I asked Pace fondly in an undertone.

"No, but these chickens will lay blue eggs, Fletch," he said with a grin. "Blue eggs!"

We refilled the emptied cart with two crates full of beeswax and one quarter cask of honey. Pace also loaded two heavy sacks filled with tanned leather to take back to town.

Lunch was oatcakes with bacon cooked right in, and Quinn's cinnamon buns were delightful afterward. Their happiness was contagious. And by the time they were bundling Zoya up in the cart, even I liked them. A little bit.

Pace passed a few letters to Quinn to post for him in town, and I was struck with the idea that Isla hadn't heard from me in a month or more. After a quick request for them to wait a moment longer, I dashed inside to write to my sister.

Isla.

I've settled at Raven's End. Met someone here and I guess I'm going to stay. May not be back for a bit. I'm good. I'll write more later. In a rush now. Love you.

- Fletch

It was hasty and sorely lacking in details, but Zoya was already bouncing on her heels next to the cart, and I didn't want to hold them up any longer. I would pen something better later and give Isla a proper filling-in then. This would do for now, just so she wouldn't worry

Quinn added my letter to the small bundle they had taken from Pace, and soon they were rattling down the road, with Zoya's chatter for company.

"Is it weird that I don't like to see her go?" I asked Pace, who stood next to me on the porch.

"No. I hate it. But it makes her so happy. And Quinn is basically an extra parent. They'll take great care of her. They always do."

"I suppose you can't keep her cooped up here forever, can you?"

"No."

"Why *do* you stay up here?" I asked, intensely curious now that the thought occurred to me. "It's a lovely place, but it's so far removed."

"Somebody's got to care for the forest." He trained his eyes on Zoya as she disappeared down the narrow road. His entire demeanor shifted when he turned to face me. "But I'm glad you're here to keep me company. I've got an old bottle of rum down in the cellar. What do you say we make a time of it, eh? Head up to the swimming hole and cool off?"

I grinned, finding myself unable to look him in the eye. My shoes were more interesting anyway.

"Yeah, all right. Let's have a day."

FIVE

So far as adventures went, it wasn't anything special. Pace fished out the mostly full bottle of liquor while I packed some food. I grabbed my travel pack and dumped the last odds and ends from the bottom, then filled it back up again with towels, food, water skins, and the book Pace had been reading lately. We hiked about a mile up the stream, with ravens flitting from tree to tree overhead, to where a low waterfall had carved a deep swimming hole between the mossy boulders of the river.

For the first time, I began to wonder if the ravens lived in the forest of Raven's End or if they simply hovered wherever Pace happened to be. There was something strange about the way they followed him and perched on his shoulder. How he could hold out one hand and two ravens would fly down to him.

But every time I brought it up, he just changed the subject.

We stripped down and dove into the cool water. I did my best not to blush when Pace revealed miles of pale skin. The white patches were mostly on his right arm and shoulder, and the water droplets on them shone like jewels.

We swam for hours, laughing, joking, and telling bawdier stories than we usually did when Zoya was around. We took turns climbing up the waterfall and leaping off a ledge into the pool below.

After a while, I lay on the shore, exhausted in the best way, and watched while Pace floated on his back in the water. His face was a picture of serenity, with a shadow of dark stubble on his jaw.

"You're staring," he said, his eyes closed.

How did he always know?

"Can't help it," I said.

He grinned, his teeth flashing white. "Charmer."

We stayed at the river for a long time, drying in the patchy sunlight and having a simple dinner. The rum burned down our throats, and our laughter only grew louder as the sun went down. Later, we walked back to the house in the twilight and had to rush around to the barns to close up the animals for the night.

And even though we were both exhausted, I didn't want the day to be over.

We lay end to end on our beds, with the head of Pace's bed quite a bit higher than my own. We lay in the dark, both of us pretending to sleep. I tilted my chin and looked at the edge of Pace's mattress. A lock of his dark hair curled up in a graceful arc —the only bit of him that I could see.

"Are you asleep?" I asked.

"No."

"It's too quiet in here without Zoya talking a mile a minute."

Pace snorted a laugh. "I know. I've gotten so used to it. Used to drive me crazy, but I can't sleep without it anymore."

"Yeah." I pulled the pinwheel quilt a little higher and tucked my chin down. "Tell me a secret."

"Like what?"

"How should I know? Something you never told anybody."

Pace was quiet for a long twenty seconds. "When I was a kid, I stole a string of beads from a store. They were these cheap, wooden things. But they were painted blue, and I loved them."

"You little thief," I said with a grin.

"The shop owner noticed them missing and started yelling at his shop clerk for taking them. Apparently he'd taken lots of stuff in the past, and this was the latest insult. I shoved the beads in my pocket and hurried out of the shop after my mother."

"Holy hell, Pace." I smothered my smile. "You were a little shit, weren't you?"

"I was ten years old!" Pace said with a despairing wail. "I never did it again. I felt so bad."

"Do you still have them?"

"No. I burned them in the stove after dinner that night when everyone was asleep. Couldn't bear to look at them. I've felt bad about it ever since."

I muffled my laughter into my pillow. "You're so soft. It's adorable."

"Did a lot of stealing when you were a kid, then?"

"Had to. When you got nothing, it was either steal or starve."

Pace's tone sobered. "Right. Of course."

"Only did it when we had to, though. And my brother Arlo always took the licks for it when we got caught. And usually while he was taking the blame for things, me and Darius would be stealing more stuff and running out the back. And then later we'd all share it between us."

"It's a good scam."

"We did what we had to do."

"And what did Isla think of all this?"

I cleared my throat. "She wasn't with us then. We grew up at a workhouse. She was sent to the girls' home."

"They still have girls' homes?"

It was an understandable question. Growing up in the workhouse had been tough, with not enough food and too much labor. But the girls' homes were worse. They still did labor. And often less difficult labor than the rest of us. Laundry and cooking, stuff like that. But the stories of abuse were horrendous, and more often than not, the girls didn't survive long after they aged out.

"They had them a hundred and forty years ago."

"Oh, right. Sorry."

"Not a problem," I said under my breath.

"I keep forgetting how old you are."

I smiled into the blanket. "I know."

"Was it bad? Where Isla was?"

"Nah. We got her out when she was seventeen, but she was doing okay. The place was well handled. It wasn't nice, but the matrons? They kept the assholes out. It's the only reason the place was still standing when we left it. It closed down about thirty years later. It was one of the last ones to go. It got converted to an actual orphanage after that, I heard."

"Good."

"It was Arlo that did that, you know?"

"Did what?"

"He advocated against child workhouses and girls' homes to the Council of Amau for ten years. He's the reason the investigations finally happened. He and Isla co-wrote a bunch of new laws about social welfare, and now we have orphanages instead of child workhouses here in Amau."

"No shit."

"Yeah."

Pace shifted around on his bed. "So, your family is like... You're..."

I gritted my teeth. Fuck, didn't see this one coming. Clearly I had lost all ability to control a narrative since coming to Raven's End.

"Holy hell, Fletch. Talk about having secrets."

"It's no secret."

Pace's head appeared over the edge of the bed, and we locked eyes. "Your brother is the Dragon of Amau, Fletcher."

I shrugged. "Yeah. I guess."

"Why didn't you tell me? You've lived here nearly a month!"

"I thought you knew. I never hid his name."

"Lots of people are named Arlo," Pace said. "You never said he was *the* Arlo. Holy shit. I thought "Dragon" was a title that got passed down. But it's just been one immortal man this whole time. What the fuck?"

"I don't usually tell people."

Pace raised one eyebrow and disappeared back over the edge of his bed. There was a rustling noise while he settled down onto the pillow. "I suppose not."

I chewed on my lip for a long, quiet moment. "But I want to tell you things."

The tiniest gasp came from the bed above me, so soft I might have imagined it.

"I don't know what it is," I continued in barely more than a whisper. "From the first day, I've wanted to tell you things. It just keeps happening. I told Zoya my true age in the first twenty seconds of talking with her."

Pace laughed. "She's very disarming."

"It scared the shit out of me. I couldn't believe I just said it like that, you know? I never tell people about me. It's not..."

"It's not safe," Pace finished for me.

"Yeah."

"You're safe here, Fletch."

"I know."

"But it...it wasn't? Safe, I mean. The other times you got hurt?"

My chest clenched tight. "No. It wasn't safe."

"You don't have to tell me about it if you don't want to."

"I do." I clenched my eyes shut. "I do want to. I mean, there's not much to tell, really. I'm sure you already guessed the gist of it."

"I have my assumptions."

"Yeah, so. A couple decades back, I butted into a fight when I should have just left it alone. But someone was getting hurt, and I wanted to help them. Ended up with a sword through my gut for my troubles. The, uh, the woman...The one they were trying to hurt. She got away. The asshole who stabbed me got away too. And the woman's father, he brought me home to try and help me, like you did. But it scared him when I began to heal. He thought I was cursed, and he locked me in his root cellar when I was too weak to fight him off."

I swallowed hard with a throat gone strangely dry. But I had meant it when I said I wanted to tell Pace everything, to give him the darkest parts of me, to have them held in gentle, trustworthy hands.

"He got...curious. Wanted to experiment, see how far he could push me and still live. I won't, uh...I won't go into all the gory details. But he had me down there, half-dead, for a long time. I don't remember how long. The days blurred together, and there weren't any windows anyway."

"How'd you get out?"

"Got lucky. He left me alone one day too long. Got strong enough to fight him off the next time he came in. But the kicker is, she was there the whole time. The woman I'd saved. She was there in the house, heard me screa—She heard me. She knew I was there and what her father was doing to me." My voice began to shake. "She never did anything to help. I was so angry with her, angry with myself for trying to save her in the first place. If I weren't so desperate to get away, I might have given her the same thing her father got in the root cellar. But I just ran."

Pace was already moving before I finished speaking. His bed frame creaked as he hauled himself up, and he appeared at the side of my bed. Pace knelt and pulled back the pinwheel quilt before I had a chance to object. Not that I would have objected, but was now really the time, Pace?

But he just crawled in next to me under the blanket and wrapped his long arms around my middle, squeezing me tight.

"I'm so sorry that happened to you," he said into my shoulder.

My eyes began to water at the casual intimacy of it. Or maybe the tears were already welling up, and now it was finally safe to let them go. I gripped the arm draped across my middle, tracing the white patches by memory where they arched over his elbow.

Neither of us had a shirt on, and any other time, the horny beast in my gut would have reared its head. But now, all I could think of was how warm Pace was, skin against skin. How safe. How right.

"I killed Edie," Pace said into my shoulder.

My heart stopped, and my hand froze on his arm. I had to have imagined it, right? He didn't say that. He would never.

"She was so sick," he went on in a soft voice. "She begged me to do it. She was in so much pain, couldn't even get up anymore. She just wanted it to be over. Zoya was staying with Quinn at the time. Edie didn't want Zoya to see her like that, so she'd been away for nearly a month at that point. And then she begged me, said it would be so much easier. And she was dying anyway and I—"

His voice trailed off, with tears of his own running onto my skin. I gripped him tighter and pressed my mouth to the top of his head.

"Shh," I said against his hair.

"I miss her so much sometimes it hurts. And I hate her for making me do that, but I would do it again. But I loved her. She was in so much pain, Fletch. I just couldn't—"

"Shh. I know."

"Nobody knows. I buried her that night, and Zoya came home two weeks later. I told them all she died in her sleep, but I think Quinn guessed. They knew Edie so well. They knew she wouldn't want it to drag on forever. They never said anything, though. It was just a look in their eyes."

I threaded my fingers through his hair and held him close. Tried to be an anchor for him. How long had he carried this weight alone? Years and years. Pace's breath slowly evened out with deliberate huffs of air across my chest.

"Some pair we are," he said after a minute. "I feel so broken."

"I've lived a hundred and forty-one years on this earth, Pace.

I've seen it all, good and bad. I know broken. This is not what broken looks like."

He let out another shaky breath of air and snuggled a little more into my shoulder.

My bed was not big enough for this. It wasn't made for two fully grown men, even crammed together as we were. The mattress sagged in the middle, and the wooden beams pressed against my side just a little too hard to be comfortable.

But I wouldn't have moved for anything.

I held Pace close to my side and ran my fingers through his hair in the way I'd been dreaming of for weeks. And after a while, his breathing slowed down to a soft snore, finally at peace.

Six

Something had changed between Pace and me.

It had been coming for a long time, but I'd been trying not to look directly at it. If I looked too closely, it might disappear.

Before, it had been easy chatter, small smiles, *charmer*.

Now, after waking up tangled together on my narrow bed, there were lingering looks, my fingers deliberately touching his as I passed him a cup, or a hand on the small of my back when he passed.

The air was charged with it. Static filled the space between us like the thick, undulating thunder of an approaching storm. I was the dark roiling clouds, and Pace was the steady anchor of the earth. Soon the lightning would be close enough to light up the sky, and the thunder would vibrate through us both. Any moment now...Any second. *Flash. Boom.*

Pace was at the goat barn, fussing with a gate that didn't want to close properly. I stepped onto the front porch of the house with a mug of cooling tea in my hand and paused to watch. He had taken off his shirt in the afternoon heat. The white patches blossoming on his arm and shoulder seemed to shimmer in the sunshine. He was so beautiful—all rippling muscles, sweat, and square shoulders. A hint of dark stubble brushed his jaw, abrupt against his fair skin.

His hair fell into his face when he bent over the gate. I had spent the entirety of last night with my hand in those soft strands. My fingers ached with the memory of it. I wanted to hold him again. I wanted...

He stood up straight and glanced over at me, like my gaze was a brand on his skin. The corner of his mouth lifted in a smile, and it broke the ache in my chest into sharp little points of need.

Pace dropped his pliers into the toolbox at his feet, plucked his shirt off the fence rail, and approached the house. He pulled the shirt on as he went, covering up all that skin. It was for the best, probably. I couldn't think straight, looking at him.

"It's going to need a new pin," Pace said, ambling up the porch steps.

"Hm."

Pace stood next to me at the rail, smelling of sweat and heaven. He laid both hands on the rail and leaned forward next to me. "I've got a whole bucket of odds and ends in the shed. I'm sure I can find something that will work. Rig something up with an old iron peg."

I nodded, still staring out at the goat pen, where Pace had been a moment before. The first sparks of lightning arced between us, feelers searching for the nearest point of contact. Could he sense it?

Wait...He could feel it, right?

This tension wasn't all in my head. Couldn't be. It was too real, too thick. My chest burned with it. Only the warm press of his hand could put it out, bank it back to embers. The ghost of it still lingered across my chest, where that hand had lain while we slept the night before.

I dared to glance over at his profile.

Fuck. He was already looking at me. Dark irises like pools of ink in his pale face. Once, I had thought these were the eyes of Death. Endless, gentle, unturning. But they were the opposite—full of life. Life like I had never known before in all my decades. And I found myself getting lost in them.

"Fletch," he said softly.

My knuckles had gone white from clenching the porch rail so hard. Pace covered my hand with his and rubbed his thumbs over the bones of my hand, as if to soothe the tension in them.

I turned my palm over to intertwine our fingers instead. Pace smiled and eased into my grip, like our hands had been made to fit together.

Flash.

My body pulled toward him like a magnet. "Pace, I—"

He smiled softly. "I know. Me too."

I closed the distance between us without meaning to. His mouth was warm and soft against mine, and sweetness blossomed through my whole body at the first touch.

Boom.

Pace gasped against my mouth and squeezed my hand a little tighter. He pulled me in by his grip on my hand, and then he was everywhere. His arm around my neck, his fingers in my hair, his chest pressed against mine in a searing heat.

This was it. This was the point of everything. This was why I'd been given the gift of immortality. Without it, I would never have lived long enough to reach this forest, this porch, this kiss.

In the corner of my mind, I heard my forgotten tea mug clatter to the floorboards. My hands had more important things to hold. I gathered his solid bulk against me and deepened the kiss with a whimper.

Pace smiled against my mouth, gasping for breath. "I've never kissed anyone with a beard before."

I grinned and rubbed my facial hair against the sensitive skin under his ear, just to hear him laugh about it and feel him squirm against me. Another breath-stealing kiss stole the laughter from his lips.

It was everything I had imagined and more. Gentle caresses of his calloused fingers and his firm body under my hands. Sighs, smiles, teeth, and tongues. It was more than that too. There was a comfort, a rightness to it, more than just pleasure or excitement. Touching him felt like coming home.

It was achingly sweet, that first time between us. We took our time exploring each other, mapping out freckles, scars, and kiss-wet skin, like two men who had all the time in the world.

It wasn't always so sweet, though.

In the weeks after that first lightning strike, we came together fast and slow, hard and gentle. Sometimes, it was more teeth than anything, with biting kisses that made me gasp. Sometimes, it was as sticky smooth as the honey from his hives.

But every time, it ended the same: one of us plastered across the chest of the other, gasping for breath and whispering affection into the other's skin.

I never wanted to leave. I'd spend the rest of my decades there until Pace grew old and withered. I would have him until his last day, when he left this world for the one beyond. And then I would find a way to follow him there too.

Two weeks after Zoya left for Wainstown, Pace and I lay naked on the big bed we now shared. It was late morning, long past time for us to be out working the small farm. But we lazed about anyway, telling secrets and sharing stories that hadn't been aired in years. Decades, in my case.

Zoya would be home soon, and our honeymoon would end rather abruptly when she did. We missed her, of course—Pace especially—but we also wanted to make the most of the time we had on our own.

"Do you ever think about fate?" I asked.

Pace pressed his mouth against my bare shoulder. "Sometimes."

Two ravens flitted in through the open window to poke about in the kitchen, looking for any scraps we might have left out. I had already gotten so used to them I hardly noticed the ravens anymore.

"I think it might be fate that brought me here."

Pace shifted to look up at me from across the pillow. "Why do you say that?"

"I came here because I am one of only five immortal humans. I came here because I wanted to meet the Raven King. Death himself. I figured if anyone could tell me about my immortality, Death could."

"You didn't come here to ask for your death?"

"No, no." I let out a heavy sigh. "You said once that you'd seen him?"

Pace traced a finger through the hair on my chest. "Once or twice. Living so close to his forest, it would be strange if we never saw him."

"Has Zoya seen him? She's not scared of him, is she?"

"Yes, she's seen him too. She talks about him sometimes. At first, I was worried because why would he ever approach her? Why would she look for him? But I think he's just curious about humans sometimes. She's not afraid of him. Or anything at all, really."

"I just wanted to talk to him," I said. "I was afraid. Still am, I guess. The thought of death terrifies me, but that fear calls to me too. I wanted to stand my ground and stare death in the face. A bad motivation, I suppose. He'd never have come to me with ideas like that, would he?"

"I don't know."

I sighed. "And instead, I found you. The man who saved me from death and took me in."

"Hmm."

I caught his gaze and found myself falling into their inky black, as usual. "You're the love of my life. Did you know that?"

Pace's expression melted around the corners.

"And I've had a very, very long life. So that's saying something."

He smiled so sweetly, and I leaned in to kiss it off him. Pace let me do it, leaning in, as if we could get any closer.

"I love you, too," he whispered. "I didn't think I would ever again, but I do."

SEVEN

In all my romantic daydreams about lightning and thunder, I had forgotten about the weather that follows close behind.

The metaphorical storm hit on a sunny afternoon. I was deep in the shed, digging through the scrap bin for something I could repair the tanning frame with, when I heard voices out in the yard. At first, I thought Quinn must have brought Zoya home unexpectedly. I dropped an old shelf bracket back into the bin and headed toward the door of the shed.

But as I approached, it hit me that the voices were unfamiliar. Pace said something indecipherable, and then a stranger spoke. A man, his tone deeper than Pace's but choked with tears.

"She just can't take it anymore," the stranger said. "Please, you have to help us. I can't do it myself. They said you could help."

I edged to the door to peer through the crack. Pace stood near the front porch of the house. A stranger huddled close. He was a tall white man, hunched like he carried the weight of the world in his large travel pack. The man had tight-curling hair, cut short, and an expression like he could collapse inward at any moment from grief.

Pace laid a hand on the man's shoulder in a comforting gesture

I had seen before. This all seemed so familiar, actually. Pace had done the same for Mistress Harper just three weeks prior, and she'd had that same look of mourning on her face.

"Please," the stranger said again.

"I can't," Pace said gently, his expression broken. "If she wants it, she'll have to come here. She must ask for it herself."

"I don't have a cart. I can't get her here. You could come to her. Barer Township isn't far. You could be there and back in a week."

"I'm so sorry, Lon. I can't leave here with all the ravens. She must come to me."

"That's not fair!" Lon shouted.

The man clenched his fists at his side, and my heart stuttered in my chest. He wore several hunting knives and a hatchet strapped within easy reach. It would only take half a second for his grief to turn to anger, and he'd have a weapon in hand. Pace would be in danger.

No. No, no, no.

I crept out of the shed on silent feet. Lon was turned slightly away. If I moved slowly, he wouldn't see me.

"How is it fair that only people who can walk or people who live near Raven's End get to benefit?" Lon shifted from one foot to the other. The anger had already started.

I sidled along the wall of the shed, wishing I hadn't left the shelf bracket behind in the scrap bin. It wasn't a proper weapon, but it was something.

"I hear you." Pace put his hands out in a placating gesture. "I understand better than you might think. I've been where you are. But these things aren't meant to be fair, Lon. They just are. I'm so sorry."

"She deserves to die with dignity!" Lon shouted, color high in his cheeks. "She can't move! She can't even sit up since the fall! Can't feed herself or do anything but stare at the ceiling all day. It's been two years, and she's begging me, man. Don't you see? What am I supposed to do?"

Something about this was starting to click into place in the darkest corners of my mind, but I couldn't think about it yet. I couldn't...not yet. Not until Pace was safe. He should be backing away, should be putting distance between himself and the broken man before him. He should be...

Fuck. Pace was so fragile. Any one of Lon's knives would just go right through him.

Pace looked close to tears himself, and that broke my heart even more. "I'm sorry. I can't help you."

"That's not good enough! I didn't come all this way to leave empty-handed!" Lon shifted his weight again, a move I had seen often enough in the past.

I launched away from the shed and sprinted toward them right when Lon reached for Pace. In the same movement, Lon pulled a utility knife from the strap on his pack.

Fuck, fuck, fuck.

I rammed into Lon at the same time he grabbed Pace's arm. Pace stumbled off balance.

Lon and I hit the ground and skidded through the gravel, awkward with the large pack still strapped to his back. I grunted with effort and wrestled Lon beneath me, but he was a stubborn fucker and had a tight grip on the utility knife. He twisted and screamed his rage, and in a quick move I absolutely should have seen coming, he managed to jam his fist into my gut, just below my ribs.

"*Aurgh*! Fuck you, you crusty old fuck knuckle! Damn it!" It didn't hurt quite yet. My body was too tightly wound to *feel* the utility knife sink into my flesh. But I knew it was going to be a bitch healing, and that was supremely irritating.

Lon froze, as if managing to actually stab someone had shocked the hell out of him. He wasn't a bad man. Lon was just grieving, confused, and hurt. He let go of the utility knife, leaving it hanging out of my gut, and raised his empty hands in alarmed surrender.

"Fletcher!" Pace shouted from behind.

He pulled at my shoulders to get me up, and I let him do it. All the fight had gone out of Lon, and he lay on the ground, his hands still up. The danger was past.

"I'm fine," I growled.

"You're *not* fine," Pace insisted. "Let me look at it."

"I'm fine!" I said again, probably harsher than was necessary. But the wound was starting to hurt properly. I yanked the knife out of my gut with a hiss of pain. Blood soaked my shirt immediately and ran down my side, ruining my pants. I held up the bloody knife for Lon to see. "I'm keeping this."

Lon nodded, frantic, his face white as a sheet.

"You should go," Pace said to Lon. "There's nothing we can do for you here."

"Yes. Yes, sir. I'm sorry."

"If you can get your sister here, then we can talk again. But—"

I glared at Pace. "Are you fucking serious?"

Pace ignored me.

"But otherwise, there's nothing I can do. Go home, Lon. Be with your sister."

Lon said nothing in reply. He scrambled to his feet and hauled ass down the road, his pack rattling.

Pace and I stood side by side on the gravel, watching to make sure Lon really did leave. Fuck, my side hurt. This was such bullshit. How did this keep happening to me?

"How bad is it?" Pace asked.

"It's not that bad," I said, my voice tight.

"Stitches?"

"Fucking—No!"

Pace rolled his eyes at me. "You're bleeding a lot, Fletch."

"Just a bandage. Real tight. No stitches, fucking—Don't you remember the last time? No stitches!"

"Fine! Fine. Let's go. Come on."

He led me onto the porch and inside. I pressed my hand over

the wound. It was bleeding way too much. The bastard had hit something important. For anyone else, it could have been fatal. Hell, it might be fatal for me too. I still didn't know how close I could get to death without crossing the line.

It was such a mess. Pace hissed and swore under his breath, and I did my best to hold still and let him take care of me. By the time we got the bandage on, half the floor was littered with blood-soaked rags, and we were both covered in it. But though the blood seeped through and the bandage was wet to the touch, it didn't spill over. It would hold.

Pace made me lie down on the bed and rest while he cleaned up the aftermath. Then he brought a damp rag and a bowl of clean water to mop me up.

"He really got you, didn't he?" Pace murmured, wiping down my hip and abdomen.

"I've had worse."

He met my eye, and something about the open care in his expression loosened the anger clenched tightly in my chest. "Well, it's no tree branch. I'll give you that."

I snorted. "Fuck you."

"Maybe let's give it a couple of days?" Pace said with a smile.

"Give me twelve hours."

Pace laughed.

But the knot in my chest was more than just pain, fear, and adrenaline. And as beautiful as it was, Pace's laughter wasn't enough to soothe it.

"What was he asking for, Pace?"

His hands froze for half a second, then Pace rinsed the rag and sat on the edge of the bed. His eyes settled on my chest, and he chewed his lip.

After a long moment, he finally spoke. "He was jealous."

"Lon? Jealous of what?"

"Not Lon." Pace's hands remained relaxed on his lap. The

white patches on the right side were tinged pink with my blood. "Death."

What the ever-loving fuck was that supposed to mean? I waited, brows drawn close together.

"After...After Edie...I sat up from her bed, and he was here. In the house. The Raven King."

My expression hardened, but I didn't interrupt.

"He was just there. In the corner by the basin. And he said... He told me...He said I stole Edie's story from him. That she was supposed to come to him and tell her story and then he'd repay her with a death. He said if I was so ready to do his duty for him in his own forest, then he'd let me."

"Pace, what—"

"And then the ravens came. One hundred and one, he said. One death each. If someone came looking for the Raven King, their path would bend toward me instead. And I'd have to listen to their stories and bear witness to their pain. Then they'd take a raven with them so when they were ready, the raven could give their death as promised. And when the last raven had gone from the forest, when all one hundred and one deaths had been dealt, that's when I'd find my own end. And the Raven King would take up his mantle once more."

I stared at Pace, blood rushing through my ears so loud I could barely hear him speak.

"I should have told you sooner—" he began.

"Get out."

Pace's mouth snapped shut as if I'd slapped him. It probably would have hurt less if I had.

"Fletch, I—"

"Just go, Pace. I need you to get out. I need—"

"Fine. Okay."

"You said to tell you if I needed space. I'm telling you!"

He was already up and walking toward the front door. "I know. I'm going."

Pace left the house and closed the door behind him. By the creaking sounds of the porch, I could tell he didn't go further than the rocking chair by the rail.

Alone, I stared up at the ceiling, willing my heart to slow down. That damned cobweb was back in the corner just over the bed. A nice big one. I glared at it, annoyed that it would probably hurt too much to raise my arms to get it down.

Pace was a death dealer.

Damned cobweb. They had always grossed me out.

He didn't tell you. He lied to you.

There was an entire forest outside where that spider could build its nest. Why in our—

I swallowed hard.

Our house.

I had moved in with a death dealer, and he had let me do it.

No, that didn't even bother me so much. I had seen much stranger things in my time. This was one of the darker things, I'd admit. But still...

No, it was the lying. He had kept this massive secret from me, and he let me fall in love with him. Pace had handed out at least two deaths that I could recall since I'd been in the house. The first time had been when I'd woken up in his bed. Zoya had made me a tea party and said, *"He's outside. He has a visitor."*

How many deaths had he dealt out to strangers with his daughter just right there? Did she even know? How many secrets was he keeping?

Someday, when I'm gone, Zoya will take over for me. Yes, she's seen him too. She's not afraid of him. Or anything at all, really.

I rolled out of bed without thinking about it first and swore at the pain in my gut. The bandage was holding so far, but it still hurt like hell.

I slammed open the front door and stood on the porch, breathing hard.

Pace stared up at me, his eyes cold. Unmoved.

There were so many questions I wanted to ask, but I could answer them all myself.

Why didn't you tell me?

You might have hated me. I was afraid.

Why do you do it?

It's not like I chose this, Fletch!

How could you dare?

You forgave me when it was Edie. How are these people any different?

"You could live forever," I said, my tone combative.

Pace blinked several times, completely thrown by my statement. "What?"

"If you didn't give away the ravens, your end would never come. Does that mean you're immortal too?"

Pace set his mouth in a tight line. "I wouldn't do that even if I could."

"Why the fuck not?"

"People aren't supposed to live forever, Fletch."

Oh. That hurt. He wasn't wrong, but it was a fact I had carefully avoided for over a century.

"I've done some rough math." Pace rose from the chair. "People sometimes come all at once, but the year Zoya turned three, no one came at all. It's hard to judge these things, but it's reasonable to think I'll have a good, long life, Fletcher. A relatively normal life."

"Fuck you."

His expression hardened. "Don't talk to me like that."

I turned and pounded my fist against the doorframe with a roar of frustration, but I barely felt it over the stab of pain in my gut.

"Fletch, don't. You'll hurt yourself worse."

"Get off." I shrugged him away. That kind of caring had fooled me before. *Liar, liar, liar.*

Pace let his arms fall to his sides. "People have been coming to

Raven's End forever, Fletcher. Long before I was born. And they'll keep coming after I'm gone."

"That's not what I'm upset about!"

"Then what is it?"

I rounded on him. "Doesn't it hurt? They tell you their stories, you said. How can you bear it?"

"Of course it hurts!" Pace pressed a hand over his heart. "It guts me, Fletcher. But these people...They hurt so much worse. They don't come here because they're sad. They come here because they're at their absolute lowest. Bearing more than anyone was ever meant to carry. At least with me, they're passing their pain to another person who actually cares about them instead of one of the Old Kind."

"The Raven King isn't a man. He's a spirit. A ghost. He's not *you*."

"I know, Fletcher! I know!"

I had no idea what I was saying. If I could just force Pace back into the mold he'd been in before, then everything would be good again. A carer. One of the good ones. Someone who wouldn't betray me, lie to me, keep secrets. Such massive, incredible secrets about horrible things that I didn't understand, that I didn't want to think about.

"He doesn't understand what this does to a person! He can't!"

"What difference does it make? I made a choice to let my wife die with dignity the way she wanted. The way she asked for. But because of where I live, I caught the attention of one of the Old Kind. I should have known better, but what can I say, Fletch? I was in a bad place. And now I'm living with the consequences."

"This isn't right!" I shouted.

"Okay? Go tell *him* that! By all means! Go tell him that every time someone comes here, I have to go hide and cry into my shirt and then come out and pretend everything's okay so Zoya doesn't worry. Go tell him that every time I hear a noise on the road, I panic, thinking of all the pain that people are bringing me. Go tell him how much guilt I feel for thinking of my own pain when they're hurting so much worse!"

I clenched my eyes shut and leaned against the rail.

"I try—" There was a thud when Pace leaned back against the house. "I try to talk them out of it. I always invite them inside, offer them a place to stay. Something good to eat. I listen to their stories, just like the Raven King told me to. It breaks my heart, but I listen. And sometimes? Most of the time, actually? It works. It's enough to get them to think twice. To hesitate. And then they'll get going and talk themselves out of it. Those people go home with a jar of honey and a bag of eggs instead of a raven, and...Hell, Fletch. I live for those days. Because it means I'm making a difference here. I think that's the Raven King's true purpose as well. To let people stare Death in the face and decide if it's a friend or foe. To tell their story and let out their pain."

I clenched my fist against the railing. "I just don't—I don't get how they could even think of it."

"I know you don't, love."

"I get it, Pace. I mean, I don't, but I do. I don't even know what I'm arguing about here. I just know that I trusted you. And you lied to me."

"I know. I'm sorry."

"You should have told me, Pace!"

Pace said nothing, just took it.

"I gave you *everything!* And you handed me back lies! This isn't a secret you can just keep from someone you claim to love! You've been crying about it? Hiding it? Alone? I could have been there for you, Pace! I could have helped you! And you hid it from me! What else are you hiding?"

"Nothing, Fletch! Nothing. I swear."

I blinked back the tears "How am I supposed to trust you?" I wanted so *badly* to believe him. But I had also wanted to fall in love with him. I had done it so fast, so blindly. All it took was him being nice to me for one fucking day, and I had painted him into a pretty picture. The perfect man. Simple, sweet, caring.

But no one was like that, and I hated that truth more than any other.

"I just wanted—" Pace ran his hands through his hair in agitation. So incredibly soft. "You came here, and I thought at first you were one of them. That you were going to carve out a little more of my heart and leave again. But you stayed, and you tried, and you healed. Someone who could not die. Do you have any idea how miraculous that was for me? And you liked me for *me*, not for the relief I might give you. And you were so strong and funny and—"

His words cut off when I wrapped him up in a hug.

He said the next bit directly into my hair. "I just wanted to be *me* for once. In love with someone beautiful and good. Happy. For a little while."

"You could go on forever, just like me. We could be happy forever."

"The only way for me to live forever would be to stop listening to people who need a friend more than anything. I can't do that."

"They can talk to someone else," I whispered into his shoulder.

Pace gripped me tightly, careful of my stab wound. Always so careful. And with his gentlest voice—the one he used to tell me he loved me—he said, "I'm not afraid of Death."

Fuck. That hurt too. Because I was absolutely afraid of him. But he was hurting Pace, and that was worse.

I pulled out of the hug. He had left a light jacket over the rail near the steps. I yanked it over my bare chest and the bandages wrapped around my stomach.

"Where are you going?" Pace asked.

"To tell *him* a few things." I stalked off the porch and away from the house.

EIGHT

I walked for what felt like forever. Raven's End was a huge swath of hilly forest alive with birds, squirrels, turkeys, deer, and a thousand other things. The verdant trees muffled everything near the ground, but they gave voice to the wind. It rustled in the canopy high above while I tramped through the leaf litter, ignoring the stabbing pain in my...Well, in my stab wound.

Eventually, I had to stop. One, if I walked forever, I would pass right through Raven's End on the northern border. Two, I was getting lightheaded with blood loss. I'd already soaked through my bandage and Pace's jacket. It was stupid to be running around like this so soon after a serious injury.

I sat down with a huff on a boulder near the top of a large hill. The trees opened below me, giving a grand view of Amau to the east. It was a beautiful spot. A shame I had come with such a heavy heart.

They said if you sat quietly enough and for long enough, the Raven King would come. So I focused on my breathing and watched the clouds scuttle by, making patterns of the sunshine on the fields below. Slowly, the sun began to creep toward the west. Hunger gnawed at my stomach, but that was probably part of the trial. How patient could I be? How long could I endure the discomfort?

The hours crept on. I played the conversation with Pace over and over in my head. Every which way I looked at it, Pace was a victim in the entire situation. Beginning to end. But also...of all the people to be singled out by the Raven King, Pace was probably the only one who could have taken the curse and turned it into something good. Something worth doing.

How many people had he saved just by talking to them? By being there in their darkest moment?

"Sixteen," said a deep, resonant voice on my left.

I stiffened. In my periphery, a shadow moved.

"...so far, that is to say," the shadow said.

"Sixteen what?" I whispered.

"Sixteen lives the caretaker has saved since the day his wife departed." The voice was rich as thick molasses and as sharp as smoke. "It has been fascinating to watch, for I did not know such things could be done."

"How could you not know a life could be saved?" My own voice was much too harsh. It was not wise to goad the Old Kind.

"I am not of Life."

With a great force of will, I turned to look directly at him. A tall figure, black as night, stood in the shadow of a tree, its hunched back toward me. It wore a black cloak that muffled its shape, so it was hard to tell if it truly was a giant raven like the tales all told. It shuffled to the side with quick, jerking movements and the rustling of feathers. It seemed to feel my gaze because it slipped further behind the tree.

"I have looked for you many times, adventurer," the figure said, "but my eye does not find you. I looked for you today, but still, you were hidden from my sight."

"You can see me now."

The figure moved back into view, just enough to reveal a beady black eye set in a face of fine, black feathers. A raven's eye but much larger. Taller than a man. Dreadful to look at. The eye roved over me, never quite still.

"You are afraid of me."

I clenched my fists at my side and said nothing.

"If you fear me, why do you seek me?"

"You should let Pace go free. The job you set for him is not meant for humans. It will break him."

The Raven King made a clicking sound from behind the tree. I almost didn't want to see the great beak that had caused it.

"The caretaker took up my mantle. He stole a story from me."

"People make mistakes. This is not just."

"You do not yet know justice, but you will learn it. A witch will show you the way."

I recoiled from the words. "You would prophesy to me? You are Death. You are not Future."

"I am the future of all things."

"Not of me."

The Raven King emerged a little more from behind the tree, and this time, I caught the movement of his great beak when he clicked it. "Am I not?"

"Let Pace go free. Release him from this curse."

"The caretaker stole from me. Now he must repay the debt. One hundred and one stories. One hundred and one deaths."

"He only took one story from you. Only Edie's."

The Raven King eyed me. "It is an even trade."

I swore under my breath. The Old Kind were not human, and they did not deal in human quantities.

"I watch his work." The Raven King shifted in that unnatural way until he was almost completely hidden behind the tree again. "Humans have paid me their stories for millennia. Since the beginning. And they always leave with their death. An even trade. But when they pay the caretaker, they often choose not to complete the deal. I wish to understand why."

"What difference does it make? You're getting even more stories than you bargained for."

"I wish to understand."

The Raven King melted into the shadow of the tree, and I blinked hard, trying to make him out in the advancing gloom.

"It is fascinating," the voice said right in my ear.

I startled away from the massive black beak that had appeared over my shoulder. The Raven King stood over me, and for the first time, I got a good look at his entire form. He truly was a raven taller than any man. The Raven King wore a black cloak that blended with the shadows along the ground, but it fell open in the front, revealing the sleek breast feathers and the sweep of one massive wing. Its eyes were uncanny, always moving, taking in everything at a dizzying pace. His gaze settled on me but continued to bounce back and forth over my face.

"I am not of Life, but I crave it," the Raven King said. His voice did not come from his beak, but rather echoed through the forest, as if it vibrated directly from the shadows between the leaves. "That is something you understand, I believe."

I swallowed hard but made no reply. My gut wound began to seep again with the pounding of my heart.

The Raven King stepped closer with his great black feet. His talons were six inches long apiece. "You understand that much, do you not? You, who have lived so many lifetimes. You have robbed me of a story as well."

"I didn't choose immortality," I said quickly. "I owe you nothing."

The Raven King seemed to mull this over, his eye roaming over my face. "It is no matter. As you said, the caretaker is giving me more stories than I bargained for. And when he is gone, the child will continue the work after him."

My heart stopped in my chest. "Not Zoya."

"The child will grow to be a farmer. And when her father puts down my mantle, she will take it up."

"No!" I shouted. "You can't! She made no bargain! I won't let her!"

The Raven King stepped closer and quirked his head to one side. "Who are you to demand anything of Death, adventurer?"

"Who are you to demand anything of a human?" My vision shook with anger and fear, and I hardly knew what I was saying. Who I was speaking to. "Zoya has stolen nothing from you! You cannot take from her what she does not give freely."

"She will give me anything I ask for. Just like her father does." The Raven King's molten voice scratched into my ears like beetles. "The deal is struck with the caretaker. One hundred and one ravens. But I will amend it with the child. Her ravens will be without number, and she will serve me forever."

"Fucking—" I bit back tears of rage and clenched my fists at my sides.

Think, Fletcher. Think. Death was right. Zoya was a kind soul, a carer like her father. It would be the work of one conversation for the Raven King to convince Zoya she could save people as a death dealer. She couldn't be allowed to stay at Raven's End. Not after she grew up. Certainly not when Pace eventually died.

"Take me instead." The words were out of my mouth before I could think about them.

The Raven King's rustling movements stopped. He peered at me with his great, beady eye. "I do not believe you would be suited to the work, adventurer."

"No. Take my story. You want it so badly...It's yours. But you have to release Zoya."

The Raven King studied my expression. "You would give me your story? Willingly?"

"I will give it to you when I am ready. I will take a raven. And *when I'm ready*, I will die, and you can have my story then. No sooner. Just like all the others. And in exchange, you will never speak to Zoya again, even if she looks for you. And when she comes of age, make her leave here and forget so she never comes back."

I thought fast, unable to leave anything to chance. The Old Kind were the sort to take every inch given and then some.

"Let her keep her childhood memories of her life here and of her father, but make her forget the rest. Let her leave here thinking she's left nothing behind so she never comes back. Never even looks back. You can do this, can't you?"

The Raven King clicked his beak. "It can be done."

I swiped my sweaty palm against my pants and held out my hand to seal the deal. "Do we have a bargain?"

The Raven King's eyes darted down to my extended hand, and for a wild moment, I thought I'd gone mad. He had no hands to shake with, so it was an absurd gesture. But with a flash of movement and a bright stab of pain in my hand, the Raven King accepted the deal. His sharp beak sliced a gash into the heel of my right palm, and blood welled to the surface like liquid rubies.

"The bargain is struck."

I lifted the jacket to expose the bandaging around my stomach, pressing the oozing cut against the bandaging there to staunch the blood. "Good. Then I'm leaving."

The Raven King's eye followed me as I walked past him. "We shall meet again, adventurer."

"Yeah," I muttered. "When I'm damn good and ready."

NINE

The walk back to the house went by in a blur. I kept my hand pressed against the wool bandaging until it mostly scabbed over, but the pain in my palm didn't let up. The way these things worked, I was willing to bet this would be one scar that wouldn't disappear. It was a true wound inflicted by one of the Old Kind—a mark of the bargain we had struck. For the first time in over a century, I would have to heal like everyone else.

Pace was in bed when I got back. It was past dark, but he wasn't asleep. The lamp was lit on the bedside table, and it looked like he'd been reading. He sat up with a start when I came in.

"You're back."

"Yeah." I sat on the edge of the bed and didn't push his searching hands away.

"Fletch, what is this? You're hurt again." He pulled my right hand toward him and angled it so the cut was more visible in the light. "Oh, Fletch. What did you do? What did you agree to?"

"How do you know I agreed to anything?"

Pace held up his own hand. Sure enough, tucked neatly just inside a patch of white skin was a faint scar the twin of my own. I hadn't noticed it before.

"What did you bargain for?" he asked again, resigned.

I let out a great sigh and leaned so far that I collapsed onto the bed. I rolled over and curled into him, inhaling his comforting scent.

Pace's arms went around me, familiar and sure.

"I couldn't save you," I said against his chest. "But I could save her."

I told him the details of my conversation and bargain with the Raven King, and it wasn't until I got to the part where I wanted Zoya sent away that I realized what I had done.

"I'm so sorry," I said in a rush, clutching his shirt. "I should have spoken to you first. She's your daughter, and I just made a bargain over her like I had the right. But I couldn't let him take her like that. I couldn't let—"

"Shh," Pace said into my hair. "You did the right thing. You did exactly the right thing. Thank you. She'll be free now."

I shifted to look him in the eye. "I'm sorry we fought earlier."

"I'm sorry I kept a secret like that from you."

We had fallen in love so fast, so rashly. But still, I loved him.

"Can I stay here? Can I stay with you? To the end?"

Pace nodded and pressed his mouth to mine. "Yes. Please stay. As long as you like. Forever."

For the first time in a very long time, my days were numbered. But also, I had finally found my greatest adventure. I had found home.

Quinn brought Zoya home a week later. Zoya zoomed through the house, her dark curls escaping from what had probably been a very tidy braid at one point. She nearly broke both of our necks with her excited hugs and then darted back out again to greet each chicken, goat, and raven one at a time. The bees she steered clear of, but she did give them a polite shout on her way through that side of the yard.

Quinn stayed for lunch again, restocked our supplies, and brought me back a letter from Isla. My sister had about a thousand questions and threatened to come find me herself if I didn't answer every single one of them.

I smirked at the letter, folded it up, and put it away on the shelf, unanswered. I'd quite like a visit from her, come to think of it. So let her come find me.

The wound in my gut healed like Lon had never come to Raven's End, but the Raven King's mark on my palm scarred over to a faint line and stayed. Sometimes, I looked at it and wondered what my story's end would be. But then Pace would say something smart or flick water at me while doing the dishes, and I would come back to the here and now with a smile.

People still came to Raven's End, just like always. Sometimes they came a lot, but for years at a time, we saw no one at all. Pace listened to every single one of their stories, but now he didn't have to hide about it afterward. He let me hold him while he cried into my shirt. He yelled and carried on, and that was hard. But the worst were the times when he lay dry-eyed on the bed for hours afterward.

I usually took Zoya swimming or foraging those days and gave him time to process. And when we returned, Zoya would tell him all about our adventures, and the smile would come back to his handsome face.

Zoya grew up fast. *Too* fast. I swear I only blinked one day, and there she was—a grown woman with fire behind her eyes and the warmest heart of anyone I had ever known, aside from her father. She started walking down to Wainstown by herself to spend long weekends with Quinn and their son, Remy. And not too long after that, when Remy decided he was moving to New Haven to make his fortune, Zoya announced she was going with him.

"You're sure, Bug?" Pace asked.

Zoya's smile was just like his, though there was something else there I could never quite identify. It was probably a bit of Edie coming through in the shape of her eyes.

"I love him, Daddy. I have to go."

Pace squeezed my hand, and my old scar seemed to burn under his palm.

In Zoya's mind, she probably thought she would come home to visit sometimes. Send us letters, let us know how her life was going...But Pace and I knew better. The time had come for my bargain with the Raven King to be fulfilled. Zoya would walk away from Raven's End and think she had left nothing at all behind. And as hard as that was, it was for the best. She would be free.

It took a long time for Pace to come back to me after Zoya left. He was there, but he was a shadow of himself. Eventually, though, he started talking about her again. We pulled out journals we had kept over the years, retold the stories, and remembered her with joy.

The years passed slowly. Pace didn't age over the decades, though his white patches continued to shift and dance slowly across his skin. The pair of us were stuck in time, and we made the most of it. We built a bigger bed but slept crammed up against each other anyway. We expanded the apiary, spent lazy afternoons swimming naked in the dappled sunlight, and made up endless, ridiculous adventure stories to regale each other with. Isla visited every year and stayed for weeks at a time, and Quinn was a regular face at our table.

And month by month, year by year, people came to the house and took away a raven. The great black birds dwindled to a few dozen, to twenty, to ten. And soon, there was only one left. It sat in the rafters, copying us in its croaking voice, and waited until its time would come as well.

I watched it warily at first, but as the months went by, I began to forget about it.

Until the day we heard footsteps on the gravel road.

Pace and I looked up and caught each other's eye. The time had finally come. Just like we always knew it would. We'd had over forty beautiful years together, and now Pace's penance had come due.

He hugged me tightly, and I kissed him with everything I had.

"I love you," I whispered against his skin.

"I love you."

"Thank you for everything. For this life I've had with you."

Someone knocked on the front door.

Pace smiled, dry-eyed and serene. "Stay here, okay? Don't come out and watch."

I nodded my agreement. He kissed me again and went outside.

I sat on our bed for an hour, staring at the last raven in the rafters. I couldn't hear what they were saying out there, but it didn't matter. Pace was listening to his last story. And while it was possible the stranger would change their mind and leave without a raven, I didn't let myself hope for it.

And sure enough, just as the bars of afternoon sunlight began to creep up the wall, the raven took off with a rustle of wings and flew out the window.

The stranger's footsteps crunched away from the house and down the road, and then there was silence.

I got up and went to the front porch, then froze.

There, on the rail, stood a raven. It was different from the ones that had been following Pace around all those years. It was a newcomer. This one had patches of white on its right wing, bright against the midnight feathers.

My heart stuttered in my chest. Pace was gone, but at the same time, he would be with me always, wouldn't he? Right to the very end. The Raven King had a little kindness in him after all.

I approached the porch rail, and the raven watched me with curious eyes. He hopped a little closer to me with the scritching of talons on wood.

"I, uh—" I cleared my throat. A single tear rolled down my

cheek and into my beard. "I suppose it's time I had my next adventure. What do you think?"

"*Adventure,*" the raven repeated.

"Right. Exactly." I wasn't ready to follow Pace into death just yet, but I would in time. Just like I had promised. "Let's go find the stupidest possible way for me to die, eh? How long do you think it'll take?"

The raven eyed me, then flitted up to sit on my shoulder. It ruffled its feathers.

I sniffed and scrubbed at my face with both hands. "Let's go find Isla first. Maybe she has some bright ideas. We'll leave first thing in the morning. And don't worry. I'll send Quinn up here to collect the animals. They can manage it all. Then off to Mitsmooren. What do you say?"

The raven preened its wing feathers. The white patches shone in the afternoon light.

"Pretty," I whispered.

The raven's cunning little eye caught my gaze.

Charmer.

Thank You
for Reading

If you enjoyed this book, please consider leaving a rating or review. With your support, I can keep daydreaming for a living.

You can find convenient links to all the popular review sites on my website: annacackler.com

Content Advisory

This book contains scenes that may be distressing to some readers. Below is a list of these topics, drawn up to the best of my knowledge at the time of publication. A regularly updated list can also be found on my website: annacackler.com

If, while reading this book, you come across any sensitive topics that need to be added to this list, please reach out to me at anna@annacackler.com and put CONTENT ADVISORY in the subject line.

~

The Glass Wheel
Death of a parent, depression, grief

Bluewater
A tertiary character is burned alive near the beginning of the story, but it is not a graphic scene and the character is drugged to not feel pain or fear.

Starsong

Child abuse—an adult man is beaten by his father on the page, and their history of child abuse is implied.

Raven's End

Mild gore, previous assisted death, death dealer, suicide, swearing

Acknowledgments

I am so grateful to everyone who has helped me make The Sibylline Saga a reality. I could not have done this without the network of support from both family and from new friends I've made along the way.

Many thanks to those of you who helped me name the Athorum: Gerry Robinson, Jim Meeks, Ashlyn Van Benschoten, Sallie Montuori, and Bear C. It was so fun to brainstorm with you all the ways this mythical cure-all came to be. And thanks to Maria Luihn for giving Lon his name in Raven's End.

I'd also like to thank my many early readers, who helped me polish the series: Zhade, Elizabeth Plass, Brittney Willbanks, Enos Evans, Pam Cemen, and Carla Evans. I couldn't have done it without your feedback and encouragement.

And thank you so much to Lyndsey Smith at the Editing Forge for her tireless work in giving this series its final polish.

There are three other people who have supported me through the ups and downs of being an author. It began with my mother, who told me stories every night and shared her love of books with me. Thanks, Mom, both for the excellent start and your ongoing support and encouragement.

Thank you Chelsea for listening to me ramble and vent with infinite patience. You say you envy my confidence, but that's all fake. You kept me sane when I was barely keeping it together.

And thank you to Kevin, my very best friend and the best husband anyone could ask for. I can't express how much your support and your faith in me has meant.

This series has been an absolute labor of love that began when I was just a teenager. I am so incredibly proud of it and of myself for getting this far. And I'm can't wait to see what comes next, because this is only the beginning.

The end.

This is such a surreal moment for me. After writing this little afterward, I'm going to upload some files, write an email for advance readers, and do some other housekeeping work—and bing bang boom, the Sibylline Saga will officially be a part of my past.

It only took 23 years.

If you read the afterward from book one, you'll know I started the very first drafts of this series when I was fifteen years old. Sitting in high school science class, writing scenes on notebook paper and then folding them up in a very specific way to keep in a box under my bed. I didn't even have my own computer back then. I had to share one with the whole family.

Once, while staying with my dad, I wrote about 20 pages and saved them on a floppy disc to take home. Apparently that had been an important floppy disc with all of my dad's banking records on it. Oops.

Seems like it was just yesterday, but I was just a kid.

Okay, I have got to get it together. It's nearly midnight, I just finished the final proof edit of Raven's End, and I'm feeling a bit sentimental, okay? Give me a minute here. Maybe now isn't the best time to be writing this...

Or, no. You know what? This is the absolute BEST time to be writing this, because I have no filter right now. Let's dig in deep, chickens.

The Glass Wheel was my love letter to spinning.

I've read too many books in the past with some FMC (female main character) bitching and moaning about how she doesn't want to sit around spinning/mending/sewing/weaving. She wants to go outside and [insert "boy" activity here].

Well you know what? I'm the FMC that would rather sit inside and spin. It's AWESOME. It's relaxing, pretty, and vital work. Fabric and thread were some of the most valuable assets in pre-industrial times. Being able to make good thread and fabric was a highly revered skill. It was important.

And don't even get me started about how the patriarchy managed to turn the word "spinster" into an insult. Being a spinster was one of the few ways a woman could be financially independent, and they turned it into shame. What the actual fuck balls?

I'm sorry about the swearing. I wasn't lying when I said I have no filter right now.

Anyway. So I wrote The Glass Wheel in answer to all that. I had an FMC that loved spinning, who was good at it, who used it to support herself and her family on her own terms and took pride in her work. Yes she still lived with her father, but they were a team. They loved each other. It was *their* farm.

The Glass Wheel was also the moment when I realized how deep fiction can gut a person.

I always intended for Aurora to be grieving, but I didn't set out to write such a striking allegory for depression. I have some experience with depression—entirely to do with the autistic burnout I didn't realize I was sinking into while writing the story. (I've learned a lot about myself since then and am taking much better care of myself now.)

Aurora was so tired because I was so tired. She became obsessed with her task and let everything else fall to the wayside. Anything to avoid feeling all the bad things. Anything to pretend things were fine.

It was supposed to be about spinning, but instead it was about me. I exaggerated it quite a bit for the sake of the story, but the roots were there.

To anyone who finds themselves a little bit in Aurora's story, I see you. Take care of yourselves, loves, however you can. Even when it's hard.

All of my stories are a little bit me, deep down. Bluewater is my bullheadedness. Ayana is me when I'm mad. She's the me that refuses to back down, who isn't ashamed to say, "No." I've softened a bit in my adulthood, but I can say I've burned a few bridges in my time.

Starsong is my faith. I'm not a religious person, but I have such faith in humanity, in the magic of the world around us, in the simple beauty of starlight on a clear night. In family and in love.

And Raven's End...well. I'm not sure I'm ready to tackle what Raven's End is. I wanted to write a love story, and I think maybe I've hid behind that love story to peek at what scares me most: leaving my loved ones behind to carry on without me. Or worse, carrying on without them.

Thank you to everyone who has made it through to the end with me. You've taken a part of me with you, and I hope you've found a little joy, a little comfort, and a kindred spirit between these pages.

And now—finally—this is the end.

On to the next adventure.